A KINGDOM FALLS

Born and raised in Eastern Canada, John Owen Theobald moved to the UK to study the poetry of Keats, and in 2009 received a PhD from the University of St Andrews. He lives in London, England.

The Ravenmaster Trilogy
– BOOK III –

A KINGDOM FALLS

JOHN OWEN THEOBALD

ZEPHYR

First published in the UK in 2017 by Zephyr,
an imprint of Head of Zeus Ltd

9 7 5 3 1 2 4 6 8

A catalogue record for this book is available from the British Library.

ISBN (HB) 9781784974428
ISBN (E) 9781784974411

Typeset by Adrian McLaughlin

Printed and bound in Germany by CPI Books GmbH, Leck

Head of Zeus Ltd
First Floor East
5–8 Hardwick Street
London EC1R 4RG

WWW.HEADOFZEUS.COM

For Noori, Claire, Avery, Emma,
and all the future leaders of the resistance.

And for Tracy, who was always
too good for this place.

TOWER OF LONDON

1. WHITE TOWER
2. CHAPEL

3. BARRACKS
4. HOSPITAL

5. ROOST
6. TOWER GREEN
7. KING'S HOUSE
8. CONSTABLE TOWER
9. SALT TOWER

10. BLOODY TOWER
11. MAIN GUARD
12. CASEMATES
13. TOWER SCHOOL

14. TRAITORS' GATE
15. DEVELIN TOWER
16. BRASS MOUNT

17. WEST GATE
18. MOAT
19. RIVER THAMES

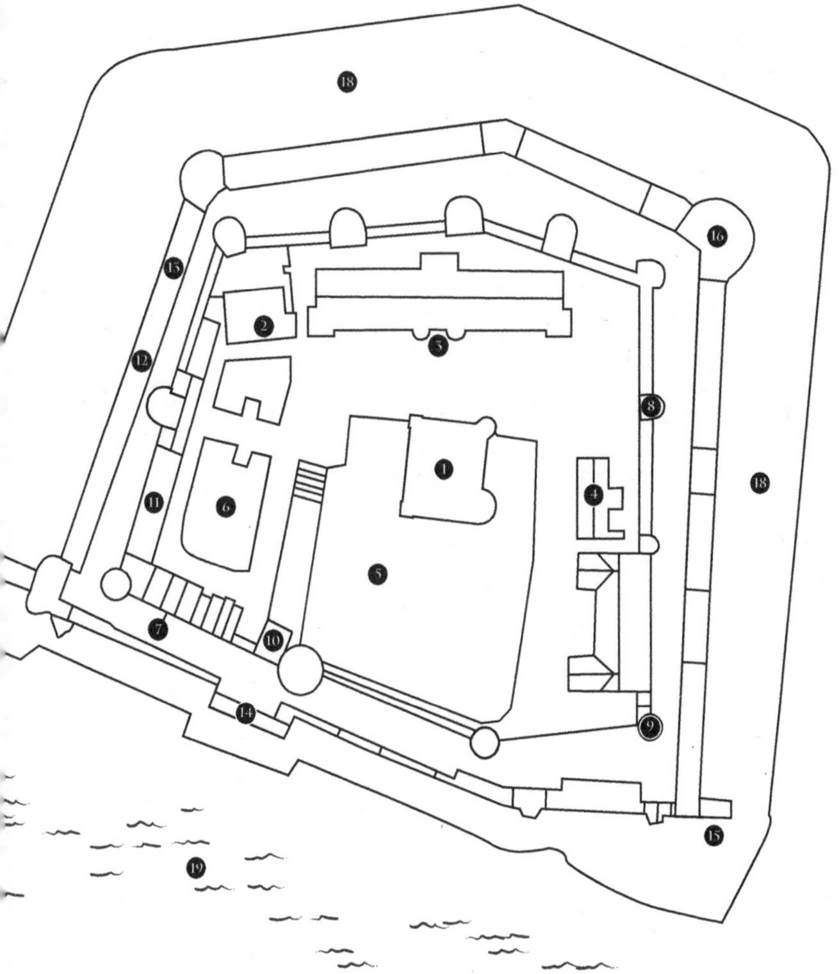

18
16
15
2
3
12
8
1
18
4
11
6
5
7
10
14
9
15
19

'Dark is a way and light is a place.'

Poem on My Birthday, Dylan Thomas

'By the thousands, wheel through winter air,
Above sleeping dead of yesteryear,
Across the fields of France
No passerby forgets.
Be our voice of duty,
O black funereal beauty.'

Crows, Arthur Rimbaud

I

LANDING

1

TIMOTHY SQUIRE

6 June 1944

We float in silence through the night. It is the silence of the abyss.

Twenty men sit facing each other across the narrow fuselage. I turn my head away to the porthole. At first it's an enormous wall of black, but I can just make out shapes in the light of the moon: other gliders headed to other targets, also crowded with soldiers and vehicles.

I look back at the men inside – decent blokes, most of them. D-Company, first boots on the ground. The thought hits me like a brick: Timothy Squire, one of the first soldiers in the greatest invasion ever attempted. *Only a year ago, I was working as a builder down at the docks.*

A voice rises up, as Bishop, one of the younger soldiers, tries a Cockney tune to mask the fear.

I don't want to be a soldier,
I don't want to go to war;

I'd rather hang around
Piccadilly underground

Some of the lads join in, but swiftly fall silent, and again we are soundless men, stuffed in a glider with a jeep and two anti-tank guns.

I rest my boots lightly on the plywood floor, trying not to think of what would happen if we were shot from beneath – how the whole thing would cave in and crack into pieces. I try not to think of what might happen if the tow rope snaps, and we ditch into the North Sea. I try not to think at all.

With shaking hands, I ease the buckles strapping me in. No matter what happens, I will not be belted in here to drown or burn.

I glance over at Arthur Lightwood, the other sapper and my best mate through all this, ready to make a joke, but his eyes are squeezed shut. It barely looks like him, under a camouflage helmet, his face black with stove soot. I must look the same. Not as ugly, of course.

I can't worry about us being shot down. *Just do my bit.* We will land ahead of the armies, find the bridge, and disarm the bombs. *I'm a sapper, I can disarm a bomb.* That's all. Then we hold the bridge until the reinforcements arrive.

A man couldn't ask for better reinforcements. In a few hours a whole continent of British and American troops will be crossing the sea, tens of thousands of trained soldiers. The greatest bloody cavalry you could ask for.

I look back at the window. I've got to see something, otherwise this rolling will have me sicking up in my helmet. Clouds hide the stars, I can see only the haze of the full moon.

'All right!' Major Roland's voice blasts into the stillness.

The glider is ready to be cut loose and there is no going back. A powerless glider falling to the earth. The well-defended earth.

I think again of 'Rommel's asparagus' – great sharp poles erected against glider landings. Major Roland had no bright ideas about avoiding these. *We'll try not to land on them.* My heart throbs in my chest.

My mind flees to happy, easy, warm thoughts. Anna Cooper on Tower Green, the ravens croaking on the battlements, Dad dusting off his beloved suits of armour. The earth unmoving under my feet.

With a great heave we are cut loose. I count – six heartbeats before gravity rushes in. Seconds have never passed so slowly. My stomach drops to my feet, but I keep my eyes on the porthole.

I can only see a broad shape, dark against the darkness, but I know what it is: the great bomber that towed us here is heading back. There goes Cecil Rafferty, swanning off back to England. Back home. His job is done, ours is about to begin.

Once Rafferty's plane has vanished, my shoulders sag with relief.

I told him to watch out for Anna, to make sure she is safe from her father, that sneaky German who's turned up in her life in the middle of a bleeding war. *We shook hands on it, Cecil Rafferty and I.*

She'll be safe, I know. Relief is followed by the suffocating thought that I will never see her again.

Forward motion jolts my head down. The pressure builds in my ears, pushing against my skull. We are falling, fast. No time to spare a thought for Anna or Cecil Rafferty. The dive builds, our speed growing, as we plummet into the howling darkness.

And the abyss swallows us whole.

We plunge towards the ever-hardening shape of land below.

Thankfully, Rafferty and the bombers seem to draw the anti-aircraft fire away, which now erupts from the darkness.

As the glider veers left, I can feel the crosswinds. We are turning in a great circle. My stomach heaves. We should be over Cabourg by now. Are the pilots bloody lost?

There. I can see it. The rivers, flashing below, and the canals like ribbons of silver. I can see the bridges. So can the glider pilots, apparently, as we swing suddenly towards the road bridges. I hear a sound, a great explosion, but it is distant. Not us.

Not yet.

'Brace up!' the co-pilot calls out.

The glider buckles. In the swaying darkness, people

pitch forward and back. From underneath each wing giant flaps are deployed, acting as a brake against our speed.

But it's not enough.

We're falling too fast. We've done this countless times in training and we've never come down like this. The bleeding glider's got a parachute and we've deployed it for less. Soot-covered faces stare at each other wildly in the howl of wind. The dark French countryside is 600 feet beneath us. My eyes are glued to the wooden side of the glider. *I will not die inside this box.*

My rifle butt can take out this wall, if needs be.

The dive builds. Someone, I don't think it's me, screams. I grip the seat, clench my teeth, press my eyes closed.

Let out the parachute, man!

'Stand by for ditching!' calls the co-pilot.

Everything jars. And with a great splash, we land.

The plywood box, God love it, does not snap in half.

But it is sinking.

We won't be able to get the jeep or the guns out. We are supposed to unbolt the tail of the glider and swing it back, unloading the weapons, equipment, and vehicles. In the training exercises, we could get the tail off and the jeep out in two minutes flat. But now the tail is under water.

So are we, floating in the river, clinging to a drowning wooden box.

We hit the bank, and the men are already clambering out. I am so heavy with supplies I worry I will sink alongside the jeep, but I make it to the shore, spitting and swearing.

Rigby, one of the pilots, seems to have hit his head, hard, on the landing. Though he looks ready to faint at any moment he manages a smile as Lightwood and Hamilton, the other pilot, help him scramble on to the bank.

'You'll be all right, mate,' I say. Plastered with muddy water – his helmet is God knows where – his face under the mud is white as the moon. The soot meant to disguise his face has completely washed away.

'I'm cold,' he whispers.

I swallow hard, forcing myself to speak. 'You'll be fine. Let's get you out of this swamp, huh?'

He makes no response. I watch his heaving chest before forcing myself to look away, and take stock of the eerily silent landscape. The marshland is flooded, the water waist-deep. *It's not meant to be this flooded.* At least we're out of the glider, where everything shook like hell.

Major Roland looks at us, not at all sure he likes what he sees. He seems to have broken his glasses in the landing, but I know his searching look has more to do with the state of the unit than any vision problem. 'Come on, chaps. Time to get moving.'

We try. Rigby is not looking good, so we have to take turns holding him steady as we go. If only we had the jeep. Not that it would be able to move in this, but the poor bastard wouldn't have to stagger through the swamp. Everything smells of wet grass and mud.

The world seems to grow darker with each step. *What am I doing here?* I've never been outside England before – only once, to Aberdeen for training. I have no idea where I am, in a country run by the bloody Germans, with a rifle I've only ever fired at a wooden target. *You signed up for this, mate.*

The air is humid, and the quiet – the stillness – is like nothing I have known before. Morton, a portly fellow who was meant to drive the jeep, is dripping sweat next to me.

The Yanks can't be far behind. The Ox and Bucks lads who make up D-Company are some of the finest soldiers in the British Army, and Major has got this whole operation sorted.

I question the truth of that after five minutes pushing through the water. The weight of my gear is crushing – food, grenades, fuel, a small Tommy cooker. All that running he made us do back in Dorset – the miles and miles – doesn't seem to have helped much; then again, we were always running on dry land.

Other key points from training come back to me. *Take no prisoners. Two shots only: one to the stomach, one to the heart. Never look him in the face. Do not stop for wounded comrades.*

Well, we've broken that rule. We're practically carrying a dying man through the swamp. The water is getting deeper as we move ahead. We're going to get lost. *We're already bloody lost.* Behind enemy lines.

If you're lost, make duck calls.

The thought of the duck calls we learned is enough to make me laugh – a snorting, giggling sound.

Captain Pascoe turns. 'Squire. Knock it off.'

But I can't, and I go on sniggering until Lightwood wades over and grips my arm. 'Stop scaring the lads, Squire. They think you've lost your marbles.'

I notice the keen look – he's not sure they're wrong. The giggling finally dies into coughing. *I'm fine. I'm fine.* We won't have to kill anyone. Rigby will pull through. We just have to reach the bridge, and disarm it. That's all. And then the Yanks will arrive.

I nod to Lightwood and he drifts ahead; not too far ahead, I notice.

I'm fine. I'm doing a sight of a lot better than Rigby, who looks a few seconds away from slipping under the water and not coming back up.

Over the noise of splashing and panting, I can hear the hoot of owls in the distance. My skin crawls at the sound. I march on through the warm water, tightening my fingers around my rifle in the darkness.

Surely we've been walking for a month and a half before Major finally holds up a hand. It takes my whole soul not to collapse in the muddy water. The swamp slants dangerously around me, but I manage to focus as Major's voice reaches me.

'McCormick, did they get the other bridges?'

McCormick, who's in charge of the wireless, is silent. 'We lost frequency in the jump, sir.'

Lightwood steps forward. 'But… they won't know when we've got the bridge. Won't they think we've been shot down?'

Roland sets his jaw. 'I don't know what they'll think, Sapper. Keep moving.'

We have to complete the mission and send the success signal before 06.00 hours. Just how the hell are we going to do that?

The fields are less flooded here. We rush in, running in a crouch, still awkward if not as painful as it was in training. The lads spread out and – always – keep moving. There are no trees for cover, just swampland and distant fields.

I strain my eyes but see no cows. *They'll be asleep, of course.* But cows mean safety, of a sort. Cows mean there are no mines nearby. Gallagher, a mountain of a man with the eyes of a hawk, holds up binoculars but says nothing.

Finally, he speaks. 'There.'

Another hundred feet and I can see it, too. *The bloody bridge.* It doesn't quite look like the photographs – it's definitely a swing bridge, but I can't see the steel lattice that should be there.

But this is it. The men prepare their grenades, guns at the ready.

We reach the bridge, noticing too late the German sentry on the parapet. But his face is pure shock, and before anyone can even fire, he runs. His helmet sits abandoned. There is no sound.

The lads gaze around, uncertain, looking for the trap. Rommel will have set a trap. Where is the barbed wire?

'Squire. Lightwood,' Major calls. 'Get on these bombs.'

Lightwood gives a crisp salute. The fussy nature of the armed forces suits him. He's been saluting and standing to attention like he was born to do it. The whole thing puts my teeth on edge. I understand it, of course, in a time of war we need order and all that, but how is it going to hold once these Germans start firing on us?

Snapping to, I rush ahead, with half the men behind me, Lightwood making for the opposite side with the other half. My legs are wobbling.

The lads tie me in and lower me down on a rope. For once, they don't make a bollocks of it. In fact, I swing under the bridge smoothly. My boots slip, finally finding the struts of the bridge, and I start to climb to the middle. *A good bomb is always set at the weakest point. The weakest point is always the least accessible.*

Once I find the fuse, it should be smooth sailing. Major Roland forced me to master countless types of fuses and bombs during the gruelling months of training.

'Hurry up, Squire.'

'I'm... trying...'

Where are the blasted bombs? No luck that there's a detonation wire I can simply cut. Whatever it is, it's definitely not a 'hellbox'. But where are the wires? *That German will come back with a regiment if I don't hurry up and get this sorted.*

Gunshots split the air. A man drops from the bridge,

plunging into the river. Dead. I can tell from the cry that it was Bishop. Return fire lights up the night.

Silence.

'Just one,' someone cries. 'I got him.'

'Back to work on the bombs!' Major calls.

The Germans will have a better guard. It *must* be a trap. *The first sentry ran in the other direction. He's not going to keep this secret for us.*

'Squire, what do you make of the bombs?'

Search me, but I can't find the bloody thing. I look across at Lightwood, dangling in the darkness opposite me. He shakes his head.

I swallow, my throat tight with fear. 'There are none, sir.'

'What's that, Sapper?'

'The bridge isn't rigged to blow, sir.'

In confused silence, the men start pulling me up. I clamber on to the bridge and see Lightwood leaning against the rail, his figure telling us all we need to know.

Something's wrong.

'What do we do now, Major?'

'Form a perimeter defence round the bridge.'

A defensive position? For how long? We need to find the proper bridge. *The bloody swing bridge with the steel lattice.* The whole invasion might count on it. We *can't* set up shop for the night.

But that looks to be exactly what we're doing.

'Sir,' comes a whispered voice. 'I don't think Rigby's in a fit state. We might be losing him.'

The men help drag him over to the hedge that will

apparently serve as our defensive position. He is unconscious. Bishop is killed; Rigby well on his way. Our wireless is gone, so the others will think we're all dead, and they'll think the bridge is lost. And that German sentry is likely to bring all his pals back. Things can't get any more grim.

'What if he doesn't wake up, sir?'

Major doesn't answer. At that moment, all heads turn to the west. Into the deep night flies a huge red glow, lighting up the sky. The German sentry has carried his message.

The flare climbs into the night.

7 June 1944

A grey dawn breaks. We all stayed awake throughout the remaining night. A difficult act, considering Major's ban on cigarettes until sunrise. Now that the fear of giving away our position has passed, matches blaze and fag tips glow all around. Puffs of smoke mix with the morning mists.

We take turns washing our faces clean of soot in the river. It's almost enough to make one feel human.

My stomach is still queasy – maybe from the landing; maybe from nerves. The air is thick with the heavy scent of damp earth and swampy grass. The Germans did not come for us. Maybe that flare was for someone else – one of the other glider units.

'How's he doing?' someone asks.

There is no answer, but I can see Rigby from here, propped up against the ditch, eyes closed.

A huge noise, distant, fills the empty air. Guns. *Naval guns.* The Allies are here. Our reinforcements, but not close enough to help us. We're on our own.

The sun rises, burning off the mists; it is already threatening to be a hot day. That gets Rigby to open his eyes and look around. I'm not sure he knows what he's seeing, though. *Christ, we need to get him a doctor, fast.* I crush out a fag, and consider lighting another.

'To the east,' comes a whisper. 'Someone's out there.'

A figure is moving unhurriedly across marshy fields. A child – a girl. A French girl, likely as not, though it could be a scarecrow by how thin she is.

'Squire,' Major whispers.

'Sir?'

'Get over there, find out what's going on.'

What's going on? 'I don't speak French, sir. Send Hudson—'

'Just go over, hands up in peace. Ask her where the Christ we are. If any of the men go, they'll scare her off. You're close to her age. Go, Squire.'

Close to her age? This bloody... 'Right, Major.'

I hold up my hands and walk, slow even steps. The little girl has a bucket, which makes me think of Anna, feeding those blasted birds at the Tower. *Feels like a different life.*

The girl doesn't run. She just stares at me. Likely she thinks I'm a German. I have a French phrase book in my shoulder bag, but if I go reaching in there, she'll head for the hills.

'Hello. Hi. Do you know where we are?'

'You are British.'

'Yes. Can you tell me where I am, exactly?'

She peers over at the ditch where the men are hiding, clearly not afraid. 'You are the landing?'

'We are lost. Can you help us?'

There is something about her, like she's sizing me up. *Bloody French.*

'The Germans shoot anyone who helps the Allies.'

'You're not helping the Allies. Just tell me where we are. Please.'

This is taking forever. Major will be having kittens.

She keeps looking at me. 'You say you are not the landing and you are not the Allies. Why should I help you?'

'Because we're lost. Please, *merci*, tell us where we are.'

She shakes her head, amazed at my stupidity. 'The Dives.'

'This? This is the Dives River?' I say. 'Are you sure?'

'Of course.'

'We're on the wrong bloody river…' I trail off as she tilts her head at me. 'Do you know how to get to Robehomme?'

'*Robehomme?*' She pronounces it without half the letters. 'It is very close. I visit there with my pa on market days.' She gives me that long look again, before sighing loudly. 'I will take you.'

I swallow, glancing back at the ditch and the twenty cowering soldiers. *How will this go over?*

As I approach, the girl walking quietly by my side, the men watch us cautiously.

'Right,' I say. 'This here is the Dives River crossing, Major.'

'Meaning we're ten miles from our objective,' he says, nodding to himself.

My throat tightens. 'Meaning we're at the wrong bridge.'

He turns to me, eyes hard. 'Meaning we'd better get moving. Leave the girl.'

'I know the way,' she says.

'The marshes are flooded. You'll be drowned like a rat.'

'*Rat?*' she raises an eyebrow.

'He only means that it will be dangerous,' I intervene. 'And you don't want to be seen helping us. Thank you. Please go on with your day and say nothing about meeting us.'

She shakes her head but seems to accept this. When I glance back, she's filling up her bucket in the river. *Is she really going to drink that?*

'Wait!' I call, before hurrying back in a sloshing run.

'Squire!' Major shouts after me.

I reach the girl, who is looking at me with wide eyes. *I must be quick.*

'I don't want to get you in trouble,' I say, panting. 'But there is a British soldier – one of our men – he is badly hurt. We may have to... leave him behind. If there is anyone you could tell...' I trail off.

She says nothing, but I nod and hurry back, my guilt somewhat lessened.

'Do that again,' Major says as I re-join in the men, 'we carry on without you.'

'Yes, sir.'

We wade three hours across flooded fields towards Robehomme. How did the glider pilots mistake the River Dives for the Orne? *Swollen by the flooding*, someone muttered, but I'll need to hear a better excuse. *We landed on the bloody thing*. What happened to the maps? I thought this all had to be perfect? We may have lost the whole invasion.

I take my turn carrying Rigby, who is coughing and sputtering. When we finally put him down, I meet eyes with Major Roland. *Do not stop for wounded comrades.*

'We'll come back for him,' Major says firmly.

I nod, but I don't let go of Rigby's hand. I shake him, not gently, but he's out. *And we're going to abandon him in a swamp.*

We prop him up against the trunk of a thick tree, and Robinson puts his water next to his leg. And then we turn and leave. *Someone will come for you.*

The sun is hot enough to roast a French chicken. I keep my eyes skinned for machine guns posted in wheatfields, but there is nothing.

There is, however, a distant farm building used as a hangar for German planes. I can see a Messerschmitt 109 and a bigger transport plane waiting inside.

Again thoughts of Anna slip in. She can be a bossy old stick sometimes, especially around the ravens. But I just want to see her face again, hear her whistle to the birds, watch her face light up bright as her hair. Anna told me she loved me. She gave me back my Grampa's watch for good luck, and made me promise to come back. The watch always feels heavy on my wrist – I never did get used to wearing it. *But I'll take all the luck I can get.*

I'm coming back home to you, Anna. I promise.

As the morning lengthens, bombers appear in the western skies. I see the formation, recognize our own planes. I've studied enough aircraft spotter guides to tell the make and model from just the outline. The cavalry has come, but not for us.

There's going to be a hell of a fight on the beaches; but our mission is to secure a bridge that the men will need once the battle is won. We pause, smoke in silence, and hurry onwards again. No help is coming, for us or for Rigby.

We'll have to keep rowing our own boat.

2

ANNA COOPER

7 June 1944

The tall grass waves golden in the morning light. Here I am, in a field in Wales, standing next to a wooden bi-plane. Only a year ago, the thought of me flying a plane – even a basic wooden Trainer like this – would have been impossible to imagine.

A lot has happened in a year.

A lot has happened in the past day.

My head throbs as I double-check the petrol tank. The headaches are growing worse. Now darkness doesn't even help. Nothing helps. *Shove aside the pain, focus.* I've got more than enough fuel to get back home.

Last night I watched the endless planes fly across the sky, heading to France. The huge invasion force, staining the sky black with smoke. Britain and America, teaming up to invade France, kick the Germans out, and push all the way to Berlin and end this dreadful war.

It has finally begun.

Thousands upon thousands of ships, barrage balloons waving amid the armada, stony-faced men setting off to save the world. And I sat on the riverbank, watching the brave soldiers float into the sea.

What do I do now?

'Cup of tea?'

I turn to the voice – so strange and yet so familiar. A man stands in the doorway of the small cottage. A man I know mostly from a photograph. *Wilhelm Esser.*

Father.

Only two years ago I was certain I had no father; that he had drowned when I was five. Now he has returned, full of warnings about new German weapons. A man – a German – I know nothing about except the lies Mum told me. Now she's gone, and Uncle's gone, and this man – this stranger – is all the family I have.

And I must leave him behind.

He is watching me, seeming to read my thoughts. 'You *stole* that aeroplane. You will be arrested if you go back.'

I force myself to meet his eyes. 'I *borrowed* that Trainer. And I will take care of Commander Gower. Just tell me everything you know about these weapons.'

He finally nods, adding a new crease to his heavily lined face. 'I will tell you everything. But won't you have a cup of tea first?'

I take a small sip of the hot tea, savouring the real milk.

The old couple who own this cottage seem almost unaffected by the war. They live in the farmhouse across the field, and they did not raise an eyebrow when I introduced Father, his accent unnoticed. They fed us a dinner of mashed swede and carrots (they are not *completely* unaffected by the war) and once Father had offered some payment, the smiling farmer was happy to let us stay as long as we like.

People have grown used to accepting unlucky strangers into their homes.

I still remember when I heard, four years ago, that I was being sent to a new home. I can replay it all – sitting in the hot room, with the headmaster and the lady from the Women's Voluntary Service. How they told me Mum was dead, killed by a bomb, and that I was being sent to live at the Tower of London with an uncle I didn't know, while bombs rained down on us.

I look over at Father, sipping his tea at the low wooden table.

'Tell me about these weapons you built for Hitler.'

He sighs. 'I was offered a job, by an old friend who studied engineering with me in Berlin. We had studied rocket technology together.' Father drops his head. 'But when Hitler came to power, the research centre was forced to stop thinking about space travel. His research – our research – was used to build something else.'

He pours more tea into my cup. The sun is hot at the window, and the small kitchen suddenly feels even smaller.

'This is a weapon the world hasn't seen before. Hitler

wanted something, in case the war went wrong, that could save the day. Even back then, we called it the Miracle Weapon.'

I laugh, a harsh sound, unfamiliar in my own ears. 'I lived through the Blitz. We can take any weapon Hitler could throw at us.'

'This is different,' he cautions.

'What do you know about the lives of those on the other end of your bombs?' I swallow. 'Did you know what was happening here?'

'The moment I learned about the bombing of England, I ran away to come here – to protect you.'

'I didn't need your protection. Yeoman Oakes and the Warders at the Tower took me in, but I protected myself. You should have come back to protect Mum.' I think of Mum, crying behind the closed door, playing the violin he left behind. My voice hardens. 'She killed herself, you know. I'm not sure if anyone told you the truth. They told *me* she was killed by a German bomb, that her bus to work had been hit. But she gassed herself in the stove. Everyone lied to me, even Uncle Henry.'

She killed herself. I am not afraid to say it. But in truth, the thought terrifies me. She had these terrible headaches, too…

He nods stiffly. 'Your uncle was only trying to help, Anna. So I am.'

Since I was five, he has been just a stern face in a photograph, and some half-remembered music. Now, whatever else he is, he is alive.

'Well, I don't want anyone's help. Just please tell me how we can stop this Miracle Weapon.'

He gives a reluctant nod, but he does not have a chance.

A great bang rocks the door.

The smiling farmer is back. And this time he has a gun.

'Keep your voice down,' I say.

'You know,' Father says, amused, 'I lived here for years and no one recognized me.'

'That farmer sure did.'

He makes a noise that could be agreement and stops talking. I was able to convince the farmer – after several long minutes – that Father was in fact Dutch, not German. He finally relented, but it was clear we'd overstayed our welcome.

Together, Father and I walk among the London crowds. Father is wrong. Just as Hitler expected an invasion, Churchill anticipated a reprisal. Children and pregnant women are being evacuated from the city. Sandbags are stacked high in front of warehouses once again repurposed as air raid shelters.

We *are* ready. No matter how fancy these rockets are. I realize my hands are shaking and stuff them in my pockets. *We are ready. We have to be.*

These are people who have lived through war. Many are old – there are few young people among the crowds – and most are women. Women in summer dresses going to pray at the tomb of the unknown soldier – typists, perhaps, worried about their sweethearts, brothers, neighbours, friends.

Queues of women wait to get the evening papers, others to give blood, and others line up for fish. Some are quite elderly, others pushing prams. Wait, watch, and do what we can from home. It's the women's lot.

There is still food, at least. As we flew over to Wales, I saw every patch of dirt was used to grow food. We will feed ourselves, never mind what the war has to say about it.

'I can get rooms easily enough,' he says again.

'No. I can't risk you getting arrested.'

'Are you not taking me to a prison?'

I give him a withering look. 'It's the only place you'll be safe.'

'I thought you were trying to keep me away from this place.'

As we turn towards the Tower of London, I glance down at the docks, the ships still crammed in. More people will be fleeing to safety, I suppose – Canada, America.

Turning away, we march onwards to the Tower gate.

'Just pull your hat down. Lower,' I say as we cross the bridge and enter through the West Gate. We stay close to the inner walls. Most of the residents will be in and around the White Tower, so we need to keep as far from there as we can.

'The Warders will be on the look out,' I remind him in a whisper. 'And they *know* what you look like. I need to get you safely inside and then explain everything to Oakes.'

'I'm sure he'll be thrilled.'

The Tower is quiet, the Warders at their posts. Even the encampment of the Scots Guards battalion, usually a hive of noisy activity, looks mostly empty. I breathe a sigh of relief.

On the Green the new trees planted after the Blitz are now almost head-high. Yeoman Stackhouse stands by the roost, carrying on a one-sided conversation with a raven. He doesn't even see us pass by.

We follow the twisting alley towards the Casements. I steal another glance at Father. When he came to see me for the first time, during the Blitz, he seemed hunched, stooped. Now he stands tall. For the first time, I catch a glimpse of the strong, proud man from the old photograph.

Suddenly there is a voice behind us. 'Take one more step and it will be your last.'

Yeoman Oakes has a weapon at Father's head.

Father glances from the corner of his eye but does not move. 'I believe that's a ceremonial mace, Gregory.'

'I'm sure it's up to the task. Shall we find out?'

A raven jeers from the Green. I put my hands up, stepping towards Oakes. 'Yeoman Oakes. I have brought my father here. He might be able to help us.'

'Anna.' He doesn't take his eyes from Father. He is going to raise the alarm, and bring the whole Tower down on us.

'This man has deluded you into thinking you can trust him. Let me take care of him.'

'No, Yeoman Oakes,' I say. 'You don't understand. Put the mace down, please. I promise I will explain.'

'I have seen the damage caused by this man's lies. Your uncle, to his last days, remained convinced he was a good man. But you must trust me.'

Another raven calls out. They seem to be enjoying this little spectacle.

As Father speaks, his words are slow, cautious, and he keeps an eye on the mace as though it's a snake. 'I am trying to help.'

'Hitler not all he was cracked up to be?'

Father manages a small smile. 'He is a monster. And I helped him. Helped him develop a weapon.'

The mace is lowered an inch. I can see that Oakes's face is softening. *We might get out of this after all.*

At that moment, Yeoman Sparks appears. 'Good God, Gregory. That's the White Tower mace.'

'And this is a German spy.'

Oakes's face has hardened again. If only Sparks hadn't picked this moment to come round the corner. What can I do? Once the Warders have been alerted, there is no hope.

'I can explain,' I say, keeping my voice low. 'All of this. Just, please, can we move inside?'

The four of us stand uncomfortably inside the empty room. This building once housed Tower School, but it was badly damaged during the Blitz. No one will come in here.

'Anna, I am sorry, but this man is a Nazi.'

'I just need him to stay here – under your watch – for a little while.'

'Anna, that is impossible.'

'I need to be able to speak with him. He knows valuable things.'

Oakes sneers. 'What does he know?'

'He has information about upcoming German attacks. I have to pass the information on to the Air Ministry, but I need him to be safely hidden away.'

'I can't allow him to stay here,' Oakes says, but I can see him wavering.

'Please, just trust me.'

7 June 1944

Oakes, Father, and I stand on the south battlements under the stars. Father makes quiet remarks about the constellations; Oakes says stubbornly silent, despite his shared fascination for the night sky, and aggressively drinks wine.

I have learned some of the constellations, the Great Bear, the Big Dipper, Cassiopeia. Now that the blackout has been lifted, and people no longer fear to put their lights on, the stars are harder to see. But I know they are there.

Oakes is a tall man who radiates strictness. I remember

how imposing he was the first time I saw him, in his blue Warder's uniform and cloak, like the painting of an old king. Now I tend to see the laugh lines at his eyes, and the bald spot that has finally claimed his hair.

'So you will go to the Air Ministry?' he asks.

'Yes. I will tell them everything. Will Father be safe here, Yeoman Oakes?'

He is quiet for a long moment. 'He will be safe. I will speak to the others.'

'Thank you, Yeoman Oakes.'

'You have to call me Gregory, dear,' he says gently.

'Thank you, Gregory,' my father says in a quiet voice.

Oakes stares at him, unsure how sincere he is. 'Anna, would you care for another?' he asks, wandering over to the bottle. I nod and he loudly fills both of our glasses. Father, empty handed, wears a smile. The night air is cold and clean.

The wailing of the aid raid siren shatters our stillness. Raids are much less common now, but they still happen. Or something sets off the sirens. There comes a noise I catch, then lose, then catch again. *What is that?*

As I listen a loud buzzing can be heard over the siren. A strange engine noise I can't seem to place.

A dark object slides into view, angry flames trailing behind it.

'That's not a plane,' says Oakes, abandoning his wine glass.

'No,' Father says.

Oakes curses. 'We need to find a shelter, Anna. Now.'

'We don't have time,' Father says.

Oakes grips his arm. 'What is this?'

The buzzing sound grows to a steady drone. 'A V1 flying bomb.'

'What do we do?'

Father watches the sky. 'Hope.'

Oakes stares at me in horror. Father turns away, his steps strangely calm, and walks across the battlements to get a better view.

I can see it clearly, caught in searchlights about 2,000 feet above. Moving *fast*. So this is Hitler's vengeance. The bomb speeds closer, the great noise building. It is deafening.

Oakes moves to stand in front of me, a shield.

The noise vanishes. And so does the bomb.

Searchlights stab the suddenly empty sky. The bomb is dropping to its target, seconds from impact.

I remember being with Mum in the old sitting room, when the air raid siren wailed and we fell into our practised routine: filling the sink, dragging down the mattress, placing cotton-wool earplugs.

'*No one is brave, Anna, not truly. We only do what we have to.*'

I take the most basic precautions – back against the wall, hands over face, thumbs in ears and fingers over eyes.

The silence is total. I hold my breath as I count. Four seconds. Five seconds. Where is it? It could be anywhere. Just above us, or racing silently to some unsuspecting target? Seven seconds. Eight seconds.

Please, God.

Nine seconds. Ten seconds.

The world explodes.

The blast of scalding heat knocks me into the floor.

As I find my feet, gazing around, I see all the windows have blown out of White Tower, the doors rocked off the hinges. Warders cry out; people are covered in glass and blood. The bomb didn't even hit us, and the large crack in Martin Tower has opened wider.

The ache in my head strengthens. I am going to be sick. Staggering to the battlements, I peer over to the Thames below. Again, the docklands have got the worst of it.

Smoke curls among the ruins.

We would never have made it to the shelter. Even if we'd listened to Oakes and run the moment we heard the siren, we'd never have got close to safety. The thought settles on me like a weight. *No one down there made it to a shelter either.*

Oakes is white as a sheet, his eyes red.

'Those buzzbombs are nothing,' Father says.

'Sure as hell didn't feel like nothing.' Oakes glares at him.

'Compared to what is coming next...'

'What do you mean? Speak up, man.'

'Rockets.'

Oakes turns to Father, his eyes filled with anger. 'How do you know this?'

'I worked on the rockets,' he says quickly. 'That bomb you saw. The rocket you will never see. They fall from the edge of space, without a sound, faster than sound. There is no defence.'

'And the damage?' I force myself to ask. 'Is more than this?'

'Each warhead weighs 2,000 pounds. The rocket is 50 feet high, and carries a ton of explosives.'

I stare at him, anger rising up in me. *He helped build this weapon that will threaten so many lives. My father.* 'How many of these things do they have?'

'Thousands upon thousands,' he says, then adds, 'England will run out of things worth destroying before Germany runs out of rockets.'

Father swallows before beginning in a slow voice. 'I was a propulsion specialist, alongside my friend. The Reichswehr made us an offer. They would support the development of liquid rockets, but only if we would accept military terms and move the whole operation behind the fence of the military facility.

'We could not refuse – his financial situation was perilous. We argued but there was no choice. If we wanted to build and test a rocket, we had to become a military research programme. Conditions and restrictions were part of the cost.

'Once the war broke out, the SS took control.'

Oakes glances at me. 'I thought the Nazi war machine was spent. I thought Hitler was desperate, that defeat was closing in.'

Father nods. 'It is. He is desperate – and all the more dangerous. He will fire all of these rockets, destroy as much as he can.'

'Then let us hope the invasion keeps moving swiftly,' Oakes says.

'We can't just wait,' I counter.

Oakes turns to me. 'No. There is something,' he says, and folds his hands. 'The Chislehurst Caves. People lived in there during the Blitz. We could be safe there.'

Father seems to be considering the idea. I heard all the complaints about 'shelter slugs' during the Blitz – those people who refused to leave the shelter when the All Clear sounded, who refused to do their part and get on with it.

'Yeoman Oakes,' I say firmly, 'I am not hiding in some cave. We will find a way to stop these rockets.'

8 *June* 1944

'You've come to talk to me about the rockets?'

Sir Archibald, head of the Air Ministry, looks up from his great wooden desk. He has a thin face and a dark moustache with just a hint of grey. He has a stern look that matches his position as one of the most powerful wartime leaders in Britain.

'I'm just passing on information, sir. From my sweetheart. He's a sapper, and he knows all about bombs.'

'Oh,' he says, visibly relieved. He is a serious – and busy – man, and has little time to discuss weapons with a woman. 'Well, where is this bomb expert now?'

'Normandy, last I heard, sir.'

He nods, his attention already turning back to the papers scattered across his desk. 'Well, tell him not to worry. We've landed reinforcements in France and we are sweeping towards Paris as we speak. The Nazis have never seen a Blitzkrieg like this.'

'Yes, sir, it's just that—'

'You see, the Germans are in a defensive position – and with the Russians pushing from the east...' he shrugs, 'we're not worried about German attacks.'

'But the rockets will be – he thinks they will be – used as a last desperate act. They have countless rockets, and they won't stop firing them. They are very powerful.'

'My dear, I must tell you that we know all about these so-called V2 rockets. Don't look so surprised. Last year, we bombed Peenemunde into the ground as soon as we heard what they were building there. If they still have some rockets floating around, it's not worth the effort it would take to track them down.'

'Of course, sir.' I swallow. 'Ah, well, he did ask me to mention liquid oxygen.'

'What's this?' he says.

'It's how the rockets are fuelled, sir. It means they must rely on convoys to transport the rockets to fire from mobile sites. So… if you could recce the delivery systems – lorries and shipping – you can follow them to the source. He also mentioned that the rockets are assembled off-site and transported to secured locations by means of lorries.'

'Indeed? That is a surprisingly thorough knowledge of the enemy's weapon,' Sir Archibald says. 'Your sweetheart is a fine man. But I'll need every available aircraft supporting the ground offensive. Don't worry, dear. We have guns set up to deal with the incoming missiles.'

'But you can't shoot down a rocket – it's faster than sound, there'll be no time to even see it approaching, sir.'

He stands, a tall man despite the stooped shoulders. 'I appreciate your concern, and your eagerness to help. But do not worry, if they launch something like that from France, our men over there will stop them. I promise.'

'But—'

'My dear, the war will be over before Christmas, and you won't have to worry about rockets any more. And please thank your sweetheart for delivering this knowledge. We could use more young men like him.'

I feel myself shrinking. 'I will, sir. Thank you.'

'They did not believe you?' Oakes asks, casting a suspicious glance at Father.

I shake my head, but I feel my face flush red with

embarrassment. 'They know all about the rockets, but they don't think it's a threat worth targeting.'

'Well, we will keep petitioning them,' says Oakes.

I exhale slowly. 'That's not enough.'

I lived through the Blitz, and lost many people I loved. My friends, my uncle, my mother. These rockets are coming, and they will be even more deadly. I can't let it happen.

Oakes shakes his head. 'You heard what he said. There is no defence.'

'Then we need an offence. We need to track them from the air and destroy them before they ever get set up.'

'You?' Father stands.

Oakes gestures for him to sit. 'Please, Anna. You mustn't consider such a thing – it would be suicide.' He trips on the word, before rushing headlong into the rest of his advice. 'I mean, it would be foolish, and you would not be permitted.'

He's right. I am an Air Transport Auxiliary pilot only. The RAF will not let us fly an aircraft with weapons. The women of the ATA have flown everything – from bombers to Spits – but we are not permitted to engage the enemy.

'I must try,' I say.

'Anna, you can't. Not alone.'

'I won't be alone.'

3

TIMOTHY SQUIRE

7 June 1944

Damn Cecil Rafferty. It must have been his fault – perfect Mr RAF Pilot with his slicked-back hair. I remember when Major introduced us to our posh pilot, and the words sting as I hear them again.

'Don't worry. He's one of the RAF's finest. He'll put you in the right spot.'

Ha.

It doesn't matter that the glider pilots took over after the bomber let go of the towline. Obviously, Rafferty had already led us astray. That bastard has made a right mess of things. When I see him next, I'll wipe the public-school smile off his face.

For now I crawl though the marshland, brushing aside invisible strands of spiderwebs, the stink of rotting flowers in my nose.

Before long I can see a tall church and a road of stone houses. The small village looks quaint, with French men and women going about their days, but the SS have been running these towns for years. It is not safe.

As we get closer I can see most of the shutters are closed. *I don't envy the people inside.* It is hard enough to breathe in this airless heat. The place actually reminds me of Disley, that speck of nowhere Dad evacuated us to during the worst of the Blitz. I couldn't run back to London fast enough. If only I could run home now.

We can't go into the village. Besides the fact that the lads are seeing a German sniper in every shadow, we know the SS will execute anyone who helps us. I hope that girl doesn't get caught; I hope she can find some help for Rigby.

We need to get to the bridge, now. I remind myself of the instructions. *Don't accept anything offered by the French. Food and drink might be poisoned.* Have they really gone to the side of the Germans? They've been here for years now, but still… The bastards *invaded* them.

None of the villagers so much as looks over at us. No one even glances up; no one speaks. The Frenchmen hurry, stiff, to wherever they are going. As I watch, I begin to understand. A war has been fought here – fought and lost. London would look mighty different if Hitler had invaded us.

A boy races by on a bicycle, screaming in French.

'*Ils atterrissent! C'est vrai. La mer est noire de navires!*'

'What is it? What is he yelling about?' Captain asks.

Hudson nods, someone making sense of it. 'He's talking about the invasion. He says, *They're landing! It's true. The sea is black with ships!*'

The villagers seem happy to hear it, though I worry that may not last. About an hour ago I saw our bombers circling a city in the west – Caen, likely as not. They will have levelled it. Plenty of Germans in there, but plenty of French people too, I'll wager.

We move round the village, crossing the farmland and heading north. I inhale deeply: the countryside, the fresh air, the sun shining high in the sky.

A great rumbling noise echoes behind us.

'What's that?' I say before I can stop myself.

'Tanks,' says Gallagher, binoculars to his face.

'Tanks?'

'Major,' comes Gallagher's stern voice. 'They can't miss us.'

A long moment of silence as Major weighs our options. 'Into the village. Quickly.'

We turn back, running at a jog, heads down, until we pass into the churchyard, moving swiftly past the chipped gravestones.

Major holds up a finger and we stop. I am completely still, straining to listen, forcing my breathing to steady. We look faintly ridiculous, burdened with our packs and supplies, skulking in a churchyard. In front of us is a war memorial, a heavy stone cross. I stare at it, waiting. *Waiting for the tanks to pass. If they see us…*

And if some Frenchman has seen us? How can we trust them not to turn us in?

A heavy, metallic voice reaches us. The message is in many languages, even English.

'Stay indoors. Stay indoors.'

It is a German loudspeaker van, making its rounds through the village. *The tanks are coming next.*

It seems impossible that all the horrid things from life can suddenly seem like a lark. Sapper training was a nightmare of daily drills, kit assessments, weapon inspections. Being confined to quarters for days at a time leading up to the invasion. I never thought I'd miss any of that rubbish.

Unable to stand still, I step onto the stone memorial, peering back into the distance. I can see them, coming along a road from the east. Squat, invincible iron brutes of machines, reeking of diesel and oil even so far away. *Tigers. The most deadly of the German Panzers.*

No one makes a sound.

After an age the long column of tanks and motorcycles passes, but we stay motionless through the fading crunch of the caterpillar tracks. They're headed to the beaches.

Can our tanks best theirs? Tigers versus British Centaurs and American Shermans?

'Squire. Time to move.'

Well, we can't stay here, squatting behind some gravestones. Staying close to the houses, we slink through the streets towards the farmland ahead. Shadows of faces move behind windows, but all the villagers stay safely inside. We just need to pass through and keep heading west until we reach the bridge.

We are almost free of the bloody place when a harsh whisper comes.

'*Germans.*'

We sink beside a farmhouse. I peer round the wall, squinting, trying to see what Gallagher saw.

'More coming,' he says, breathless. 'A patrol. From the north. Coming in here.'

And so they are. I can see the bastards from here, waving to their mates headed to the beaches. Go on, lads – join your pals. Why are you coming this way?

We just have to stay quiet, hidden. Luck has sold me down the bloody river. Cowering, again – this isn't quite what Major Roland trained us for. Run, fight – move, move. Not hide, duck, whisper, pray.

The line of new Germans appears, moving swiftly into view. A squadron, chanting a song as they march towards the village. Helmeted, machine guns slung over shoulders, they look more like an escort than…

'Sweet Christ.'

McCormick punches my arm, but the Germans don't seem to have heard me. And I'm not certain I won't yell out again. What I am seeing is beyond belief. I know the man at the front of that group, would know that face at a mile.

It is Cecil Rafferty.

As I squint I see he has his boots tied around his neck, hands over his shiny head. A German soldier is behind him, submachine gun at his back. And twenty more soldiers are on his heels.

I knew I heard an explosion.

They shot his bomber down; likely captured him as he parachuted out. Somehow he still looks like a lord, out for a walk on his estate.

Engines announce more new arrivals from the north: motorcycles, with machine guns mounted on the sidecars. *It's like bloody Piccadilly Circus in here.*

The motorcycle soldiers wear the grey uniform of the SS. And they've come to take over control of Rafferty.

'Major,' I whisper. 'What can we do?'

Roland shakes his head. 'Stay out of sight.'

'That's Cecil Bleeding Rafferty they've got.'

'I don't care if it's Winston Sodding Churchill. We have an order. *Get to the bridge and take it.* Not to engage with enemy troops. Now stay out of sight, Sapper.'

'But, sir—'

'Quiet, man. For Christ's sake.'

Get to the target. No stopping. No fighting. No helping.

Motorcycles turn into the village, one by one, and Rafferty is gone. But the patrol is not. And one of the ugly bastards is looking right at me.

We run, gunshots sounding behind us. The knot in my throat gives way to a scream. Stupidly, the unit has split in at least three directions.

Captain Pascoe is leading our retreat, with me and Lightwood on his heels. We stay low, stopping frequently to listen for sounds of the hunting Germans. Pressed up against the side of a house, my ears ringing, my thoughts scrambling, I look Lightwood in the eyes. *We're trapped.*

We should've stayed with Major. I heard him cursing us as we ran but, well, Pascoe was faster so I followed him.

The view down the alley is a right mess. We are outnumbered many times over, and the patrol is spreading out to surround us. The familiar nausea is rising in my chest. We need to move, now. Captain Pascoe gives a stiff nod.

I remember what Dad said the first time I got hurt playing football. *Always keep your head up, son.* I take a deep breath, sink low, and stay low; but with my head up and my eyes skinned. We slip round the corner, and hurry back towards the churchyard. Hopefully the others are there, waiting.

We may have lost the rest of the unit, but we also left the ugly bastard in our dust…

Until he suddenly emerges from a yellow door in front of us, firing like a maniac. I dive behind a wall, scraping my knee on the hard cobblestones.

'That's the same bloke,' I pant. I don't know how, but I know it's true. Frenzied shooting echoes down the alley. *That ugly Nazi should be well behind us.* 'What the hell is going on?'

'Tunnels,' says Captain Pascoe, his face sheet-white.

'Tunnels?'

'They've dug tunnels under the houses, likely running through the whole town. We need to get out of here, get to the bridge and wait for reinforcements.'

He takes out a grenade, and gestures for me to do the same. Finally, something we learned in training will come in handy. I fumble the grenade from my pocket. My thumb holding the safety lever, I thread my finger through the pin and pull it firmly out.

'Ready?' he says.

'Ready.'

With a wordless scream, we each hurl our grenades towards the gunfire, and under the cover of the blast we make our move. Fire and smoke rages behind us.

Oh how proud Major would be. He's never seen three soldiers run so bloody fast.

We race through the rippling cornfields. It is impossible to see anything through the tall, waving grass. Germans could be hidden anywhere in there. I thought war meant blasted lands, men hiding in holes – then at least you could *see* the bloody enemy when he charged you.

The farmer's field is chaos. Sounds of gunfire and screaming churn in the air. My bones turned to water hours ago. I wish hopelessly for a shield, like the ones Dad took care of in the White Tower – silver, engraved with three red lions.

No, a shield wouldn't help, not here.

There are more and more guns, machine guns and rifle fire. We are running, falling, rolling into bushes, racing back towards the distant marshlands we came from. Bullets thump and sink around us. Smoke and dust hang in clouds.

'Over here, lads!'

I dash madly towards the voice. A sweet British voice.

Our boys are packed in a ditch like sheep.

Captain Pascoe, once leading the charge, is now a few steps behind. Lightwood and I reach the ditch first, and just in time to see Pascoe fly through the air like a doll.

I've tumbled into the mud, and now stare into the haunted faces of the men who came in that glider. *Those of us who are left.*

'About bloody time, Squire!' Major yells.

Nausea rushes up, but I don't have time to be sick. The lads are planning a charge. Oh, I remember this bloody poem from school. 'Charge of the Cock-up Light Brigade.' Everyone bloody dies. On my knees, I stare at Lightwood, certain this ends badly.

Major Roland calls out. 'Remember your training! Stick together. Let's deal with these bastards!'

And, bless the mad sod, he scrambles out of the ditch and rushes ahead, keeping low. But keeping low isn't enough. Rifle fire takes him in the head, puncturing his helmet. Major slides to the earth, dead.

Hamilton cries out, leaping to his feet his gun already firing. He only makes three steps before a rifle bullet drills a hole in his chest, knocking him back into the ditch. His eyes turn to glass as he sinks to the mud.

Lightwood roars and moves to climb out before I grasp his arm, yanking him back. He tumbles on top of me, cursing in shock, but I squeeze his arm tighter.

'Stay down, man.'

I'm not certain he's going to listen. The others definitely

aren't. Cries rise up as they storm out in a mass of guns of grenades. Bodies flail and fall, while Lightwood and I huddle in the ditch, just able to see the few feet around us – which is swiftly becoming a butcher's yard. Gallagher is done, and a machine gun tears McCormick clear in half.

My eyes snap shut, but it's too late. I vomit again and again, my throat burning. When I open my eyes, tears blur my sight. Shrinking as small as I can, I curl up in the ditch.

Bullets shriek above. Tensing, I harden my muscles to become somehow stronger, thicker, an impossible shield of flesh and bone against the mechanical rage of the guns.

My eyes closed, teeth biting into each other, I pull my body tighter and tighter into a circle, a ball, a nothing. The earth explodes all around me. Without a thought, without noticing, my voice rises up, a high pitiful howl which I cannot stop, which doesn't come from any part of me that I can control. Some great violent uncontrollable surrender.

The guns fire on, and my spirit howls.

'Squire.'

Lightwood crawls towards me. He looks at me, eyes wide. Above the guns have stopped. The sun is low in the sky. How much time has passed?

'Lightwood,' I cough. 'You smell like a rotting jockstrap.'

Laughter burbles to his lips, but then he is choking, gasping, sobbing. He does not stop.

My thoughts are dangerously slow. Is the battle over? Have the Germans left? Or are they making their casual way over here to finish us off? I think of Mum and the horrid letter she'll get from the Ministry of War. But right now it's Lightwood who looks like he's about to split. I lean against him, our backs pressed against the muddy wall of the ditch.

'Lightwood, mate,' I say, my voice cracking with thirst. 'You ought to meet this girl, Anna's friend. Florence Swift. She's proper pretty. A damn sight too smart for you, but you could try your luck. You two would hit it off in a heartbeat.'

He doesn't respond for a long moment, and I worry that I've lost him. *No, damn it, don't give up. If you go, I'm gone. We'll be blathering like babies in here. Be strong, mate.*

There *are* tears in his eyes, but he blinks them away. 'Had a girl once, back in school. Helen. She was smart. Funny too. Imagine what it would be like, having someone funny in here instead of you?'

I muster a laugh, but it comes out as more of a cough.

Silence falls. The adrenaline that kept me running for hours has turned sour. Where is everyone? Dead, I remind myself. Since we've landed we've lost Bishop, Rigby, Pascoe, McCormick, Hamilton, Major Roland – the whole bloody unit. And Rafferty is as good as dead.

In between shell bursts, the field is quiet, the wounded having screamed themselves hoarse, the dead silent. Hamilton's body is in the ditch with us. I stare at him, lying still, his shin bone sticking out of his trousers.

'Lightwood,' I say. 'Give me your hand.'

'What?' He eyes me, wary.

'Your hand. Please, mate.'

He inches closer, slumps against me. 'You going to read my palm?'

I don't answer. Instead, I take his hand, hard and calloused, and hold it in my own. His fingers are cold, lifeless, like squeezing a dead fish.

'We're not going to die in here, OK?'

He nods, but his eyes are blank. I squeeze his hand again. 'Lightwood. I love you, mate. You're my brother, OK? I'm sorry about all the mad things that got us here. You've really got to stop listening to me. But I'll get us out of here, somehow. We're not going to die here, all right? Christ, man, can you hear me?'

'You always did talk rubbish, Squire.'

His voice is a dry rasp, but his hand grips back until it hurts.

'I promised Anna I would come home. I *will* come home, and so will you. All right?'

Lightwood and I stay crouched in our foxhole as night falls. This is a disaster. A full-blown cock-up. We're trapped in a ditch not two miles from the village, which has knocked Quarter's office off top spot of worst places in the world. Hell itself would be to spend another moment in this blasted place.

The first-aid box in the bag slung around my neck comes

into my thoughts: bandages, and two needles of morphine. *One for pain, two for eternity.*

Unless the patrol has given us up for dead?

Still, we stay put, terrified our first move will be our last. From our hiding place we can see the lights to the north. At night German bombers arrive to blast the ships at anchor. I stare up at the bombers, flying low. You can almost feel the heat of the exhaust. Anti-aircraft tracer fire lights up the night. Then comes the well-spread, massive explosions. The biggest fireworks I've ever seen, but the last thing I want to do is watch. We sit in the ditch, waiting out the darkness.

I stare into the packet with three fags inside, which is all the tobacco I have left in the world. I light one, trying to remember a time I hated the taste of these things. The smell wards off the putrid stench of rotting bodies all around us. *The rotting bodies of my friends.*

Lightwood though keeps me from thinking too much about the others.

'We can't get caught,' Lightwood says. 'I've heard all the stories. They'll snip off our balls.'

'All right, mate.' I cough. *Snip off our balls?*

I know what he means, though. Major told us they send out men to prod the corpses, make sure no one's faking being dead. The bloody cigarettes might give us away, I think, but still puff the thing down before I crush out the end.

What do we do? What can we do? I run through our options. We don't have any. All we have are two smoke grenades, a Mills grenade, pistols, one rifle (Lightwood lost his in the panic), and a knife. Hardly the stuff to battle a German patrol.

I think of Anna. She won't be surprised. *Landed at the wrong bridge; killed on the first day.* They don't put that sort of rubbish on medals. Not that I did any worse than Lord Rafferty. Shot down and taken prisoner and God knows what else. What a tit.

And Anna is all alone, with that good-for-nothing Nazi father stalking her. I should have left it alone. Once I discovered her father was hiding in the city, I should have gone to the Scots Guard, or at least told Oakes and the Warders at the Tower. Instead I brought her right to him. A raving madman.

Rafferty might not be dead. Not yet. He'll have information they want – maps.

'What about the bridge?' says Lightwood, who is starting to look like his usual ugly self again.

'Forget the bridge. The Germans bloody well know we're here now.'

'What then?'

I search my mind, but it's the only idea I can find. *Sod it all.* We can't let the Germans catch us hiding in here, we need to move. And why not go for it, and get properly out of this hell? We can go home, go back to work at the docks, if Quarter will have us.

A daring rescue mission. Well, they won't be expecting that from us.

'Back at that farm building,' I say, slowly. 'There were two planes. One was a transport plane.'

Lightwood looks at me. 'You've pulled off some mad plans before mate, but there's no way you can fly a bloody aeroplane.'

I cough, clutching the cigarette pack. My heart is galloping in my chest. This could be even worse than the glider. Might even be worse than running back into that patrol. Lightwood has lived through too many of my schemes already. He covered for me when I sneaked out of the base on a motorcycle to see Anna. God, it was me who messed up the fuse that got us both kicked out of sapper training in the first place. He deserves better than this.

Well, I don't see a lot of other choices. A sapper's got to use his head – or what's left inside it, at any rate. I'm not sure I've got the strength left to do this, but like hell I'm going to let him know that.

'No,' I say. 'But I know who can.'

'Rafferty?'

'Rafferty.'

'Posh bastard,' he says. He coughs blackly. 'What if the planes are gone by now?'

'They won't be. Trust me.' *It's our only choice.*

I rise to my knees, peering over the lip of the ditch, scanning the field for suspicious German soldiers. There is no one living in sight.

'Well?' he says.

I turn to Lightwood, who's looking at me expectantly.

'You've got a plan for springing Rafferty, haven't you?'

I nod, raising the packet of fags and offering it to him

before taking the last one for myself. If we're going to attempt something this mad, we'll need a cigarette first. 'I do. And you're not going to like it.'

4

CECIL RAFFERTY

8 June 1944

The thin sludge slips through my fingers as I try to eat it.

I'd laugh if my throat wasn't so raw. Even with the liquid of the sludge, my throat is too dry. I need water, and soon.

'You like your meal, Tommy?' The mocking voice behind the bars comes from the SS officer who caught me and has become my gaoler. He is quite devoted to his task, certain I have information he can use. He seems to be a man of some military importance – an SS colonel, maybe even a general. I do not look up, but I can see the highly polished boots through the bars.

'And how is your leg? Must have been a rough landing.'

I don't answer his taunts. *Let the little Hitler rail.*

'Our first British prisoner. You must be very proud. We are taking you to the Gestapo, and you will tell them everything you know about the invasion plans. Oh, how you will talk.'

The boots disappear. I empty the bowl into my mouth. My RAF training has prepared me for considerably worse than this.

If we are marked to die, we are enough
To do our country loss; and if to live,
The fewer men, the greater share of honour.
God's will, I pray thee, wish not one man more.

Shakespeare, at such a time. Well, Father would be proud. Mother would expect me to be brave. Elizabeth would expect nothing less from her big brother.

Anna, though; my mind wonders what she would think. She would think me a great fool. *She will not think of you at all. She chose that little runt, Timothy Squire, who's off with his division having a nap on a bridge.*

Anna decided I was a bit dotty, asking her to get married. I didn't behave quite properly and she saw that. Far too many of the lads are married now, and practically all of them are engaged. It was a year ago, but I can still feel the heavy sense of shame. I acted too quickly, impudently. This damn world is changing.

I remember that night at the Lansdowne club. A small party, and the nurses and WAAF girls sat like puddings the whole evening. But Anna danced, alongside her friend, the American girl. The lads all watched, grinning like cats. She looked young, not a day over seventeen I'd wager. She was marvellous.

We kissed, during the dancing, and I invited her back to

the bar in my hotel for a goodnight tipple. She went cold as a fish and shook my hand goodnight. *I knew I was in trouble from that moment.*

I was with Nell, the Cleopatra of East London. As jealous as, too. Nell lectured me like a Mother Superior the next morning, though I was still drunk for most of it.

I lick my fingers clean, then stare out of the bars in the heavy silence. A distant woman slips off into the shadows.

Who are these villagers, living under Hitler? Could London end up like this? Oakley Park, the family estate? People just quietly going about their business. Father and Mother? Elizabeth?

Not that I can do anything about it, locked away in here with the rats. No, the rats can get out. I am the only one trapped here – until the Allies reach me. In truth, some of the divisions should be here already. Not that the Gestapo could make me talk, whatever they try. But a division flying the Union Jack would be a happy sight indeed.

I thought for certain they had come already. As soon as the SS came on their motorcycles, a battle broke out. I heard the guns, waited, but nothing happened.

An explosion shatters the silence. For a moment I don't move, worried that I imagined it. But no, the Germans are yelling, a motorcycle engine coughs and fires up. This time, the Allies have come.

I drag myself to the bars, straining to see out, to see anything. There seems to be a great deal of shouting, but little else. The guards have scattered, no doubt taking up defensive positions. *By George, they've truly arrived.*

With a surge of hope I rise to my feet, my broken leg throbbing, and cling to the bars waiting for the rescue squad – maybe it's the unit I dropped off, or the lads that landed at Caen.

Nothing happens. I strain my ears, certain the Sherman tanks will be part of the eastward push. But I can't hear anything.

Then a small hand clangs the bars, and a British soldier is there, leaning over, panting heavily. He looks to be alone.

'Good God, man.' I exhale deeply. 'Where is everyone?'

The soldier is still catching his breath, head down. *Where are the others? Where are the tanks?*

'Can you blow this door?' I ask.

Finally the face turns up at me. I take a step back into the cell, my leg screaming in pain. No words come.

Timothy Squire.

'Happy to let you stay as long as you like, Rafferty – but we can't risk you telling Hitler all our plans.'

Telling Hitler…? I force myself to breathe. Timothy Squire, a little sapper, comes to a fortified village alone? Madness.

'Where is the cavalry?'

He doesn't answer, instead rummaging around in his pack. He pulls out something and holds it up to the lock. A safety pin.

'I am the cavalry.'

'Oh, for God's sake... *This* was the CO's plan, to have a junior sapper come and try to pick the lock? I may as well sit back down and wait for the SS troopers to come—'

With a smooth click the lock opens, thuds to the ground.

Timothy Squire swings the gate open. He doesn't even have a rifle.

'Can you run?' he asks.

'No.'

'Well, let's go.'

I take his outstretched hand, and together we stagger down the cobblestone alley. My leg sends fire through me. Moving is torture beyond whatever the Gestapo had planned.

'Where are they?' I ask.

Timothy Squire drags me on, a damn sight faster than necessary.

'The others, Squire. Where are they? I thought the whole unit was here.'

'So do the Germans, hopefully. Let's keep moving.'

'What? Is it really just you? How did you make that explosion?'

'I didn't.'

This urchin. How does Anna put up with him? I pull up, stopping us. Enough is enough. I will not be played like a sodding pipe.

'What? The two of us, with no weapons?'

He cuffs at his running nose. 'I've got plenty of weapons, mate.'

'Safety pins?'

The rev of a motorcycle. Squire's little ruse is up. They'll be coming now – all of them.

'We'll get a hundred yards before they shoot us,' I say.

'You want to go back? I'm getting out of here.'

As we run, the occasional head peers out of a window before retreating. It'll be harder to find just the two of us – they'll be looking for a proper unit of soldiers – but we'll be spotted soon enough, limping through the empty streets. *Why in the devil didn't they send more men?*

'Why?' I ask finally, as we collapse against the side of a house. The wall is rough-hewn stone, but at this moment it is more comfortable than swan feathers.

'You talk, the invasion fails.'

I resist the urge to punch him full in the mouth. Barely. 'Talk? You think I'd tell the SS the invasion details?'

'I think the SS would get those details from you, and every other little secret you've ever kept. Don't get taken alive.'

A yell from behind us gets us moving again. I'd love to see how long Mr Tough Bollocks East End would last in an SS cell. Soon the pain in my leg pushes all thoughts from my mind.

'What's your grand plan here?' I manage to speak around the panting. 'You play the hero, and then Anna falls madly in love with you?'

'That's your first decent idea, Toff. I suppose you are capable of them.'

The sound of motorcycles is now behind us *and* in front

of us. We're running towards a row of cottages, and they're surrounding us.

Squire pulls me round a corner, straight towards a small cottage with a yellow door. He barges inside, and we fall heavily on to the wooden floor.

I scramble to my feet in the sudden dimness. We are standing in a surprisingly clean front room.

'What the hell are we doing in here?'

Squire is staring around like a fool. What is he doing?

'Look, you toff!' he says.

'For what?'

Footfalls on the stairs and a man in a vest appears in a torrent of French.

'Back upstairs!' Squire points his finger. 'Now.'

The man is gone as swiftly as he appeared. Squire continues scanning the room.

'What are you looking for, man?'

'Something – ah!' He kicks a heavy rug across the floor, uncovering a hatch.

'The cellar? That's the first place they'll look—'

'In.'

He shoves me down, leaping in after me, and pulls the hatch closed. Stale air rushes to greet me. My leg roars in fury.

Even in the darkness, one thing is certain – this isn't a cellar.

Squire has his knife out. 'Quiet, and follow me.'

'What is this place?'

'Our way out of here.'

We race down the tunnel in a crouch, splashing in puddles. No one else is down here – yet. A sharp smell of mud makes it difficult to breathe deeply. Other hatches can be dimly seen above us, connecting to other houses. It appears the Germans have taken advantage of tunnels once part of medieval stone quarries and built their own connecting tunnels.

We stop, both gasping in the damp, airless passage.

'What are we looking for? A lot of good it will do us to pop up into a house filled with SS soldiers.' I swallow, forcing myself to stay calm. I lean against the wet stone, taking the weight off my leg for a blissful moment. 'You don't know the way out, do you?'

'Not yet. But I will once we get close enough.' He shakes his head, turns and looks at me. 'Any guesses?'

I close my eyes, struggle to block out the pain, the exhaustion, the stupidity of this boy and his schemes. 'The smell – it doesn't smell like there's any air close by. Maybe we should have taken that last turning.'

I open my eyes to see him nodding. 'Fine.'

We double back, and the air does smell clearer as we move on. Unless this is bringing us back the way we came. A glance at Squire shows he's thinking the same thing.

If we somehow survive, I will always have nightmares of black walls, horrible dripping ceilings, and rank heat.

German voices well out of the darkness. *They are coming.*

We dash round a corner but Squire abruptly pulls up, and I slam into him, almost spilling us both into the water below.

'That way,' he pants, pointing down the other branch of the tunnel.

'How do you know?'

Behind us the German voices grow louder. Yelling – they must have heard us.

'The smell,' he says, abandoning whispering and splashing ahead. 'Vinegar.'

'*Vinegar?*'

A bullet whizzes off the wall behind me.

'Run!' he yells.

I run, my leg a blaze of pain threatening to black out my thoughts. *Run, keep running*. There are just enough corners to keep us alive, the German guns unable to find a clean shot. Yet.

The air is getting thinner and I realize I can't keep up. *Sorry, Elizabeth. I'm not the hero you think I am*. I slip in the mud, my leg finally giving out.

'I'm done,' I hiss. 'Just go.'

'Get up, you tosspot.'

He hauls me dripping to my feet. I can't go on. I am positively knackered. But with each gulp of air, I too can smell vinegar. Another bullet fires, the blast a terrifying echo along the tunnel.

'There!' Squire yells, racing forward. 'Phosphorous!'

Phosphorous? A German is on my heels. I am going to die, in a tunnel, racing after a street urchin from East London.

Any moment now I will feel the German's bullet in my knee – they will shoot for the knees, to question me again, before executing me. I run headlong into a huge cloud of white smoke.

Instantly I hold my breath, but I am lost in a world of white.

So too are the Germans behind us, cursing and swearing – but still firing into the strengthening mist. My hands are shaking madly, my head is staring to spin – only the pain in my bloody leg keeps me alert. Am I being poisoned? Suffocated?

'Lord Toff!'

Dazed, I peer through the roiling fog, seeking the voice. Above the dense white cloud I can just make out something. The last thing I could have imagined.

I reach out my hands, feel the receiving grip as I am hoisted up through the hatch. Even as I am pulled free of the tunnel, and the heavy hatch slams shut behind me, I still see it.

The grinning face of Timothy Squire's little bodyguard, Arthur Lightwood.

As he pulls a desk over the hatch, Lightwood glares at me. All sign of the black eye I gave him is gone, but apparently not forgotten. In fact, I can still remember the punch he gave me. *Cheap shot, of course, after he rugby-tackled me to save me turning Squire in a punchbag.*

At least he's got a bloody rifle.

'What the hell was that?'

'Smoke bomb,' says Lightwood.

Squire sheaths his ridiculous knife. 'Like I said – phosphorus.'

'Where are we going?' I say, looking between them. 'Tell me now, or I don't move another step.'

Squire looks down at me with red eyes. 'I've just seen my mates torn to bleeding shreds by these bastards. I don't care if your leg is hanging by a thread. Stop whinging, you're coming with us.'

'Are you threatening me?'

Squire gives an elaborate sigh, shoving a chest of drawers on top of the hatch for good measure. Fingers of smoke leak up through the floor. And voices – they'll find a way up here soon enough – phosphorous or not.

'A hangar, just east of here,' he says. 'Saw it on the way in.'

'You saw a hangar?'

'I saw inside a hangar,' Squire says. 'And there's a transport plane.'

I grit my teeth; the weight of this news sinking in. *This is all starting to make sense. The sod* did *have a plan.* 'You need me to fly us out of here.'

'Well, we didn't pick you up for your good looks.' He tries a smile. 'Think you can fly it?'

'Of course I can fly it.'

'Then let's get moving.'

Lightwood forces a smile of his own. 'Maybe try not to drop us in a bog this time.'

We move swiftly from the house, Squire and Lightwood between them holding me up. We are just outside a churchyard at the outskirts of the village. The nearby fields have been blasted to ruin, the grass scorched away by grenades and torn up by machine guns. But there it is – a hangar in the distance, not a mile away, and untouched by the battle.

'Halt.'

A group of German soldiers steps out from round the corner. An ambush. We're surrounded; it's over. For the second time in as many days, I raise my hands in surrender.

The Nazi leader steps to the front, holding a submachine gun.

'Tommies, you cannot escape—'

A great blast of red, and the leader's dented helmet crashes to the ground, then his lifeless – his headless – body thumps the cobblestones. There is a shout and the second man falls.

Silence.

A new solider steps to the front, all smiles. 'You are British, yes?'

Squire finds his voice before I do. 'Yes.'

'We are Polish.'

And the man laughs. They all laugh. I still haven't found my breath, but I slowly lower my hands.

A Polish squadron under the charge of two German sergeants – apparently their loyalty isn't as strong as Hitler would hope.

'So this is the great invasion?' The Polish soldier says amid the continued laughter.

'More are coming,' I answer. 'I promise.'

He nods and kicks the dead man's gun towards us. 'Go. You killed them. We may chase you again.'

I grab the heavy gun, and we're off again, the two smaller men holding me up.

'No chance that was part of your plan,' I grunt.

He has the nerve to smile. 'A little luck is always part of the plan.'

A roar of motorbikes close behind us, followed by screaming voices. The Germans have found their dead men. Gunshots ring out. *Looks like they found the killers too.* I say a quick prayer in my mind for the brave Poles.

Motorbikes thunder closer and I glance back to see the grey uniforms – not forced Polish recruits this time. The SS officer and his men have arrived.

We race for the hangar.

The SS officer can't be shaken off. Squire keeps looking back, which slows him down. Soon, even I have lumbered ahead of him. Exhausted, we run in silence, staring only at the farm building – so close now, barely a cricket field away.

'Squire,' pants Lightwood.

'What?'

'The planes.'

'What about them?' Squire asks.

'There's only one.'

He keeps running but he's turned white as a ghost. He is looking at Lightwood. 'There were two.'

Lightwood's voice is still low. 'There's only one.'

I squint at the plane crouched in the hangar, recognizing immediately the contour of the body and shape of the wings. 'That's a Messerschmitt 109.'

Lightwood reaches the hangar and I'm barely a step behind. I slow to a stop at the sight of the plane. *Timothy Squire. You ignorant little urchin. You've doomed us all.*

Squire has basically arranged my execution. And his own, but that's little comfort. I turn to Lightwood, for a moment feeling genuine pity.

'OK, Christ.' Squire is finally showing some panic. 'OK. Rafferty, you take Lightwood and get out of here.'

I stare back, feeling like this all must be some dream. 'It's a 109,' I say slowly. 'A single cockpit fighter – barely fits a man with room to reach the controls.'

'Surely you can fit him somewhere—'

Gunshots settle the debate.

'No one's getting in that plane,' I say.

'You are,' Squire says. He turns to Lightwood, handing over a pack of food and weapons. 'Take everything. Christ, I'm sorry, mate. Run. In the other direction from this plane – they'll be after him.'

'No,' he says. 'I'm with you, mate.'

'Get stuffed,' Squire says. 'You're getting out of this one.'

I shake my head. 'No one's going anywhere. They'll catch us first.'

'I have a plan,' he says, rummaging through his pockets.

'A good one.' He pulls free a paper – a map? – and for a second a smile breaks across his face. 'If this works, I might just make good after all. Now get moving, both of you. Rafferty, keep an eye on Anna while I'm gone. Lightwood, mate, I'll see you back at the Fox and Hounds.'

And with that he runs back towards the approaching motorcycles, paper held high above his head.

Lightwood hits me, knocking me out of my daze. His eyes are red. 'Fly that bastard out of here.'

It's a 109, similar enough to ours. The gents at the aerodrome have taken apart a few, compared engines and wings. I can fly this plane in my sleep. But that's not the issue here.

'What? What about you? I can't leave you here.'

'You're a rubbish distraction, Rafferty. They're going to try to take you down. I'd hurry up, by the way.'

'And you're just going to run in the other direction? This is mad.'

I turn back. Of all the absurd things I've seen today, this clinches it. Timothy Squire, hands raised, surrounded by a semi-circle of SS soldiers. He is holding up that map in his hands.

'I'm not leaving him behind,' I say, surprising myself.

'You have to,' Lightwood says, nodding. 'They'll kill us all. Fly.'

He's not wrong. Whatever Squire's game with the map is, it's not working. Machine-gun fire pings off the plane.

I stare at him, Squire's little bodyguard. He won't last an hour, no matter how many bombs he has. He doesn't even have a rifle.

There is nothing I can do.

'Fly, you tosspot!'

I throw Lightwood my gun and hurl myself on to the wing, reaching for the cockpit. With fumbling hands, I find the latch, shove open the canopy and tumble inside. The pain that shoots through me cuts the world to black. Another bullet tings off the plane.

I force the darkness away, focus. I know I can do this. I *have* to do this. I wrench the canopy closed and my hands go to the control column, finding the switches, and the engine roars to life.

Through the windscreen, I gaze wildly at Lightwood, meet his grim stare. Glancing past him, I see Squire, the little sod of a sapper, facing down a circle of SS.

I taxi to the middle of the hangar; the black spiral of the propeller is small and furious compared to the great paddle blades of a Lancaster bomber. Can this plane get out of here in one piece?

With a bang the throttle kicks in. The plane jumps wildly as it picks up speed, the heavy rattle of the rotors drowning any other sound. It's got some guts after all. The Messerschmitt lurches free of the hangar.

The nose of the plane lifts, straining, off the ground. I rise, the wings, the tail, the wheels – lifting in full flight over the ruined field – and in one horrifyingly slow moment, I am the easiest target in the world.

But the killing blow doesn't come. Or not for me, at any rate.

When I finally exhale, the only sound is the wind. I say

a silent prayer for Timothy Squire and his bodyguard. The last sound I heard as I took to the skies was the bang of a revolver.

II

A NEW FEAR

'Now in my dial of glass appears
the soldier who is going to die.
He smiles, and moves about in ways
his mother knows, habits of his.
The wires touch his face: I cry
NOW. Death, like a familiar, hears
and look, has made a man of dust
of a man of flesh. This sorcery
I do. Being damned, I am amused
to see the centre of love diffused
and the waves of love travel into vacancy.
How easy it is to make a ghost.'

How to Kill, Keith Douglas

5

ANNA COOPER

9 June 1944

Without even a glance at Stonehenge during the descent, I land smoothly at Hamble airfield. The afternoon sun is strong and warm.

I nod to the flight engineer and make for the crew room. Hamble is the only all-women ferry pool, and I smile to see the female drivers, officers, and engineers bustle across the site. This place already feels like a second home to me. I make my way towards the small, single-storey brick building, but before I get there, I see who I'm looking for.

Joy is in the hangar opposite.

It is strange to see her in her flight uniform. Only a year ago we were huddled among rocks, surrounded by our burning Spitfires. Joy has only just recovered, having spent months in a hospital bed in Taplow, being treated for a broken back.

'Well, your friend calls you Magpie, doesn't he?' She smiles. 'And magpies are always stealing things...'

'I didn't steal the plane, Joy.'

'Better hope Gower agrees. She's certainly been wondering where you flew it to.'

I look at her, feeling a smile twitch at my lips. 'You didn't tell her?'

'You asked me not to.'

'Thank you, Joy.'

I squeeze her in a hug. Joy has been my truest friend since I met her a year ago. She taught me how to fly, among other things. She's the only black female American pilot in the ATA. The laws in America won't let a black women fly a plane, so when the war broke out she came here to fight with us. Since she learned how to fly in her father's air circus in New York, she knows all sorts of techniques they don't teach us here.

'All right, Coop,' she says, breaking free of the hug. 'I only just got out of back surgery.'

'Oh God – sorry, Joy. I wasn't thinking—'

'Well, nothing's changed then.' She smiles, flashing white teeth. *Americans*. It isn't fair – they have the best sweets *and* the best teeth. 'And I'm pretty much fixed up now. Good enough to fly, at any rate.'

'Good,' I say, holding her look. 'I need your help.'

Joy and I cross the tarmac, keeping our voices low.

In the distance, off-duty pilots sit in chairs beside the

river. It was from that spot Joy and I witnessed the start of the D-Day invasion, when the first boats poured south down the Hamble and towards the sea. We watched, coffee forgotten, as the men went to war.

'Well, out with it? You've got something up your sleeve.'

I look at her calmly. 'Rockets.'

'Rockets?'

Joy knows all about Father, and has let me know she thinks he's not trustworthy. 'You need to take any information to the British commanders.' I can hear the frown in her voice.

'I spoke to the Air Ministry. They claim to know all about it, but they have identified a more important threat.'

'Bring your father to them.'

'Joy, they will arrest him, maybe execute him. He has told me everything he knows.'

'Where is he?'

'Somewhere safe. Far away.'

Father will stay at the Tower, hidden away – locked away, Oakes likely prefers to think of it. He may also treat Father as if he were a prisoner. But he will be safe.

She eyes me. 'And just what are you planning to do with this information?'

'Rockets are coming. And we're going to stop them.'

'Are we now? You think Fighter Command is going to let female pilots join an RAF squadron? You may have tricked Gower into thinking you're not cracked, but the old men in the RAF won't see it that way.'

'No, they won't.'

I have safely delivered dozens of Spits, but I still hear

Gower's earlier warning: *The first time a female pilot burst a tyre – after a year of clean flying – the RAF grounded all ATA flights.*

'So?'

'So,' I say. 'We'll need to form our own squadron.'

The crew room is empty except for Minx and Barcsay playing bridge, coins and bills stacked beside them. With the invasion under way, the need for transporting aircraft has fallen off dramatically.

'Why?' Minx says, not looking up from her cards. Cigarette smoke clouds the room. 'Even if we save the empire, they'll still take away our planes the moment the war is over.'

Mayfair Minx and Countess Barcsay, two of the most glamorous ATA pilots – posh socialites turned war volunteers – have grown used to the action and urgency. *I hope.*

'You'll still be able to fly, Minx. You have your own plane.'

She squints at Barcsay's card a long moment before pressing down her own. Minx still *looks* like a society girl, glamorous in lipstick and painted fingernails. She was given her name from the newspapers, who used to print photographs of her dancing in clubs. She is also one of the first women to fly a Liberator bomber.

'Call me mad,' she says. 'But I'm not sure I'll be satisfied just flying to parties. I might want to do a little more.'

'Well, you can start right now.' I swallow, trying to find my best leader voice. For some reason, all I can think of is Flo, my best friend from school, and the commanding tone she used to pick players for netball. 'I'm forming an all-woman squadron.'

The crisp snap of a card fills the silence.

'Why not?' Barcsay flips long blonde hair. She is a horse riding champion and Countess of some place in Europe I can never remember the name of. 'Everyone knows about the Night Witches.'

Minx gives a snort. 'Yeah, but the Russians are mad as hell. And they have those poor girls flying cropdusters. You're talking about Spitfires, I assume?'

I nod. 'We've flown Spits in formation before. Together we've banked hundreds of hours flying. And Joy is an excellent teacher.'

Minx raises a perfectly manicured eyebrow. 'What can Joy teach me that I don't already know?'

A moment of quiet as I try to find the words. 'Precision diving.'

Minx slowly folds her cards away. The game has been abandoned. 'Bringing the circus to us, are you, Brooks?'

Joy smiles. 'If you can handle it.'

I turn to hide the relief on my face. Barcsay's voice follows me to the door. 'Where are you going?'

'To scour the base. We don't have many pilots left. And we're going to need the best ones.' And the best pilot in the ATA has just quit. I keep walking, calling over my shoulder. 'Someone find me Bella Jensen.'

After a few hours' sleep at Mrs Young's cottage, my billet when I am posted to Hamble airfield, I am ready to head back to base and put my mad plan into practice.

I button the dark blue uniform, two stripes on the shoulder – one narrow, one broad – watching myself in the mirror. Commander Gower's opinion of me seems to have soured. She was grateful when I warned of last year's attack on the Castle Bromwich factory, but only allowed me to join the rescue pilots at Joy's insistence. She forgave my destruction of the Spit as an act of heroism to save Joy, and even promoted me to second officer. That was us even, I suppose.

But my 'late return' of the Moth – a model not even scheduled for delivery elsewhere – seems to have put me in her debt once again.

I put on the peaked cap. The hat *does* make me look older, even if I no longer need to lie about my age.

My head still throbs. The pain is getting worse. Mum said her headaches became worse as she aged. How long before I have to sit in an utterly dark, utterly silent room, while someone brings me vinegar-soaked towels? How long before I have to endure the constant visits of a doctor, always offering some new remedy that never works?

How long before the pain becomes too much to handle? How long before my thoughts start to turn black? *No, they are simple headaches, not some curse passed down from*

Mum to me. But I can't lose the feeling that there's a clock inside me, ticking away to some dark future.

I take a final look in the mirror.

This is who I am, no matter what happens. A pilot.

Father helped created these murderous weapons; it is up to me to try and destroy them.

The only question is – how will Gower react?

As I walk on to the tarmac in the grey morning sun, they are all there. I can scarcely believe it.

'Coop.' Joy nods to me.

I look over the faces. Joy, Bella, Canada, Barcsay, Minx, all wearing caps, sunglasses, and full flying uniform and slacks. I remind myself that it was Gower who fought the RAF when they insisted women wear skirts to fly. She said the same thing then that she said when she fought to have women pilot fighter planes. *Damn the rules, this is war.*

'Bella, glad to have you back.'

Only two days ago, she quit in protest of the ban on female pilots joining the D-Day invasion. Now she gives a wicked grin. 'I was promised I could be in on the action.'

'More than you might want.'

'I'm in,' she says, firm. Bella, like many of the others, had a glittering past life. She was a ballerina before she became an expert on Spitfires, and only the small gap in her teeth reminds me she is not perfect.

Minx laughs. 'But you so enjoy being on leave.'

'My last leave was a disaster.' Bella sighs, but her smile suggests otherwise. I am usually chided for not taking part when they talk of their 'dirty weekends'. People go to bed with each other much more easily during war. It might be the last time they do, Barcsay always says. But we have more important issues at hand.

'We're all in.' Minx says with a stiff nod to me. The others nod too, and I see the flush of excitement in their faces.

'Well, all right,' I say, trying to maintain a calm face. 'Let's do it.'

The six pilots, in full uniform, slacks, caps, and boots, march towards the office. I can feel the eyes of the engineers and ground crews.

Once, I used to hear Flo's voice in my head, filled with good sense and caution. Now I only hear silence. I force myself to breathe steadily, and knock on the door.

Commander Gower opens it. Pauline Gower is an impressive woman, with two thick bars of gold on her shoulder and gold wings on her left breast. Her voice is soft, her manner casual – but she didn't become Britain's first female commercial pilot, holder of multiple international flying records, and Commander of the Women's ATA by being soft and casual. She takes us all in, her eyes lingering on Bella before turning back to me.

'Anna Cooper,' Gower says dryly. 'What can I do for you today?'

'We have it on good authority that the Germans are about to begin launching supersonic ballistic missiles into London from northern France.'

Gower leans forward at her desk. 'What authority is this?'

'My father.'

She raises an eyebrow. 'Your father works for British Intelligence?'

I take a long breath. 'German rocket development.'

The room falls silent. I can feel Minx and Barcsay exchange looks behind me, but I keep my eyes locked on Gower's. Eventually, she gives a stiff nod.

'And you've passed this intelligence on through the correct channels?'

'I have, Commander. But the correct channels are not interested.'

'Because they doubt the source?'

'Because their plans have already been made. They need all their bombers – and the American bombers – to deal with the ground offensive. The threat of rocket attacks will not alter their plans.'

Gower and I talk while the others listen in various states of anxiety. They didn't sign up to be connected to a German, and possibly viewed as a spy.

This is the only way. If I had told them the truth earlier, they never would have agreed to join me.

'And what exactly do you know of the targets?' Gower asks, still looking only at me. 'Is there likely to be a main site?'

I almost collapse with relief, but force myself to stay

upright and focused. *She is taking me seriously; don't make her change her mind.*

'We don't know, Commander. Allied bombers already destroyed Peenemunde – where my father worked. They may have other bases, including large-scale storage sites. But the launch sites are designed to be mobile.'

'Mobile launch sites?' she repeats. I sense her disbelief returning. 'So there could be countless units, spread out across cities and mountains and forests?'

'Yes, Commander. Exactly.'

'Exactly?' she almost chokes on the word. 'How is that positive?'

'A single launch site would be heavily fortified, perhaps a bunker – far beyond what we could destroy with the Mark XVI Spits.'

Now her eyebrows reach her hair. 'The new Spitbombers? I assumed you were angling for a recce mission, which is a mad enough idea on its own. Just what it is you have planned?'

'To destroy the mobile launch sites, or at least the convoys of fuel trucks. The Spits will be the perfect hunters.'

She is silent for a long time, before looking around at the other pilots and then back to me. 'None of you have the skills.'

'Barcsay will teach us to use weapons. Joy will show us how to dive bomb.'

'Not things you learn in an afternoon.'

'Which is why we'll need to practise.'

'And you want my planes to practise with? And then what? Maybe some of you are capable enough to learn these skills in time – we don't have control over the air space. More invasion forces may be crossing, and intricate aerial traffic patterns will be a problem.'

'We only ask for a chance to train. And, of course, we would never attempt an actual mission until it was safe and we had your express permission.'

'And you are of course aware that unauthorized training on RAF planes is illegal?'

I swallow hard. 'Damn the rules, Commander Gower. This is war.'

We have been taken off transport duties. Instead, we will be training. Gower didn't say she supported the idea – or even that she believed me about the rockets – but she is willing to let us conduct practice drills with her best planes.

'For seven days,' she said. 'Maximum. And if they are needed elsewhere – and they likely will be – I need them back that instant. And I don't think I need to explain what will happen if there is so much as a scratch on any of the planes…'

We have the Mark XVI Spitfires, and seven days to work with them.

Spitbombers, they're called, fighter planes modified to carry a bomb rack. Once the bombs are equipped, the 500 lb bomb is carried beneath the belly of the plane, with a 250 lb bomb beneath each wing.

I stare at the Spit as I approach, wondering how the real

bombs will affect the weight and the steering of the plane. For training we are only using small smoke bombs.

Gower cautioned us that the planes were not designed to carry these add-ons. In fact, she thinks turning the Spitfire into a fighter-bomber is an insult to a perfect machine. Far more importantly, she warned us that once we enter into a dive, we must never exceed the 'maximum permissible airspeed': 457 m.p.h. I laugh at the thought, remembering with terror the speed during my first ever flight in a Moth, which has a blistering top speed of 90 m.p.h. But most of all, I'm thinking about the fit the RAF will have if they find out what we're doing here.

Suddenly I am the Flight Leader of a squadron. Even though I am the youngest and least experienced, I was the one who brought us together. Of course, the girls may not listen to me now that they know about father. With every side look, I feel sick with guilt. He helped build these weapons. *I will help destroy them.*

I shake off the thought as I climb the wing to the cockpit and slide open the canopy.

The sword can't be put back in the stone now.

First thing on the agenda is Joy teaching us to use the instruments. Female pilots are not allowed to learn to use the control panel – a vile and idiotic rule that has led to multiple deaths and countless abandoned flights. In a climate of endless clouds, in the middle of enemy bombing raids, no pilot should have to fly blind.

Gower had already decided to look the other way on this, and she has also lifted the ban on women pilots flying armed craft. Perhaps the escalation of the war effort demands it. Perhaps she no longer fears reprisal from the RAF. She's got much bigger worries now.

Once we've mastered instruments, we'll move on to practising formations and then swiftly on to the more difficult manoeuvres – and then dive bombing.

'What are we called?' Minx says with an exhausted smile.

We are back in the crew room at the end of a punishingly long day, which ended only when the last of the light was sucked out of the sky.

'What do you mean?' I say.

My mind is still on our manoeuvres. During the Blitz, I remember watching the fighters, spiralling into the clouds above the city. It was always hard to tell who was the hunter and who was the hunted. Now we'll have to be both.

Bella lights a cigarette. 'Well, we need to have a name, don't we? The Flying Devils?'

I remember with a grin that once Bella couldn't be bothered to learn my name – Megan, she kept calling me.

'The Mad Pilots?' Barcsay offers, her blonde hair flattened with sweat. 'The Suicide Sisters?'

Joy laughs hoarsely. 'Coop's Chicks?'

The girls have not mentioned anything about my father's identity as a German, but I notice they all look at me a little differently. Now, though, they are giving me their usual smiles.

In my own exhaustion, I can't match their easy tones, but the words somehow come out calm. 'The Ravens.'

For too long we've been caged, our wings clipped. Now we're really part of it. Now we're going to help end it.

Joy nods, and forces herself to stand. She holds both hands against her sore back. 'Works for me. Come on, Ravens, let's get some sleep. We're back up there at sunrise.'

6

TIMOTHY SQUIRE

10 June 1944

A dark room, not unlike the one I sprang Cecil from, and I'm stuck here. Fat chance he's going to return the favour.

The stone walls are cold and smell of ripe apples. My skull throbs. I am lying on my back, staring up at the night sky through the bars in the top of the door. A fat moon hangs there. It isn't night again, is it?

They captured me in the afternoon, I remember that much. Pain makes it hard to think properly, but I know the burning lines across my shoulders and neck are courtesy of the butt of that Nazi's rifle. They took my compass, map, tea, first-aid kit, Grampa's watch – Mr SS took everything. To Rommel himself, he said.

Those last moments play over and over in my thoughts. A warning shot was fired into the earth in front of me.

'Don't shoot!' I cried out. 'Please. I have this.'

As the SS man swiped the map from my hands, I twisted to watch the 109 lift into the clouds. *Rafferty's gone.* My eyes tried to track Lightwood through the fields, but there was no sign. *Take all my luck, my friend. Whatever I have left, it's all yours.*

'Where is the rest of this? The rest, or I shoot you now, little Tommy.'

The SS leader stepped into the middle of the circle. He unsheathed a knife, cut at my trouser leg. I did not object, did not move.

Unfurling another paper, he looked from the two papers to me. Then he held the knife to my throat. 'What is this? Huh?' He pressed the knife against my skin. I could feel the bite of the steel. 'I cut the Jews' throats from ear to ear. I will do the same to you. What is this?'

He shook the papers in anger, but something written there caught his eye. He stared for a long moment, a wide-eyed look taking over, then sheathed his knife with a snap. 'Baums!' he called. '*Kommen.*'

A German rushed over. '*Obergruppenfuhrer?*'

He showed the papers to the other German, and after a moment the same wide-eyed look came over him. He turned back to me. 'This is true? These documents?'

I didn't answer, only bowed my head.

His eyes gleamed with victory, with lust. He barked out some orders, and a man on a motorbike arrived.

'*Bringt das zu Generalfeldmarschall Rommel. Jetzt. Schnell!* Say thank you to the little Tommy. Germany is about to win this war.'

I can see him now, pointing at the two maps. Unbidden, snatches of an old song rise up. *Timothy Squire is a rotten liar.* A song kids used to sing to me at school, a song I hated so much I couldn't read my comics through the tears. Now, though, the smile hurts as it cracks my lips.

Fancy that, little Timothy Squire outsmarts the great Desert Fox himself. *A rotten liar, indeed.*

One in six men were given false documents, split over two pages, of operational plans for a make-believe second part of the invasion. With any luck, Rommel is sending his best tanks away from the war to battle an imaginary army in the west.

But Mr SS will only take the bait for so long. Once the truth is out, he'll stick my head on a spike. How much longer do I have?

I don't imagine they have any *Champion* comics with Rockfist's adventures to help pass the time. I have been trying to remember them, to piece together my favourite old stories, but somehow it never comes out quite right. *I know he punches out that polar bear, but how he did he get to the igloo in the first place?*

The guard comes, and the door opens more slowly than a door has ever opened. When he slops down the food, I start laughing.

'What's so funny, little Tommy?'

I can't stop. The food, the cage, the bored guard – all I

need are feathers and I'm as good as a Tower raven. I doubt they'll let me out for the day, though.

While I sit trapped inside this cage, I can't help but think about everyone.

Dad is the wisest man I ever knew, even if he spent most of his time locked up with his books and suits of armour. When I was small, though, and too scared to be alone, he always sat beside me until I fell asleep.

Mum would be proud of me. She'd shout at me, of course, for ending up in here. But she'd be proud that I did it. Better this way than falling into the river chasing cats, like she warned me about every day when I was a kid.

I told her I'd bring her back some French cheese. She laughed, but she always went in for my jokes. I suppose all mums do.

I feel it, heavy and sharp and gnawing at my guts. *I will never see them again.*

Anna is beautiful. And she has a way of looking at you, of really seeing you, that makes your skin prickle. Wherever she is, you want to be there too, even if it means putting up with croaking bloody ravens with their great snapping beaks and talons. Where is she now?

She's where she needs to be, flying Spitfires and helping win the war – while I sit here locked in a cage.

I remember her, lying in the hospital bed, missing most of her teeth, and she still had it – this feeling, this spark… I don't know. Even when she looked like she was dying, she was full of life. I can hear her, now, laughing like Bow's bells.

I guess it's love that does that. But the idea of her being

hurt, of her being in danger, fills me with a fire, an anger that I've never known before. It's not that I want to protect her – she can protect herself, and me to boot – it's only that I can't stand to see her in pain, to see that spark threatened.

Truth is, Anna made the wrong choice. Cecil can look after her, buy her things, take her places, bore her to tears talking about whatever rich people talk about. What am I going to do? I didn't even stop her dad from messing about in her life. A bloody Nazi, and I helped bring them together! Now she's in danger and it's my fault.

At least now Rafferty can swoop in and save the day.

Bastard.

We should have stayed in the bloody ditch. Lightwood and I could have waited a few more days, then moved west – eventually we'd have found some Allied troops. Or the bloody German tanks.

We'd have had a chance, at least. But running for the bloody planes, just hoping they'd be there – madness. And now Lightwood is as good as killed, and there's no one to blame but me. There's no way he made it more than a mile before they ran him down.

No, we couldn't have stayed in that ditch. Our unit was split, maybe all killed, and we knew we'd be dead next. Lightwood was even more scared than me. I had to do something. Free Rafferty, and we make a run for it.

In that mad, bloody moment I knew he needed someone to have a plan, to have something, or he was lost. *But you listened to the wrong person, mate. You needed a leader, a hero, and you got a lying little rat from the Tower.*

Truth is, I'm far more of a coward. I signed up early because everyone else did – even Bobby Miller, who spent most football matches tripping over the ball. The sappers – the bloody engineers – seemed like the safest place to be in a war. If you know what you're doing, defusing bombs isn't so scary. But bloody slathering Germans chasing after you with machine guns – that's what I was trying to avoid.

I think of the needles. *Two for eternity.* Not that I'd take them even if I still had the bloody things. Anna would kill me if she found out.

Then again, why should I get to stay alive and not Lightwood?

I force down thoughts of how good a bed would feel, or the bunk at the unit barracks, or even the cot on the floor in the corner of Lightwood's room, where I stayed while I was pretending to still be up in Aberdeen finishing my sapper training. A broken rock would be more comfortable than this.

It is the same feeling I had when the patrol surrounded us at Robehomme. I can't think of that massacre without a raw, nauseous feeling chilling me to the bone. I worry I'll never stop seeing the bodies, the ruined faces – and the smell, the stale blood and burnt hair. *One more nightmare to add to the list.*

From my cell I can see the central square as it fills with

American prisoners in blackened faces, with heads shaved bald, guarded by German soldiers. Paratroopers, rounded up from the initial landings. I feel properly bad for these blokes.

But the sight of each new man they bring in pushes the breath from my body. I hoped I'd never see the bastard's grinning face ever again. But I look for it in every face. It was madness to hope he'd get away on foot. It is not him. It is never him.

Arthur Lightwood, you blighter, where are you?

Mr SS has clearly cottoned on to my fear.

'Oh, we found your friend. The one who helped you with your little smoke trick. He was hiding in a ditch.' Mr SS smiles, a deeply unpleasant sight. 'We thought he must be a Jew, hiding like that. But then we recognized him. Not a strong one, little Tommy. He pissed himself. I had to shoot him, the pig. Howled as he died.'

I do not look up. He is lying, to try and break me.

Snip off your balls. Lightwood's words come back to me, and I pull my knees closer to my chest.

Lightwood is still out there. *Mate, wherever you are, keep running.*

A dull ache throbs. I am starting to get sores on my arms – itchy bumps that are impossible not to scratch. I must be allergic to these bloody Nazis.

How much longer do I have?

Not much longer, as it turns out.

'You have lied to me,' says Mr SS. 'You help your pilot friend escape; you lie to me. How do you think this will end for you, little Tommy? Good?'

Slim chance of that, I'll wager. This evil wanker's not going anywhere; and he's going to make damn sure I don't either. He is always nearby, always watching.

'Not a good trade, one might think. But he did not talk. And you will. So a good trade for me, after all.' He smiles, and though his teeth are normal as any bloke's, all I see are fangs. And his eyes really are red. *But he might have a point.* Rafferty never would have broken.

'They take your fingernails first,' Mr SS says, nodding sagely. 'Then you start to talk.'

I've bitten most of my fingernails off already, mate. *Anna always hated when I did that.* I wish I could have kept my promise to her. But I'm not coming home, I know that. *My luck is all used up.* It's not like Anna's going to wait for someone who'll never come home. *That would be mad.*

14 June 1944

Every day that passes is a year. I think of England, of the watery sunshine, the stalls of food at Borough Market, the turrets of the Tower. And they'll all be telling stories about Rafferty and his shining bloody courage.

Slowly the cell door opens and Mr SS steps inside.

This Nazi is a proper creep, and today he seems more eager than usual.

'You give me this fake map, maybe you think you are very clever? Clever like a little mouse.'

I look up at him, try to hold his gaze.

'You are always laughing in here, aren't you? Well, you won't laugh again, I promise you, little Tommy. You will never laugh again.'

After he finally leaves, slamming the door shut behind him, I close my eyes, trying to erase everything he just said. When I open them again, I see a black bird landing in the square.

A raven.

My heart surges with hope. I raised a bloody raven at the Tower – Yugo, with his hungry beak. I taught another one how to talk – Ollie, who also learned from me how to always say the worst thing at the worst time. Lightwood always called me the Bird Tamer. *I can do this.*

What exactly I am going to do is uncertain. Ask it to grab the keys and toss them in here? Have I gone mad? But I am staring at the bird, willing it to look up at me, to *see* me the way ravens do.

Come on, mate. Just look up at me.

I think of Mabel. She escaped the Tower – Anna set her free, snipped the band off her foot and she and Grip flew off together. They could have gone anywhere – why not France?

'*Do you remember me?*' I hear myself whisper. 'I was well nice to the birds after Anna taught me all about you. I even helped a pair of mated ravens lay eggs. No one has done more for ravens than me… if you can just help return the gesture—'

Without harsh croak the raven struts away. *Oh, bugger off then.*

Again my back finds the cold wall of the cell. I am alone.

7

TIMOTHY SQUIRE

1 July 1944

The guards have come for me. Maybe they're alert because of last time, or maybe the town has been reinforced, but there are at least a dozen Nazis with rifles.

I am herded towards a van, guards on each side of me.

'You will tell us everything,' Mr SS says cheerfully, opening the door.

For a brief moment, I am standing under the sky. I squint my eyes in the bright light. The sky is a miracle, a proper miracle.

A hand pushes me inside and the door slams shut.

Two guards sit across from me, and once we reach the train station, three more SS soldiers join us in the car. These guards are not drinking, laughing; they are watching me, alert. One has his gun drawn. Escape is impossible.

No one speaks as the train barrels through the countryside. For the past hour I have seen mountains at the window, like great volcanoes. *Where are we?*

I memorized the maps we were given back at base, but those were of the invasion area only – and if I know nothing else, I know we've left that area far behind.

No Allied rescue is on the cards.

Hours and hours pass – a full day drifting by. The soldiers drink tea and eat sandwiches and watch me starve. It will be dark soon.

My mind wanders to the idea of playing Monopoly with Anna, sharing a Thermos of tea, listening to her cackle of a laugh – I can't think of anything more perfect.

I had my own plans for us.

A bloody great bang changes everything, and I smash into the guard across from me. Instinctively, I try to pull away from the devil, but we are spinning, cups flying, rumbling and tipping, until we shudder to a halt, a heap of blinking men.

The train has gone off the tracks.

Just like that the Germans are up, like they'd planned they whole thing, guns ready. Did we hit a cow? The train nearly tipped on its side. I strain my neck to see out of the window.

The SS soldiers call out to each other, their voices mixed with fear. Something is happening. One word I can make out and it fills me with a surge of hope. Not cows.

Resistance.

A bloody miracle is happening.

I am motionless on the floor, staring around the train car like I'm on another planet. All around me, bullets shatter windows. Everyone is screaming – German and French, all mixed together. There is a firefight going on, and I'm bound to get shot running out into the middle of it. But I am not dying in some Gestapo prison.

Time to make tracks. I crawl towards the broken door, flinching as the glass slices my hands.

'Don't move.' A bloody-faced guard stands over me, rifle pointed at my head.

A Resistance fighter leaps inside, but the guard's rifle takes him in the chest. The gun is immediately turned back on me.

I cower, unable to move. In my thoughts I see McCormick, sawn in half by bullets, Hamilton's ruined body at my feet, the blood and death of my unit, my friends. I can't move, even to save myself.

Another man in a beret tries his luck, pushing inside and firing madly. They exchange fire. Now is my chance to act fast, be a hero. But I stay, shrinking among the broken glass. The guard kills my new would-be saviour, kicking his body clear through the door.

But apparently there is a God, and at that moment, a bullet through the window takes the guard in the shoulder.

He crumples, and his rifle skitters across the floor.

This is it: *pick up the bloody gun and end this bastard.* But again I fail. Fear takes over, and I dart to my feet and run. I don't know if he reaches for me, or reaches for the gun, or even looks up. Head down, I race through the car, crashing down the stairs and falling into the rocks outside.

'*Attend!*' a voice shouts.

I lie there, panting, but I can feel the guns fixed on me.

There is silence but for my breathing. For the first time I realize the gunshots have stopped.

I stare up at a circle of men in red berets. Some guns are pointed at the train, some at me. All have the sun-roughened faces of people living outside.

A red-bearded man steps forward, beret pulled low on his head.

'Welcome to Free France.'

There is a bustle of activity as the French guerrillas try to get everyone up and moving. It is clear they expect the Germans to retaliate at any moment, though they seem to have time to strip the SS guards of boots and socks. The sun is setting behind them.

'Finally, the great British armies have arrived,' says the man with the red beard – their leader, I assume. He has a crafty look to him which – despite the fact I owe this man my life – I don't think I like.

I stand, dusting myself off and leaving smears of blood from my hands. 'Thank you. For getting me off that train.'

He flips his gun and holsters it in a single movement.

I try and fail to look unimpressed. 'You should. Without us, you'd be squealing in a dungeon.'

'Yes, well. Thank you again. *Merci.*'

Well, I can't say I like this fellow, but he sure beats the SS guards. I look back at the ruined train. 'Will German reinforcements come after us?'

He nods. 'So will the Milice. And the Milice are worse.'

I blink. *Worse than the SS?*

Before I can ask, another beret rushes over. '*Vite. Vite.*'

For the first time I realize there are people everywhere, groaning. The train was full of passengers, apparently, and the Resistance men are helping some to their feet and interrogating the rest. It seems all of them are coming along with us.

Red beard starts walking away, the others following. *What else can we do?* I would love to talk to someone else, anyone else, but Monsieur Red Beard just happens to fall back beside me.

He smirks at me. '*Un petite oiseau* told us to expect brave soldiers.'

'Wasow told you?' I say, unsure just what this Frenchman is suggesting.

He laughs, a low French-sounding chuckle. 'A little bird. Clémence, she took you and your men to the village – to Robehomme.'

I am shocked. 'That little girl is part of the Resistance?'

'That little girl saved your life. What is your name?'

'I'm Timothy Squire, sapper in the British Army.'

Maybe I shouldn't have given him my name like that, but I was caught off guard by another thought. That girl was Resistance. I've heard Yeoman Oakes tell tales of the Resistance, people who have gone into hiding rather than collaborate with the invaders. Brave people, fighters. Maybe she *did* save Rigby.

'You may call me Bernard.'

'Where are we going, Bernard?'

'We're not safe here. The Gestapo frowns on us sabotaging their trains. We left six dead officers back there. And then there's you, a very important prisoner. They'll be hunting us. With dogs.'

Oh, brilliant. How are we meant to hide from bleeding dogs?

Together we wander into the forest, and I feel the safety of the high trees. For the first time since the Middle Ages, I smile. But the thought occurs to me that I could never find my way out of here. Everything looks identical – great tall trees, no proper path – and it's a perfect maze in the gathering darkness. Our footsteps are the only sound.

I've never been in a forest before, but I know this silence is unusual. No birds singing or squirrels racing up trees. It means there must be people everywhere. I can't see bloody one of them, but I'd wager they must be hidden out here in the hundreds. And not a few of them will be watching our progress.

Well, they can't be suspicious of me. They pulled me from a bloody Gestapo prison train! Still, I keep my eyes straight ahead, my hands clearly visible. The worry must be clear on my face, because Bernard slaps me on the back.

'Come on, brave Tommy.' He laughs. 'Let's get you to safety.'

III

THE WITCH OF THE FOREST

'Set Europe ablaze.'

Churchill's instructions to the Special Operations Executive, formed to aid local resistance movements in occupied Europe, 1940

8

TIMOTHY SQUIRE

1 July 1944

There is an immense silence to the forest, despite the Resistance fighters now visible beneath the trees – mostly young men in berets, holding long rifles. We must be getting close to the main camp. The smell of gun oil and leather, dirt and unwashed bodies is strong – and cigarettes. The smell is heaven itself.

My ears are still open for barking dogs. *Bloody great German shepherds too, I'll wager. I've always hated those giant pointy-eared monsters.*

I am also aware, for the first time since the rescue, of the hard knot of hunger in my belly. We walk swiftly enough, but even still – I have to eat something and get some proper sleep sooner than later. The edges of my vision are starting to darken.

Bernard is giving me a sly look, which frankly makes my skin crawl.

'You do not seem like such a mighty warrior. I hope all

the British are not like you, yes? Or this landing will do nothing but fill the Gestapo prisons.'

All right, mate. 'You Frenchmen had your hands up for the Hun quick enough.'

A spark flares in his eyes. *Saved from the Germans, to be murdered by the French. Wouldn't that just be fitting.*

Bernard lights a fag, cupping his hand around the match. 'You bombed our navy.'

'We had to. Hitler would have used those boats against us.'

'So you take our weapons away but still demand we fight?'

'Ships aren't going to help you here, mate.'

He smiles, takes a hard draw on his cigarette. 'Let's hope you don't need a way out of here then.'

I have nothing to say to this. *Oh, I will get out of here, and I won't need your bloody ships to do it.* But I can't start a proper dust-up with this bloke.

He cocks his head at me and, damn it all, I flinch.

His laughter is swiftly becoming one of my least favourite sounds.

Again I try to walk a little behind, but he keeps pace with me. At least he's not opening his mouth, at any rate. I keep my eyes on the path, too narrow for vehicles, which leads us deeper into the forest. I am aware of a sentry off to the side, machine gun in hand. Bernard makes a sign to him, and we continue along for another half-mile, and then we are here: the main camp.

These people look underfed, and far from clean. I have

heard heroic stories of the Resistance, but seeing these men in the flesh, only one word comes to mind: *prey*. Gazelles attacking lions. They may do their share of damage, but they are the hunted.

I just need to get home. *I must get home.*

I am taken to an open drum, filled with NAAFI supplies, and my mouth waters at the sight of it. Whoever these people are, the British are helping to supply them.

Bernard hands me a chocolate bar and a package of Gold Flake cigarettes, and I worry that my eyes are watering from pure joy. 'I'd offer you soap to shave with, but we don't have any.'

I resist the urge to rub my chin, which is as smooth as ever. Just before I tell this bastard that I am practically eighteen, more people enter the circle, likely looking for food. *Or soap.* Most of them are men, but there is a woman too. They are all staring at me. *I don't care – I have food and tobacco and I'll be back among the English in no time.* I tear the foil from the packet and pull free a long, beautiful tube of tobacco.

Bernard leans in, lights my fag with a match. The relief, the heavenly taste, washes over me.

'So you wreck train tracks?' I ask, feeling suddenly blissful enough to banter with this Frenchman.

'Sometimes they're full of weapons. Sometimes they're full of soldiers.'

'So what did you use back there?' I ask. 'Bickford fuse fitted to a detonator?'

He lights his own cigarette. 'Something like that, Tommy.'

'You attach the charges directly to the railway lines?'

He nods, exhaling a cloud of purple smoke in the forest air. 'Sometimes. Other times, when we are in a hurry, we use plastics.'

'A box of RDX explosive would work better, fitted with magnets.'

A female voice speaks. 'You know explosives, do you?'

I turn to face the speaker. It is the woman, and she is still eyeing me. I must look like the devil himself. Covered in dirt and blood, starved and knackered. *Or I fit right in.*

Bernard nods to her. '*Alors, Hélène.*'

He rambles on in French for several minutes. All the while, she is watching me. Whatever he is telling her, she doesn't react. *He must have left out the part about us being hunted by dogs.* Then she calls to one of the men behind me.

'We'll stay here until morning. Put extra watch in the trees. Snipers will be here first.'

'You're the leader?' I say to her in amazement.

One thing is certain – she's proper beautiful, even in full khaki uniform with a Bren machine gun slung over her shoulder; with dark hair down past her neck and flashing green eyes.

She looks me up and down. 'I'd wear your balls for earrings, boy, if they weren't so tiny. Now come along before a Nazi sniper puts a hole in you.'

Why is everyone threatening to cut off my balls? It just occurs to me now that she is the only Resistance fighter in the camp in shiny boots and a military cap. *Of course she's the leader.* And she sounds British.

Bernard coughs, but there is laughter in it. 'Commander Wake, this is Timothy Squire, a British sapper we rescued from a trip to the Gestapo prison.'

'Is that so?'

'Yes, Commander. Are you British, by chance?' I can't help but ask, hoping I have stumbled upon a sensible person at last.

'Australian.' *Or maybe not.*

She is still looking me over when Bernard coughs again.

'We should pack him off with the villagers,' he says.

She finally nods, dismissing me.

Bernard smirks as he leads me away. 'Well, we've been living out here for years, waiting for this great landing, and you show up instead… it's a bit of a let-down, Tommy. Come on, I'll get you over with the women and children.'

He laughs and slaps me on the back, a little too hard. I don't care what this sod thinks. I don't care what any of these Frenchmen and Australians think. *I'm going home.*

We huddle round a fire, heavily sheltered to hide the glow. I learn from the other rescued passengers that the Resistance will move us along the escape chain towards a safe house in Arras. We can cross the Channel from there. *Thank you, luck.*

A friendlier Resistance fighter named Denis has brought me a chunk of grey bread, some bandages for my hands, and offered to try and find me some new bootlaces. The grey bread tastes as it looks, but I chew and chew, the crackle of the bonfire disguising my growling stomach.

As I wrap the bandages over the stinging wounds, I imagine a piping hot sausage roll. Huddled with the civilians, I light a cigarette that Denis offers me from a plain white packet, saving my own Gold Flakes for the journey north, and stare into the campfire, watching the odd swirling of flames.

A figure sneaks up to me, and I drop my fag fumbling for my knife – which the SS took off me days ago.

'Tommy,' the voice says.

'What?' I shoot back, more embarrassed than afraid. I've reclaimed my cigarette and at least some of my dignity.

'Come. She wants to see you.'

Commander Wake and I are alone, standing outside her tent at the back of the site. The campfire burns low, but I see clearly enough by the moonlight.

She lights a cigarette before she speaks. *No wonder I could smell tobacco miles away. Let's hope the dogs don't catch the scent.*

'Bernard doesn't trust many people,' she says in a casual tone. 'He thinks it's possible that you staged your own arrest and transportation to the prison.'

I swallow, aware there is no way I get out of this place without being caught. 'I am not a spy.'

I see she is wearing pips on her shoulder. Khaki tie, army

slacks, shiny boots. She is dressed the part, but her bearing is wrong – she slouches in a way that would make Major's nose bleed. *Bernard takes orders from this person*, I remind myself. *She's the commander for a reason.*

'I'm a sapper for the British Armed Forces, Commander Wake. That is the truth.'

She nods, seemingly satisfied. 'Day and night we blow up roads, bridges, rail tracks. Those bastards are heading for the beaches, and we're going to stop them. We could use your help buggering things up.'

My mind recoils at the idea. Helping Frenchmen derail trains? Spending more time with Bernard, all the while being chased through the woods by German shepherds and German soldiers?

'I am sorry, Commander. I must return to my unit, as soon as possible. Pressing action to attend to.'

She arches an eyebrow. 'More pressing than stopping the German army from reaching the beaches?'

'Well…' I can't think of anything to say to that. 'The truth is, Commander, I just – I just need to get back home.'

She'll think I'm a coward, but I don't care. I'd rather be a live coward in England than a dead hero in France.

Then why come here in the first place? A voice that sounds suspiciously like Anna's surfaces in my thoughts. *Why become a sapper, why join the invasion?* I can finish the thought easily enough on my own. If I wanted to stay home safe, I would have stayed a builder down at the docks.

Wake exhales smoke through her nose, something I am sure I have never seen a woman do before.

'I escaped from here once,' she says. 'But within two months I was dropped back behind German lines. Freedom is the only thing worth living for. I don't care if I die, doing this, because without freedom there is no point in living.'

Christ. Are all women mind readers? Anna could always pluck the thought right out of my head, but this woman is a complete stranger.

Truth is, I remember that day in Bethnal Green, when panic sent people fleeing into the Tube station. It wasn't even a real attack, only the sound of the AA gunner testing a new gun. I remember the crush of bodies, the horror of it, the corpses laid out on the street. Then the police telling each of us not to speak of it, not to create 'undue panic' – to pretend it didn't happen.

There is a reason I came here: to put a stop to this horrible war, this war that reduces us to blind trampling on our neighbours and lying to each other and ourselves. It has to end.

'I know about bombs,' I hear myself say.

'Good.'

'Well, we killed six of their men, and they've been after us for months.' She looks round the camp. 'But things will change now. It will be a while before we can stay in one spot again. But you can't feel guilty for what's to come.'

I swallow. 'What's to come?'

She smiles again, and this time it does nothing to relax me. 'Same as always. The bloody Germans come kicking back.'

9
ANNA COOPER

10 July 1944

I have come back to the Tower on leave to find it a different place. Father has been permitted to sit at the breakfast table in the Stone Kitchen, with an unspoken promise not to make himself disagreeable; but his mere presence seems to drain the energy from the room. Soon we will all feel the disastrous effects of a weapon he helped create. *Unless I can stop them first.*

Yeoman Sparks attempts to keep our spirits up. The oldest Warder at the Tower – his official position is the Gaoler – he has grown to be a grandfather figure to me.

'I know you miss your young lad,' he says in his thick Glasgow accent. 'I've known Timothy since he was a pup. He's not the type who will set the world on fire, but he's a good lad. Honest and true. Bet you can't wait to have him back.'

I cough, brushing the question aside. Toast and an egg,

tea without a spoon of sugar. Again. Yeoman Sparks is still grinning at me.

'And the war'll be over soon enough. I heard on the wireless that the Germans tried to assassinate Hitler.' He gazes at Father for an uncomfortable minute. 'Surely the beginning of the end.'

Again, Hitler's picture is in the paper, screaming from inside his uniform. What will it be like, to never have to see that face again?

Is it really the beginning of the end? People have been saying it's the beginning of the end for years. Timothy Squire told me it would be over by Christmas – every Christmas.

I have heard nothing from Timothy Squire – or about him – in over a month. It's the longest I've gone without hearing from him since we first met. When he's with me, he's also somewhere else – or seems to be anyway. Off thinking about bombs, or comic books. Now he really is off, out there, part of the invasion force. He is the most reckless boy I have ever met, yet somehow I know he will come through it all right.

'And you, my dear? What will you do, once the war is over?'

Sparks is going to hurt himself, grinning like that.

'Eat a banana.' I manage a smile. They say bananas will be back, along with silk stockings and goodness knows what else. They will get rid of the five-inch rule, and I can have a proper bath again. 'I plan to keep flying, Yeoman Sparks, unless they stop me.'

And they might. Sparks warned me, once the boys come

home they'll need all their old jobs again. Women will have to go back to the jobs they had before the war. Not that many of those jobs will remain either. I even lost my job of Ravenmaster, once a new Warder came along – and one who knew nothing about ravens.

I think of Cam Westin's mocking words, after I confronted him for trying to sabotage my plane at the ATA. *You're not a real pilot, Miss Cooper – none of you are. The second the war is over your little programme will be the first thing to go, mark my words. No one will remember it but as an embarrassment.* Cam Westin is a traitor; but he may be right.

This is who I am, no matter what happens. A pilot.

A loud knock at the door echoes through the stone room. Mr Squire shuffles inside. He is not wearing a tie, I notice straight away – I have never seen him without a tie. His face is grave, serious.

'Ah, William, what can we do for you?' Yeoman Oakes stands. I unconsciously do the same. Mr Squire, Timothy Squire's father and a curator at the Tower, never joins the Warders for breakfast.

'Anna,' he says, turning sad eyes on to me. 'I wanted to let you know that we had a visit from a telegraph boy today.'

He has something in his hands. An envelope. 'It's about Timothy.'

The silence of the Stone Kitchen rings. 'He is, it seems, missing in action.'

I can say nothing. The scene flips over and over in my mind, Mr and Mrs Squire at breakfast when the telegraph boy knocks. *The angels of death*, people call them. The look on Mrs Squire's kindly face.

Mr Squire fingers the envelope, now staring down at his shoes. 'It says here that he could have been separated from his unit, or possibly made a prisoner of war. It doesn't mean…'

All reasonable thoughts have abandoned me. *Timothy Squire*. I stand motionless, tugging at the roots of my hair with a fist.

On the bench on the Green, in full view of the sun, I sit with my hands in my lap. The dull pulse in my head has become a roar. Is it possible? Timothy Squire, who gets out of the maddest situations without a scratch – could he truly be dead? Some foolish part of me thinks that I would *know* if he was dead.

A Wife clicks past, wearing black. It is Mrs Pryor, in mourning for her son. She is the third woman in black I have seen today.

It is impossible to imagine this place without him. The Tower may be my home now, but it has always been his home. He grew up here, spent his whole life here. It makes sense, now that I think about it. A place of secret corridors and hidden passages, of walls to climb and guards to outmanoeuvre. And just below are the docks, filled with foreign travellers, spice stalls, dirt and cursing.

He absorbed the excitement of this place until he was full and carried it with him when he left. *And he will return, the same excited boy, once the war is over.*

The letter said he was *missing*, not killed in action. If he is missing, he can be found again. Sparks asks about my future – there is no future for me without Timothy Squire.

He will return.

I am due to meet Florence Swift – my oldest friend in the world – in an hour. I sit, motionless, the ravens sunning themselves nearby, until the Jewel House clock tolls.

10

FLORENCE SWIFT

10 July 1944

'I got your letter,' Anna says, smiling up at me.

I was always taller, but she has grown too. She looks different, her eyes a little sad. I remember her eyes as wide and bright and always laughing.

'You've been accepted to Somerville College. Congratulations, Flo.'

It is still mad to think that Anna *lives* here, in this great old castle. We grew up together, practically neighbours on Warwick Avenue.

We are standing in a tuck-away corner, where Anna has planted lines of crosses in the dirt. I think one of the markers is for her uncle, who died after the Blitz; the others, I am fairly sure, mark the burial spots of the ravens who died at the Tower. Once, I would have found this to be needlessly gruesome, but things have changed.

Anna seems to sense this, as her always smooth face is wrinkled with concern. 'What is it, Flo?'

'I'm going over there.'

She raises an eyebrow. 'Oxford?'

'France,' I answer, my voice low. 'I am volunteering with the nurses. I will begin my university studies when the war is over.'

She gives me a look I know very well – *she doesn't believe a word of it*. Then she snorts. 'Oxford might seem mighty dull after the Front.'

I hold her gaze. 'I know what you think. That I am some hypocrite.'

She's right to think it. I've tried many times to talk to her about how terrible the war is, how we're all to blame for its continuation. She never believes a word I say, no matter how logical, because I wasn't here when the Blitz came to London. My parents took our family to Montreal, and we stayed until it was safe to return. Anna had to stay – here, in the Tower – and she'll never forgive me not suffering the way she did.

'Flo, I don't think that.'

'It's OK. The Red Cross looks after all soldiers wounded in war. Germans, Poles, British. I will care for all the victims, and help these men get their lives back. Fighting only spreads more fighting.'

How we haven't learned that yet, I cannot fathom. One does not need to live through a bombing to see the truth of this.

She coughs, but clearly can't think of anything to say.

'I have been training, ever since the semester got out, at Hammersmith Hospital.' I add. 'Now I'm off.'

My voice cracks at the end, and all in one instant Anna sees the truth.

'Oh, Flo.'

As she squeezes me in a hug, my face feels hot. She was my best friend, my greatest friend, all through school. All my best memories have Anna in them – laughing in the back garden on Warwick Avenue, running on the beach in Brighton, sneaking into Mrs Morgan's tool shed.

Gently, we step back, looking at each other anew.

She smiles, wiping her eyes. 'Florence Swift in a field hospital.'

'Anna Cooper in a Spitfire.'

'We couldn't have dreamed this up, could we?'

'No.'

As far as I remember, I didn't dream much bigger than reading books together, laughing about boys together, and eating all the cherries in England together.

'Khaki battledress.' She suddenly laughs, and the relief is clear in her voice. 'That's what you'll have to wear.'

I laugh too, and it feels truly wonderful. *I always laughed the most with Anna.* 'Some things will be an adjustment, I admit.'

'Those afternoons, reading in the garden,' she says as we fall quiet, 'I always thought I wanted to be a hero, like King Arthur or Lancelot.'

'I always dreamed Lancelot would come and save me. From what, I don't know.' I chuckle again, my voice raw. 'Anna, I am glad I came to see you. And we will see each other again, soon.'

Once, we planned to go to Montreal after the war, and I would show her the best places to drink soda and eat ice cream, and teach her all about ice hockey. Neither of us says anything now; no promises are made.

I squeeze her into another hug, and for several long moments, she doesn't let go.

11

ANNA COOPER

10 July 1944

It is impossible to take in anything Flo told me at the raven graveyard because of the news of Timothy Squire. *Flo, off to war?* I try to imagine her coming to that decision – of her telling Mr Swift – but it is impossible.

I could think of nothing to say. Her mum must be beside herself. The family evacuated to Canada to avoid the Blitz, and now Flo is volunteering to go to the heart of it? I wonder if her two brothers have enlisted, or if her sister has joined the nurses as well. *Flo will go from china plates and plum pudding to helping dying men in a canvas tent on the battlefield.*

If she hadn't moved to Montreal, maybe we would have stayed friends, joined the WAAFs together, and maybe she would have become a pilot too. She was always so much better at everything than I was; faster, stronger. But since she left… since I stayed – nothing has been the same.

You tried to leave, a voice says. You just couldn't find a boat willing to take a terrified, penniless twelve-year-old, or you'd have been in Montreal too.

I did not tell her about Timothy Squire. They seemed to have become friends, of a sort, while I was away training with the ATA. I couldn't bring myself to say the words out loud, even to her.

I can't believe it.

I've heard all the stories. When a soldier is killed, the telegram is delivered in a blue envelope, with the word *priority* on it. It is a long letter, expressing sympathy, and notifying the receiver that the deceased's effects have been collected and will be forwarded in due course.

The letter we got is different. *Missing in action* could mean anything. He could be lost. Of course he's gotten lost – he's barely been outside East London, and now he's roaming through the fields of France?

If he's truly lost, he'll no doubt be taken in by some charming French family that we give him a good meal and send him on the right course to rejoin his unit.

A knock on my bedroom door makes me jump. Oakes waits a long moment after I answer before he comes in. It is almost like the old days, when Uncle would visit me in my room in the Bloody Tower.

'How are you, my dear?'

I close my eyes tight. 'Just a bloody headache…'

He nods, watching me.

'I'm scared, Yeoman Oakes.'

'He will return, Anna. I've seen that boy come out of all sorts of dangers unscathed. You both still have your whole lives ahead of you. This will all seem like a nightmare you woke up from.'

'What if he never comes back?'

'He will.' Despite their looking nothing alike, Oakes still makes me think of Uncle – not in those last days, when Uncle was wrapped in a blanket, and sitting close enough to the fire to worry me that he might go up in flames, but I remember him as he was before he fell ill, full of stories of the Tower and its history.

I suppose wars are fascinating when they happened hundreds of years ago, and the people who died are just names. *And often not even their names are remembered.* I'd be quite happy to never hear another war story.

'Can I get you anything, my dear?'

I pause. 'No. It's just sometimes I'm afraid that… my headaches… what happened to Mum…'

Oakes always moves faster than I think he could.

He hugs me, gently, but his voice is firm. 'Anna, no. We are all our own people. You are Anna Cooper, no one else. That is not your burden to take on. Do you understand?'

I nod, pulling back from his hug and wiping my eyes. 'I know. Thank you, Yeo – Gregory. Thank you.'

He nods. 'Just try to get some sleep.'

12

TIMOTHY SQUIRE

12 July 1944

The muscles in my legs burn. Even Major Roland's endless running drills failed to prepare me for walking, hiking, and climbing for sixteen hours straight. My feet are more blisters than feet. *Thank God, Denis found me new bootlaces.*

'We're not setting up camp?'

'They travel by night. We travel by night,' Wake says.

I heave a great sigh and keep putting one boot before the other.

The seven-thousand-strong group has headed off in countless smaller groups, platoons, each on their own mission towards our grand objective: pissing off the Germans.

Our group is a hundred, but Wake travels with a personal band of twenty men, including Bernard, Denis, a marksman named Claude – and now me. We walk at the head of the pack, prepare the camp and bonfires, and set a strong watch.

This last job is the most vital. The whole area is crawling with Germans. We have to take back roads, and send out scouts to ensure there are no patrols or roadblocks up ahead. Splitting up also hides us from roving Nazi planes, eager to drop bombs on the site of any group in the forest. Camp discipline is not so different from armed forces discipline.

Wake drills us constantly on the plan.

'How far away must a target be?'

'Twenty miles from camp,' I answer. 'Minimum.'

'How many sentries on duty?'

'Four.'

'North and south?'

'A circle. Always a full circle.'

Despite all this, the mood of the group is light-hearted – euphoric, even. *They are amazed to still be alive.*

This is mainly due to Commander Wake, who seems to know everything there is to know about German checkpoints and troop movements in the area. We move through the curving forest roads with easy confidence.

'What are the Milice?' I ask Wake. The idea has bothered me even since Bernard first mentioned the name.

'Gangs of Frenchmen who have taken oaths to Hitler. Worse than cowards.'

'Frenchmen follow Hitler?'

There is a noise in the night and we stop – a dog barking? Silence resumes.

'Of course.' She turns back to me, and the hike resumes. 'It is easier to do what you're told. Round up Jews; hunt down partisans. Soon more Frenchmen will join them. It is the pattern of subjection. Defeat, collaborate, assimilate. Pray you don't live long enough to see it happen at home.'

I nod, trying to picture such a mad scene. Anna, Flo, Oakes – surrendering, then helping, then joining the Nazi ranks. *Impossible.* But then I think again of Anna's father, that German. He would want that life for her – being ruled by the Germans, living under their bloody jackboot – wouldn't he?

The noise again – definitely a dog, maybe several. In the darkness, everything melts into shapes of green and grey. I cough, trying to keep the panic from my voice. 'Why are the Milice worse than the Germans?'

'They know the land,' she says.

The others may appear light-hearted, but I can't shake off the fact that the Milice – and the SS! – are hunting us, and we can hear bloody dogs in the distance. I keep looking behind me, my ears straining for any sound.

We march on. My body weighs a thousand tons. One idea circles my thoughts: these woods, these quiet woods, are crawling with soldiers trying to kill us.

The sun is up, but all these forest roads look the same to me, as we head south under the towering trees. It's been weeks since I've known where I am.

Occasionally, we stumble upon a proper road, and my feet sigh in relief. I make the mistake of wondering aloud about cars – my boots practically slosh with blood – and Bernard is only too happy to lecture me about why cars are never to be used. Apparently, only the Germans are permitted to drive, and to be seen in a car is to invite disaster. *Returned to your SS friends*, is how he puts it. I keep on walking through the pain.

The vineyards and villages look green and pleasant, which is a sight more than irritating. In London, we resist, and live in ruins. The French have been invaded, and their country looks whole. It's enough to make your blood boil.

We avoid towns and villages with telephone lines, and march all night, sleeping instead for a few hours after lunch and somehow no one whinges about our schedule. A schedule that is a mystery to everyone but Wake.

The sun is high – it must be close to noon – and we finally halt to set up camp. Which means a quick meal and an even quicker sleep under the trees.

'Squire. You and the Alsatian help with the firewood.'

The Alsatian turns out to be a man with a weathered face and not a tooth in his mouth, but he gathers firewood at a pace I struggle to match. Soon we are back at the camp and helping set up stones around the firepit.

The Alsatian nods as I finish lining the pit with stones.

'Always a firepit. If the Germans are upwind, they'll smell the smoke and be on us in no time.'

Bernard, after bathing in the freezing stream, is cutting

mushrooms and carrots; Claude has gone off to fill the cookpot. Soon I am toasting the grey bread over the fire, feeling my hand singe as I hold it too close.

Sentries are always set, prepared escape routes memorized. We eat sitting on logs, and bathe in the river. We sleep in tents made from parachute silk, and I am forced to share a tent with Bernard. In my exhausted state, the rough blanket will be a cloud.

After we wake in the afternoon sun, Bernard leads the group in physical fitness training, which he enjoys entirely too much. Then he is back off to bathe in the river; he is more fish than man. Breakfast is coffee brewed over the fire and stale croissants. Wake then trains men with special weapons, and then she meets with Denis, and they smoke fags and listen to the BBC news bulletin.

I take a clean shirt from my bag – thanks, Commander Wake – and slip on a tight-fitting tunic. *Bloody French.*

I use my old shirt – now officially a rag – to wipe as much of the dirt from my face before crumpling the shirt back into the pack.

Wake seems to never sleep. When I got up – after what can only have been two hours – she was there, poring over the maps, a small Colt automatic at her side, forever in the process of lighting a new fag.

She may not share her plans with us, but it's clear we can trust her. Yesterday I thought about how unfair it was that the French villages lay so untouched. Today I remember the villagers themselves, who didn't look or hear or speak. Heads down, focused only on their business.

Hoping the Germans take their neighbours instead. Keeping to themselves. Trying to survive.

Well, this is another way to try and survive – this roving camp in the forest, these men working under Commander Wake. 'Hitler has picked France to the bone,' she said as we were forced back onto a twisting forest path. 'We have different ways of fighting our own war against Vichy and the Nazis.'

I rolled my eyes then, but I feel myself nodding now. Sometimes you have to fight back, in whatever way you can.

15 July 1944

For the most part, though, time at the camp is when I make bombs – or, more accurately, plastic explosives wrapped in socks. Wake uses Nobel's 808 plastic, which looks like yellow plasticine sausages, and smells like almonds.

The Germans, I am told, are a particularly irritating group to sabotage. The Resistance work overnight removing all of the bolts on the train rails, and by the morning the Germans will have fixed it. Within forty-eight hours the trains will be running again. So bombs provide a more permanent disruption.

I have no problem admitting I'm the right man for the job. I chat away with Denis and the others as I knead the sausages, softening them up. Easy as this is for me, I am grateful to see that they have tubes of Vaseline – you have to coat your fingers in the stuff; the plastic causes a violent headache. I combine the sausages to form bigger and bigger explosives, much to the delight of the onlookers. *If only Lightwood were here. He's absolute mustard on rigging up bombs.*

Then I pack away, very carefully, the small white cones – the primary charge – and the slim metal detonators. I can feel Wake's smile.

Tomorrow, I am told excitedly, we are not simply blowing track rails. There is an approaching German convoy in desperate need of ambushing. We're running from one fight and picking another at the same time. *Seems about right.*

Anna – I can't think of her, can I? What she'd make of all this, I can't begin to guess. It seems a safe bet that she'd be angry.

Anna's done some mad things – she loved those bloody ravens after all – but there's no way she could fall in love with a toff like Cecil Rafferty. The fact that he proposed to her – Cecil Rafferty! – is almost enough to make my head spin.

And that she said no. *For me.*

We move on to L-delay units, where I explain to the newer members how the delay pencils come in three colours: red for a half-hour delay; white for two hours; green for six hours. Bernard wanders by, stopping long enough to give a grudging nod. *This is what I do, mate. You can have wearing a beret and being a wanker, I've got bomb making and disposal.*

'What do you do next?'

I turn away from Bernard to stare at the eager voice of the Alsatian.

'Right,' I say. 'The top is moulded from soft copper, and beneath is a thin wire and, important little detail, a phial of acid. What you need to do is press the copper and break the phial.'

'Releasing the acid.'

'That's it, mate. The acid melts the wire, dropping a plunger which strikes the detonator. This is why the wire is important – the thicker the wire, the longer the delay. Got it?'

The Alsatian nods. He's no Lightwood, but I feel like he's got a handle on it. Then we pack up and move on, chasing down the Germans.

David and Goliath. *Except Goliath has tanks.*

That night I find a moment to talk to Wake by the fire.

'Once France is free,' I ask quietly, 'you will send me home?'

'You ever been in a submarine? We put most people in submarines.' She takes a long drink from a bottle. 'But if you help us clear the Germans out of here, you'll get a seat next to me on a ship to London.'

16 July 1944

We slog on. South, always south, searching for our ambush. It's quite something that, with all the Nazis hunting us, and the Milice with their dogs, the worst thing in my life is this new tear in the insole of my boot. *My blister wounds had finally healed into calluses, and now this.* The skin on my heel has completely rubbed off, and each step is a throb of pain. There is no way to avoid it – limping, favouring my toes, dragging my foot – nothing escapes the bloody tear in my boot.

The landscape changes, offering a break from the thickly wooded paths that have ruined my sense of direction. Now tall hedgerows divide the farmland into smaller fields. The area slopes and climbs with hills, leading again to a forest that disappears over the horizon. But for now, I can see where we're going.

It doesn't take long to miss the cover of the trees. The sun is merciless. I am half-surprised to see the green fields, sure they must be scorched bare in the summer.

We are apparently entering an area with lots of villages, and Wake is firm in her instructions.

'About one thing we have to be absolutely clear. No one is to steal from the French – not an onion, not a blanket, not a bottle. Whatever you take from a German is fine by me, but every stolen chicken from a local farmer makes our fight that much harder. We get our supplies from coordinated parachute drops. After each drop-off,' Wake continues in a loud voice, 'you will receive money, and you will buy from the farmers at market rates.'

Everyone nods, some more slowly than others. I have heard all about how the Germans pillage the countryside, casually waltzing off with whatever they want – paintings, food, bicycles.

Wake seems to have contacts in every village, and she often wanders into towns to gather new information. When I ask Bernard if that isn't a dangerous move to let her go into hostile territory alone, he throws his head back and laughs.

In one village, they are keeping six German prisoners in the schoolyard. I can't help but think this is a terrible idea, but of course no one asks for my thoughts. Well, I've been at them for not fighting back, so I can't go on whinging now they've finally started.

And it seems France truly is ready to fight back. Many villagers try to come along when we leave, and Wake lets a good number join our ranks, including a quiet boy named Stephan. *Napthalines*, the newcomers are nicknamed – mothballs.

'They are tired of hiding,' she says pointedly.

We get no such reception in the next village, where there is nothing to greet us but silence. *Maybe the mothballs have struck out on their own, ready to challenge the Germans in the fields.* Then I see them, an old man and an older woman, maybe grandparents, hanging from lamp posts.

The smell should have been a dead giveaway, but the church is a blackened shell. No one goes anywhere near it.

'Be ready,' Wake says as we swiftly exit the ghost village. 'Every second.'

But you can't. The strain of it, the panic of seeing every movement in the distance, hearing every noise in the leaves – it is too much. You trip on your feet, or choke drinking water. You can do nothing.

So I'm not ready. Instead, I'm in a story. Not from a

comic like the *Champion*, but a serious novel like the ones Miss Breedon always had on her desk. It is an adventure, and I am going to be bloody well alive at the end of it.

As long as the wretched sun doesn't melt me to my boots.

And then it happens. We fall in with another group of Resistance, who seemingly emerge from the trees to exchange information with Wake before vanishing again in a rustle of leaves.

'All right,' she says, looking back at us with dark eyes. 'Show time.'

We scurry across the vineyard.

Our goal is to grind the Germans down, keep them nervous. In other words, let the convoy pass, fire on them, then run for our lives. *Never* play the enemy on its own terms. Never engage the Germans directly.

The thought hits me so hard I almost stumble. *What am I doing?* I've had fifteen months of armed forces training. Fifteen months in Dorset, surrounded by bloody eager lads barely older than me. Before that, I was in class, learning about trigonometry and helping feed some giant ravens. *And now I'm trying to sneak up on the greatest bloody soldiers in the world?*

I force the image out of my head. Me, Wake, Bernard, the Alsatian reach the end of the silent vineyard, and swiftly lie in the drains alongside the road.

In no time at all, the convoy of four trucks rumbles towards us. We wait, none of us so much as breathing. *I know how to fight, how to stay alive. Major taught me. I am a trained soldier in the British Armed Forces.*

'Let them go,' Wake cautions, though I'm certain no one moved an inch. I hold my grenade, pin pulled. The trucks roll on in a cloud of dust. I force myself to take a long breath, my thumb slippery on the safety lever.

They must be 50 feet past us now. It is a small convoy – no armoured cars, no soldiers on motorcycles. Just four trucks, though they're bound to be filled with Germans.

After all this time, marching and starving and waiting to get mauled by a dog, we are finally ambushing the Germans. Of course a part of me feels like this is a terrible idea – we are trying to *hide* from the bastards, after all – but the rest of me is just ready to get on with it and kick these buggers out of France.

'Now,' Wake shouts.

A hail of bullets brings the trucks to a halt. My grenade only just reaches the last truck, but the explosion catches, sending flames singing up the sides. The door fly open and a German tumbles out. A bullet takes him. The stutter of Sten machine guns is deafening.

Stick to the mission. Destroy the first and the last vehicle of the convoy. Hem them in, give them all you've got, and then make a swift retreat.

With a cry of pure rage, I toss all the bombs I have, and fire from the hip as we race across the vineyard to the safety of the forest.

I have killed men; ended men's lives. The knowledge of this should weigh on me, make me feel heavy, or at least confused. But I only feel knackered as we set up camp.

A panting scout arrives to tell Wake some news. By her reaction, it isn't good. *Is it ever?*

Wake nods and turns back to Claude. 'How long will it take to move camp?'

He sighs heavily, looking around the just settled campsite. 'Thirty minutes.'

'Make it ten,' she says. 'Their scouts have found us.'

'How many?' I ask.

'Eight thousand. So get on that fire.'

Eight thousand? We don't have that many grenades.

We douse the fire, start packing up. Wake clears out her tent, issuing commands. I follow her orders, aware that the last time I shared my brilliant ideas, I got captured and Lightwood got killed.

We run through the vineyards to a nearby forest, disappearing into the trees.

Another scout meets us, his face flushed red. 'Germans are there. East and west. We are being encircled.'

Over the next few days this becomes increasingly clear. Spotter aircraft flies above; the sounds of artillery are close. We're being encircled by an army.

'This is it then?' I say.

'No. Our goal here is not to fight to the death against impossible odds. Our goal is to fight and live to fight again tomorrow. There is still plenty of war ahead of us.'

13

ANNA COOPER

17 July 1944

To fly a Spitfire is to feel properly alive.

It was designed for a woman, Gower once claimed. It seems true – the cockpit is slim, smaller than other fighters', and perfect control of the plane never relies on brute strength.

Gower has reluctantly allowed us to borrow the Spit-bombers again, but with a warning that at *any moment* she will likely require them all to be returned. I have no interest in testing her patience.

Our extensive training programme involves air-to-air firing, divebombing, and formation practice. The last few hours have been spent perfecting echelon formation, angled slightly back from the leader, followed by a dropped-down V formation. Such defensive positions are to be maintained up to the moment when we each peel off into a dive.

'The theory of dive bombing is simple enough,' Joy says over the radio. 'Put the Spit into a steep dive, aim your nose at the target, and unleash your bomb at the same time you pull out of the dive. Easy as.'

We are using practice smoke bombs over Cornwall, and Joy's earlier lessons flash in my mind – she talks endlessly of 'vertical 90 degree attitudes' and '70 degree flight paths' – but somehow I forget it all the moment I tip my plane into a exhilarating dive at 10,000 feet.

It's hard to keep a thought in my head as I hang suspended from the shoulder straps, watching the target grow as I plummet to earth. The speed is phenomenal, as the heavy plane starts working with gravity instead of against it. In those final 10 seconds, even my breathing stops.

There is no aid to help with aiming, only your own eyes staring down the nose of the Spitfire at your impending target. In this case, a tree.

As advised, I drop the bomb at 1,000 feet – *two seconds* before impact – before swiftly pulling out of the dive and back into a climb. *Because anti-aircraft guns will be hunting you.*

I miss. Maybe 50 feet off.

'Watch your angle, Coop,' comes Joy's voice. 'You're too wide.'

Minx dives next, but pulls out, abandoning the dive with a curse. 'Sorry. My flight line was all wrong.'

Minx has another go, and this time she completes the dive, but she misses the drop by a wide enough margin that we're treated to another round of frustrated cursing.

Canada has a strong showing – despite having three fewer days of training because Gower needed one of the

Spits back – and Bella is the best pilot in the ATA, but no one hits the tree except Joy, and even she needs two attempts. By this time we are ready for a victory, and exhausted cheers erupt from the other pilots.

Once we finally land, my cramped muscles ache in protest. I wipe at the grime and sweat of the flight. The sun presses down on us, and seems to rise up again from the tarmac.

All the training seems to be taking a serious toll on Joy. As we head from the hangars, she holds her back, wincing in pain. I should tell her to take tomorrow off.

But she can't take tomorrow off. She's our teacher; without her, we'll never be ready in time. If I can go up with a headache that could blind a horse, she can go up with a hurt back.

She is smiling now at any rate, even if it's forced. 'You need to sort out those angles, Coop. There's no place in my circus for sloppy diving.' She laughs. 'Let's hit up the Mess.'

I shake my head, and am forced to pause for a moment to let the stars wink out. Sleep drags at me. 'I've got more work to do.'

Canada shuffles ahead, looking as drained as I feel. Bella, Barcsay, and Minx follow behind.

Joy and I are left standing alone on the warm tarmac. 'Training's over for the day, Coop. Time to take a breather.'

'I'll use the Link Trainer,' I say, raising my palms to calm the inevitable tide of well-meaning advice. I hate using the flight simulator – it's cramped and hot – but it's the only way to be ready. 'Just for an hour or so. You're right, I need to work on my angles. I'll meet you guys in the crew room after.'

'So you don't need to eat any more?'

I can't find the strength to humour her. 'I'll see you later, OK?'

'Anna.' The serious tone in her voice makes me stop. 'Are you sure you're feeling up to this?'

'What? Are my angles that bad?'

She fixes me with a hard stare. 'Your angles *are* that bad, but that's not what I'm talking about. You got some heavy news, you're allowed to be – I don't know, not invincible.'

'I'm fine, Joy. I am. Let's talk about it later, OK?'

As I turn off to a small side building, I can feel Joy watching me.

14

CECIL RAFFERTY

17 July 1944

Hamble airfield is a small outfit, with only female pilots and workers. Paradise Island, the lads call it, as well as some other less tasteful names.

But all that pub chat vanishes as I see the pilot crossing the tarmac.

'Miss Cooper,' I call out.

'Cecil!' She flings herself at me so hard I almost stumble. I hold her tight, my leg screaming in pain. 'It's good to see you. My God.'

'And you.' I put her gently down to the ground. She instantly seems older, wiser, more beautiful than I remember. She smells ever so faintly of lavender soap.

It is quite the thing to be standing here, in front of Anna, after all that has happened in the past year. And now I must be the bearer of bad news. No sense delaying it.

'Anna, I'm sorry to barge in on you like this – and then

to be so sudden – but do you have a moment? Is there somewhere we could sit down? There is something I need to tell you.'

'About Timothy Squire?'

'Yes.'

She ducks her head, but then looks at me with those blue eyes. 'I got the letter last week. Missing in Action.'

I look at her and turn into a coward. She lost her mother, her uncle – her bloody father is a German. How can I tell her Squire is dead, too? I remember the last moment I saw him, a prisoner on the ground, surrounded by soldiers with guns. He *is* a crafty little sod, but there's no way he could make it out of there alive.

'Yes,' I say. 'Missing in Action.'

'Do you know anything else?' She says quickly. 'You were probably the last one to see him, weren't you?'

I am forced to take a breath, but the words come out solid enough. 'I scarcely saw him at all, I'm afraid. I towed their glider over the sea, and dropped them off.'

'But you dropped them off safely?'

'I did.'

I can't tell her. It would not be merciful, not now. She's convinced herself that he's alive, and me telling her otherwise will drive her into despair.

'He will be fine,' she says, finally, but the worry never leaves her eyes. After a long pause she says. 'I'll make us some tea.'

As we begin walking, I wince as my leg flares up.

'Cecil – are you hurt?'

'No, not really. Had a bit of bother with the Gestapo,' I laugh. 'But now I'm fit as a fiddle.'

My smile drops the instant she looks away. This is going to be far more difficult than I imagined.

15

ANNA COOPER

17 July 1944

'A local peasant found me. A kind man, a brave man. He saw that I was injured, that I couldn't walk, and he offered to shelter me. I don't know where – his farmhouse, I assume. Of course I insisted the man leave me. The Germans found me not fifteen minutes later.'

Cecil closes his eyes. The last time I saw him, he proposed to me. Got down on one knee right on the tarmac in front of my Tempest Mark IV. *Cecil Sodding Rafferty*, the most handsome pilot in the RAF. The man who wooed both the stunning Nell Singer and the violet-eyed Isabel Pomeroy, proposed to *me*.

And I said no.

And here he is, looking exactly as he did on that day – his dark hair combed back, his shirt and tie crisp and perfect. The Mess hall, all women, have certainly taken notice. I've never seen so many pilots and ground crew in here at once. If Cecil notices the stares, he doesn't show it.

But something is different, and not only the stiff leg. The confident RAF pilot I knew would never hesitate to look me in the eye.

I reach out across the small table, touch his hand. 'What happened? Did they take you prisoner?'

'Yes. For two days I was locked away in a cell. But I was rescued.'

'Thank God.'

'Well,' he smiles. 'I don't know about God, but good fortune, certainly. It was a very heroic soldier who rescued me. He risked his life for mine.' He looks down again.

I watch him, try to smile. He was captured and rescued; the feeling must be confusing, impossible to fully understand.

I am glad that he is back. Please let Timothy Squire come back, too.

16

CECIL RAFFERTY

3 August 1944

Of course I should just come out and tell her the truth. But it will help nothing. Squire wouldn't want that – he asked me to protect her, made me promise to keep her safe. For now at least, it is better that she doesn't know.

She hands me a tea. I smile, taking a moment to breathe in the flavour. The cup is not white – it is blue china – so it is difficult to see the colours and the depths of the blend. My old life, the life I very foolishly used to think was my only future, was as a tea taster for Father's company. *Now I'm happy to have anything at all to drink.*

'It was a dangerous flying over in a 109,' I say. 'I had to dodge some pesky Spits over Dover. I managed to find a small base in the east, and put my landing gear nice and early in the hopes they'd guess I was one of ours. Luckily, they let me land. About a dozen men with rifles greeted me when I got out, but at least they didn't shoot me. What is it, Anna, are you quite well?'

She nods. 'Yes, sorry. It's just – that's mad, what you did. Flying a 109 over England and landing it?'

I shift in my chair. 'I suppose there's no milk?'

She laughs. 'Sounds like that Nazi prison wasn't so bad. Fresh milk. What else did they feed you, Beef Wellington?'

I watch her laugh. 'It is good to be here with you, Anna Cooper.'

She tells me how she rescued the Spitfires from the factory. How the Nazi 109s chased them through the clouds.

'I thought of you,' she says, and her cheeks flush red. 'When my engine jammed. I knew I had to jump.'

'You did?'

'I thought of your story, how you bailed over the sea near Margate. I remember being so shocked at the prospect. I was still in the WAAF then. I'd never even been in a plane.'

'I recall it clearly.'

'I just kept asking you questions about it – how it was possible. This was back in those happy days before my own parachute drills.'

I laugh, having spent my fair share of time at parachute drills. 'Elbows in. Keep your knees together!'

'Roll as you land! Roll!' She smiles, tossing back her hair with a shake of her head. 'Well, I managed to land the Spit, but it buckled and caught fire pretty quickly. I had to run as fast as I could to beat the explosion.'

'A brave thing to do, landing like that. You are a courageous pilot, Anna Cooper.'

She blushes. 'It's not as though I had a choice. I had to go after Joy. I could never leave a friend behind like that.'

My throat feels raw but I manage a smile. *I didn't leave anyone behind.* Lightwood needed me to provide cover so he could escape.

'In all honesty, I was terrified. It was one of the most frightening things I've ever done. I could barely think straight. It all sounds great now, but I was nothing if not a coward up there.'

'You have to be truly brave to let yourself be seen as a coward,' I say.

She turns fully red now, her face matching the colour of her hair.

'My father says that, and at any rate it sounds true.'

'Well, here's hoping I'll never have to do it again,' she says.

I raise my cup. 'To only landing on runways.'

Anna smiles, does the same.

'Your smile,' I say, 'is looking very white.'

She laughs. 'You can thank the rough landing for that too. Only about half of them are real now.'

The laugher settles, and she fixes me with a stare. 'No one believes me,' she says, after a moment. 'About what's coming.'

'I'll believe you, Anna.' I say, sure as I say the words that they are true. 'What is it?'

'There is something coming – a new weapon. These V1 bombs are only a distraction. There is something else, something far worse. And we have no way to stop it.'

I watch her. 'What do you mean?'

'Can you fly?' she asks.

'Not yet. A few weeks at least.'

She nods, and I see the determination harden in her eyes. 'I need your help.'

As I follow the clerk through the long corridors of the Air Ministry, I practise my speech in my head.

We finally reach Sir Archibald's office, and I offer a crisp salute.

Archibald has aged since I last saw him give an address to Bomber Command, but he has lost none of his authority.

'Well, well – Cecil Rafferty.' He shakes my hand and motions for me to sit.

'Thank you, sir.'

He settles back in his chair. 'Just the other day I was thinking, Yes, I must write to Hugh Rafferty. How is the old rascal?'

'Father is in fine health, thank you sir.'

He laughs. 'I bet he is. Always knew how to take care of himself, Hugh did. So, does the apple fall far from the tree?'

'I manage OK, sir, thank you.'

He nods. 'Now, what can I do for you?'

'I wanted to inform you, sir, of a new and I believe very serious threat facing Britain. The V2 rocket.'

'These reports do reach us, you know.' He casts me a withering glance. 'I have civilians forcing their way in here to tell me about the threat of rockets, and in one case how to defend against them, as if such a thing had never occurred to me.'

I feel my face growing hot. 'I didn't mean to suggest—'

'What do you mean to suggest, lad? I have a very busy morning.'

'Bomber strikes, sir,' I say quickly. 'On launch sites in France. We could also target storage sites, once fighters have confirmed locations via recces.'

'You are requesting a bomber mission, targeting rocket sites?'

'I am, sir.'

'As a captain with Bomber Command, I would have thought you'd know better, Rafferty.' His voice is slow, measured, and heavy with disapproval. 'Both 2nd Tactical Air Force and Bomber Command are needed as part of the battle on land. We are not to divert any bombers away from this mission. Air Chief Marshal Tedder has made that explicitly clear.

'We have a serious threat on the ground, which requires all of our focus. The answer to your request, Rafferty, is no.'

17

ANNA COOPER

7 August 1944

'He may change his mind,' Cecil says, straining to sound hopeful. 'But for now, Bomber Command is tied up with the ground offensive. I'm sorry, Anna.'

'Thank you for trying.'

'Anna,' he says softly, 'I would do anything for you.'

'Oh.'

He brushes a hand down his uniform, and clears his throat loudly. 'I'm sorry, Anna. I didn't mean…'

'I know.' I look up at him and his smile vanishes. His face is lined, serious.

I know he doesn't mean anything by what he said. He is a gentleman, and he's just being kind. He's been through hell at the hands of the Germans.

I sit on the floor of the hangar, tinkering with the new Merlin engine. Cecil's smile fills my thoughts, flooding me with guilt. Timothy Squire is out there, alive, and he's coming back – I can't think of Cecil Bloody Rafferty. Besides, I already said no to him. He has moved on to some new girl, I don't doubt.

I don't have time to feel guilty about any of this; I need to get back in the sky and work on my dive bombing. I give a frustrated twist of the wheel nut, and my spanner slips, clattering to the tarmac.

Footsteps announce a new arrival. From the dragging boots, it is a man – apparently no longer a rare occurrence at Hamble.

The man turns the corner and, blinking, enters the hangar. Well, it's hard to call Malcolm a man really. He's an overgrown boy – and he's always been a mystery. When I first met him at the Tower School, he never said a word to me other than to complain about the ravens. Then he unexpectedly turned up at White Waltham airfield to study meteorological systems, and since then he hasn't stopped talking for more than two moments together.

And today he is beaming. 'Anna, I found him!'

I stare up at him, letting my wrench fall to the floor. Is it possible?

'I found him,' he repeats. 'Hiding in a basement flat.'

'Hiding…? You found Timothy Squire?'

'What?' He shakes his head. 'No. I found *him* – Cam Westin.'

'Oh.'

My breathing slowly returns. So does anger. Cam Westin – a monster and a traitor. As a flight engineer, he sabotaged a number of planes at the ATA, including my landing gear, and I have no doubt that he is responsible for the strange crash that killed Diana Gaines.

Malcolm's arrival has stirred up some commotion. I notice some disappointed stares from the engineers hoping Cecil had returned.

'He turned up at a café,' Malcolm is saying, excitement in his voice. 'I tracked him there. He saw me. Once he looked straight at me. But he didn't recognize me. I brought three policemen with me. I caught him.'

He finished, face flushed, looking very much like a student who's confident he's aced an examination. I clasp him in a hug. 'Thank you, Malcolm.'

'I told you I'd find him.' He smiles, taking a step back. 'The trial's in two weeks. Gower will be there. And so will I, of course. Don't worry Anna, he's going to gaol for what he did.'

I nod, tears forming in my eyes.

'Thank you, Malcolm.'

Two weeks. I fight off the ridiculous urge to run home to the Tower and ask Oakes to attend it with me. I am old enough to handle this on my own. And Gower will be there. *And Malcolm, apparently.*

The thought of telling Cecil briefly flares into my mind. He knows Westin, the two are even friends. He would be furious on my behalf, and he would surely do something to help.

No, I can deal with this myself. It has nothing to do with Cecil.

Another fear slowly creeps into my thoughts. Would Cecil believe me?

I shake my head angrily to clear it. Of course he would believe me, but I don't need him to. I can handle Cam Westin on my own.

16 August 1944

'I think you ladies are starting to get the hang of it,' says Barcsay after another hard day of training. Barcsay is our resident weapons expert, and she has been relentless in taking us through firing exercises.

'I took down a few targets,' says Minx. 'So did Bella.'

Canada shrugs. 'Cooper says we're ready to go for Friday. What do you think, Brooks?'

'Brooks is better than most of us,' Barcsay admits grudgingly.

I turn to Joy, who's been silent the whole time. 'You're all getting better.'

'We *are* getting better,' I say, facing the semicircle of pilots. 'Friday, we'll do a recce of northern France.'

'Well then,' says Minx, sounding more than a little nervous, 'I'm going to get a drink.'

Hornets buzz angrily through the hot afternoon as Minx, Canada, and Bella walk away to the Mess. 'Everyone study your maps,' I call after them.

'Coop.'

I turn back at Joy's voice. She is standing still, helmet in her hands. 'Friday, huh?'

'You have other plans?' I laugh.

She narrows her eyes at me. 'We're not ready, Anna.'

I nod. 'We don't have a choice.'

'If the girls fly over a war zone, we're all going get killed.'

I shift my tired feet, taken aback. 'I thought you hated all that RAF talk.'

'I hate how they treat women like helpless babies. But they wouldn't send male pilots on this mission with only fourteen days of training.'

'I can learn the angles,' I say stiffly. 'I can. I'll use the Trainer after dinner – all night if I have to. I can do this – I'm a good pilot, Joy.'

'You are a good pilot. So am I. Bella might just be the best pilot I've ever seen, man or woman. But none of us are ready to go over there, track convoys, deal with flak, and divebomb precise targets.'

'We don't have time.'

Her face is hard. 'We *need* to train more.'

I shake my head and stare out at the planes. 'Of course you're happy to wait.'

'What does that mean?'

I turn and face her. 'You came over here because they wouldn't let you fly in America. You came here to fight for us – of course I appreciate that. But this is my home, Joy. These rockets are coming to destroy where I live.'

'I know that.'

'These people have been through enough. Too much is already gone, destroyed.' I sigh. 'If we wait around until we never make a mistake with our angles, this country will be a smoking ruin. And then what's the point?'

'Let's get to the Mess,' Joy sighs. 'And talk.'

'No,' I say sharply – more sharply than I mean to. 'I'm off to the Trainer.'

Joy snorts. 'Now? Come on.'

'You said we're not ready for Friday. But I will be.'

'Anna. It won't bring him back, going over there.'

I stop. 'What?'

There is a moment of stillness.

'I know you think, because Timothy Squire went over there—'

My voice is as steady as I can make it. 'This isn't a rescue mission, Joy. We're going over there to drop bombs.'

16 August 1944

I've decided to take Joy's advice and allow myself to relax. After a few hours on the Trainer, I took the train to London, making a quick stop at the Tower to change into the green dress I've been waiting to wear since the spring. Nell helped me pick it out, insisting the green shade 'looks snappy' with my red hair and a 'bit of lippy'.

It is a relief to be wearing a silk dress; to be free of buckles, helmets, and parachute packs. I don't even mind the heels that pinch my toes.

All week Cecil has been inviting me for dinner at the Savoy Grill, and tonight I surprised him by saying yes. Some time with him might help clear the pain in my head.

I knew rationing wasn't in effect at the luxury restaurants, but I can barely contain myself when I see ice cream on the menu, after three years without it. It's all I can do not to order it as my main.

Cecil pours me another wine and smiles. He is even taller than I remember.

In two days I will be off on a highly dangerous – and highly illegal – mission. I have to focus. I don't care what Joy says – we are ready.

'Anna, I'd like to talk to you about something.'

'Oh,' I say, looking down. What does Cecil want to talk about?

But even now that he's broached the subject, he doesn't seem keen to continue. He tops up both our wine glasses, and starts talking about his estate in York.

I think how reckless it was, that time I forced Joy to come with me, to drop in unannounced on his midsummer party – the beautiful garden, with the stand of tall poplars and a rolling valley leading to a pond. *I've thought of it, many times since. It was the most beautiful home I've ever seen, far grander than Flo's.* Music and laughter in the night air, the bloom of tiny lights in the trees, and men in white uniforms carrying trays of wine.

'And Nell?' I ask when the memory of her comes back to me. She was his sweetheart for a while, and I've rarely seen a more beautiful girl than Nell at that party. 'How is she?'

He shrugs. 'I haven't seen her since midsummer.'

'Oh.'

In truth, I shouldn't be too surprised. Nell and I became close friends after our dust-up at the party. *A girl's got to wonder whether men are worth all the fuss*, she'd said with a wicked grin. I still don't know the answer.

'We never did it properly, you know?' he says.

'What?' I say, my voice strangled.

'The midsummer party. You're meant to let the bonfire burn down, and then jump over the ashes together.'

He has a lovely voice, low and measured – though he rarely meets my eyes. *War changes people.*

'Really? Why?'

He pauses. 'True love, and all that.'

I go as red as my hair. 'I didn't know that.'

'Well, it's a silly old tradition. My sister used to do it, but since she moved to America, well, Father and I haven't quite kept it up.'

His look wrings a smile out of me. But I know I must talk to him about Cam. More and more the trial has worried me. Cecil will hear about it soon enough; I should be the one to tell him.

'Should we get another bottle?' he asks.

I shake my head. 'Cecil. I have to tell *you* something.'

He politely waves the waiter away.

'Cam Westin. I know he's your friend, but he is being charged with sabotaging ATA planes.'

'I'm sorry?'

I swallow. 'One of the planes was mine.'

'Anna, what are you saying?'

I take the last gulp of my wine. 'Cam Westin sabotaged the landing gear in my Tempest last year. I managed to land OK, but it was very close. I challenged him – he denied it of course.'

He reaches for his water. 'Anna, it must be a mistake. I've known West for years – he's one of the best flight engineers in the RAF. He would never do something to harm our own planes. This must be a mistake.'

I fold my hands on the table. 'When Commander Gower sent police to arrest him, he ran away. Now he's been caught, and his trial is tomorrow.'

Cecil is as white as the tablecloth. 'His trial? And you will be there?'

'With Gower. My word against his.'

He shakes his head. 'Please. It's a mistake. A Tempest – it's a heavy machine, and the engine has faults.'

'The engine was fine. It was the landing gear.'

'It's a prototype. I've had plenty of issues with the new planes. I just wrestled with a 109 to figure out how to get the wheels down. Every machine is different.'

'I know that,' I say, unable to hide my irritation. 'I am a Second Officer in the ATA.'

He holds up his hands. 'Anna, please – I know you're a great pilot. And of course I believe what you say.'

'It doesn't sound like it.'

'I do. Of course I do. But you mustn't go to the trial.'

'What?' I say slowly.

He stares at me, stricken. 'You can't. It's a mistake,

and we can resolve this. Let me speak to him. He will apologize—'

'Diana Gaines was killed. Her engine shut down mid-flight. One of the other girls had her engine catch fire as she took off – she managed to land and douse the flames, and guess what she found inside? Rolled-up oil rags.'

He exhales a long breath. 'I am sorry about your friend,' he says. 'But, Anna, you can't really believe that Cam is trying to kill off ATA pilots.'

'All I know is what happened. And I will tell the judge what I know.' And just like that I've lost my appetite, even for ice cream.

As I stand to leave, Cecil calls after me.

18

TIMOTHY SQUIRE

1 August 1944

More can go wrong. I mean, it feels like everything possible has already gone wrong; no food, no rest, the Germans and the Milice closing in. But until I hear the bloody yap of a German shepherd, I know there's still room for more to go wrong.

A low rumble in the distance is followed by the stink of coal. The heavy clattering draws closer, and the train barrels east into the night. What was in it? Hay? Weapons? Prisoners? Poor souls who won't be saved by dumb luck and the Resistance? I listen to the rattling echo until there is nothing but silence.

Further south we travel, the forests thinning and mountains rearing up before they are swallowed again by forests. Dull does not begin to describe it. In fifteen minutes in east London you'd walk past a harbour, three markets, and some rats so big you'd swear they were kittens. You'd also see *people*, beggars and lords and sailors and singers

– other people than the same twenty faces staring back at you, getting thinner and darker but always the same.

Never Lightwood, that horse-faced blighter. Never Anna, whose face I'm sometimes worried I can't quite recall in every detail. I can *see* her of course, her red hair and blue eyes and laughing smile, but not her exact face, not everything. *I need to get home.*

It is a cloudless night and I can see about a billion stars, along with some distant flickers and flashes – a raid maybe.

Anna told me once, when we spent the night sitting up on the Tower battlements, about a constellation called the Big Bear. *No chance I can pick it out of this lot.* Any group of these could be a bear – not that the one she showed me looked much like a bear anyway. That was a great night, though. Back when staying up all night was exciting – and voluntary.

We keep marching. In the hush of the forest, every broken twig is thunderous. Commander Wake warned us patrols are thickest on the borders. We walk and walk, but the trees don't seem to grow wide enough to give proper cover. We have Claude, whose claims have grown from being a marksman to being a sniper of great renown. And of course Commander Wake, who I am certain could dismantle several Germans with her bare hands. But if we stumble on a full German patrol, we're done for.

As sunrise comes, we exhaustedly make camp.

Some meals we have forest mushrooms – *ceppes*, they are called – or the odd bird that Claude manages to shoot. And horsemeat, which I try not to think too much about.

But the usual fare is a small bowl of boiled potatoes and turnips, and that's what we'll all settle for today. Soon, I have been warned, it will be nothing but turnips.

I sit down next to Denis. He seems a nice enough chap and a damn sight more pleasant than Bernard, who of course is never more than a few feet away. He cuts that distance in half, sliding across the log to nudge me in the ribs. A grinning Bernard is never a welcome sight.

'Denis is a homosexual.'

My eyes go wide with shock, but Denis just smiles back. 'Every man is a homosexual. If they don't know, it's only because they haven't tried it with me.'

I nod as if this is a reasonable thing to say, and bury my face in the soup. Bernard's mocking laugh rings out.

Wake enters the campfire circle with her brisk authority. 'Denis gets a clear, clean signal back to London. He controls the radio, and without that, we'd all be dead in a week. So he's the most important person here. Squire, you've got first watch.'

As the others wander off to their tents, soup finished and washing up done, I find a moment alone with Denis.

'Denis, mate,' I whisper, hoping I'm out of earshot. 'I heard what you said back there. And I was wondering – I mean, I don't want to put you on the spot…'

He raises an eyebrow at me.

'I was hoping,' I say, 'that you could send a message for me.'

He exhales, looking a little relieved for some reason. 'A personal message? Squire, this is the Special Operations wireless channel. You've seen the labyrinth of code words and protocol that go into communicating with London. I can't simply send a love note to your sweetheart.'

'No, right. Of course not. Sorry, mate. Thanks anyway.'

Red with embarrassment, I take up a position against a large oak tree on the outskirts of the camp. *Anna knows I'm OK. Somehow, she knows.* And I'll be home soon. My watch consists exclusively of seeing German shepherds emerge from the bushes. At least thirteen times I've been a second away from raising the alarm.

But no real dogs emerge.

Bernard finally comes to relieve me – at least fifteen minutes late – and I crawl away to the tents. I have been given a rather mangy blanket, and a somewhat less mangy toothbrush, and I am properly excited about both.

It is hard not to think of my bed at home. *I have been dreaming about my old bed for months.* I would love nothing more than to change out of these filthy clothes, toss my gun into the Thames, eat a sausage roll with brown sauce, and sleep in that bed for three straight days.

I fall asleep dreaming of pillows.

19

ANNA COOPER

21 August 1944

Clammy silence fills the wood-panelled room. Malcolm is walking from the witness box, having given his heartfelt account, to take a seat on the benches behind me. Gower has already had her turn, and she backed up the unusual happenings and timed them with Westin's shifts.

The judge, a round man in black robes, narrows his eyes at the pages before him. 'Despite any grievances, personal or professional, I'm having a difficult time believing someone could be so petty in a time of war.'

I stare back. I have not been asked to stand in the witness box, but this statement seems addressed to me.

'I can't explain his thinking, sir, only the consequences,' I say, forcing myself to speak slowly and clearly. 'Diana Gaines is dead. My Tempest was sabotaged. Numerous lives were put at risk.'

Turning my head, I stare directly at Cam Westin. He is

in uniform, and appears to have brought all his mates for the show. He stares straight ahead. I remember the feeling of him watching me from across the tarmac. Every day I had to work with him in the hangar, he would grumble and send me to fetch his tea.

'Flight Engineer Westin,' the judge says. 'What do you say to all this? Accusations of sabotage and conspiracy to aid the enemy in a time of war?'

He spreads his hands wide. 'I am not certain what to say, sir. One of my duties at White Waltham airfield was to teach the basics of engine work to trainees involved in the ATA programme. I believe this particular trainee holds a personal grudge against me.'

'Why is that?'

'I was attempting to teach her about engines, sir, but the mechanical concepts... well, they didn't take hold, shall we say. She grew visibly embarrassed and upset. When I suggested that a cup of tea might help the situation, she became even more agitated. She thought the idea of making tea beneath her station, and ever since I have been subjected to slander and gossip from a circle of female pilots.'

'I am a pilot – not a NAAFI girl. Get your own tea.' I say the words with more heat than I intended, but it doesn't matter. He is obviously lying, and the combined testimony of Gower and Malcolm must be enough to put Westin in gaol.

I look back at the judge, ready for this all to be over.

'Flight Engineer Westin,' he continues. 'What do you believe occurred during this so called sabotage?'

'The Tempest has a Rolls-Royce Griffon 61 piston engine, which requires physical strength to keep properly under control.'

How would you know? You can't even fly.

Westin carries on. 'I am a qualified flight engineer. And the certificate of safety for the Tempest was signed at the point of origin—'

'*You* signed that form!' I cry out.

'And the snag report completed at the other end showed the damage to the landing gear to be have been the fault of the pilot. The pilot was simply not physically strong enough to fully depress the lever; she panicked, made a number of critical errors of judgement, and caused serious damage to a new prototype aircraft.'

'I've heard enough.' The judge shakes his head. There is something stern – more than stern – in his tone. 'Dismissed.'

Dismissed?

Terrible silence stretches on. The pain in my head throbs, making it hard to focus.

'Thank you, sir,' comes Westin's voice.

Westin stands, and I dumbly do the same, but the judge calls out.

'Now just a minute there, miss. Be seated.'

I sit back down while the judge flips through papers on his desk.

'The ATA's job, if I'm not mistaken, is to transport aircraft to where they're needed, either the air base or the repair yard.'

Each word drains my body cold. 'That is true, sir—'

'So why is it that I've heard about a rogue squadron of ATA pilots flying manoeuvres out of the Hamble ferry site?'

I can say nothing. How does he know about that? Who, at the all-female air base, would give information to that slug Cam Westin?

The judge coughs. 'Commander Gower. I do hope you had no knowledge of this illegal behaviour.'

'She doesn't,' I blurt out. 'It was my plan. The other pilots tried to stop me. Gower would never have allowed it.'

The judge looks between us.

'It seems rather unlikely that you could procure the necessary aircraft without the knowledge of the base Commander?' He turns to Gower.

'I was aware of the training, Your Honour,' she answers.

'But it was all my idea,' I add hurriedly. 'I begged her to let me borrow a plane.'

'Very well. It seems you suffer from some very grand notion of yourself, miss. Did you know that the RAF banned women being attached to units because they were thought to be physically and temperamentally unsound? I dare say you have done much to prove them right. Miss Cooper, you are hereby terminated from the ATA, and your flying licence is revoked.'

I can't speak or move. I feel my hand tightening into a fist.

'Miss Cooper,' he says, gesturing to me. 'Surrender your wings. From this moment, you are strictly forbidden to fly aircraft.'

Without a thought in my head, I walk round the chairs,

and up to the judge's desk. It is the longest walk of my life. I can practically hear Cam Westin's smile.

I rip the wings from my shirt in an easy tear of thread. I place them in front of the judge, who doesn't even look up from shuffling his papers.

'And your licence.'

I slide it from my pocket across the desk, before I return to my place, trying for all I can not to look broken.

'Now then,' continues the judge, 'that almost concludes our business here. Female ferry pilots, we have more than enough of. RAF flight engineers, we need. Cam Westin, you are to report to Fighter Command Headquarters at Biggin Hill.'

'Yes, sir.'

I lose my wings; he gets promoted. Gower warned me not to go ahead with this. And now she is in worse trouble than I am.

Westin is standing in front of me. I force myself to look up, meet his eyes.

'No hard feelings, love. If I need someone to get my tea, I'll keep you in mind.'

I take the bus home in silence. Or at least as near to silence as one can be with Malcolm nearby. I remember when we first met at the Tower School; you couldn't prise a word out of him with a crowbar.

We've all changed, it seems.

'There's got to be an appeals process,' Malcolm is saying. 'For the judge to just stop you from flying like that. Forever.'

The thought of not going to France – of never going to France – twists at my gut. I wonder, just for the moment, if Joy is right. Do I really believe that I can find out something about Timothy Squire by going over there?

Maybe I'm wrong about everything. Maybe it *was* the landing gear that got caught, all on its own.

Something inside me feels frayed. It's the same feeling I had that day in the headmaster's office, when they told me Mum had died.

It's a feeling I've grown plenty tired of.

'The Ravens are disbanded,' I say quietly.

'We never even got to drop a bomb,' says Bella, pulling off her sunglasses.

'Or cross the sea,' adds Minx. 'We spent a lot of time staring at maps of France not to even visit.'

I shake my head. I am hungry, exhausted – I feel *gritty*, like I could bathe for hours and still be dirty. 'I am sorry, all of you. But the Air Ministry has got involved. Gower has been disciplined, and any unauthorized flights from Hamble will result in the immediate loss of wings for the pilot involved.'

Barcsay coughs. 'Is this because of your father… being a German rocket scientist?'

'No. I stood trial against an engineer who sabotaged planes at Hamble. I lost.'

Joy pulls me aside firmly. She is giving me that look I definitely knew she would give me. 'You didn't tell me the trial was so soon.'

'It wouldn't have mattered,' I say.

She nods, but I can see the pain in her eyes.

'I'm sorry, Joy.'

Joy moves as if to turn away, but stops herself. 'I'm sorry, too, Coop.'

'Are you?'

'Yes. We would have got there, in time.'

'I'm not giving up. I still care about saving this country, no matter what that judge says. I'm not going to sit around and do nothing.'

Joy bristles. 'I don't think you're doing this to save your country.'

'What?'

'That's not the reason, or you'd recognize how important it is to do it properly. I think you want to make a big dramatic gesture. I think you want to sacrifice yourself. I think you feel helpless, because no one will let you help.'

The girls' retreating footsteps echo through the silence.

'Then help me,' I say.

'I'm trying to.'

'No, you're not. You're lecturing me.'

'You should have told me about the trial.'

'Why? To watch you take sides with Cam Westin?'

I curse myself the moment I say it, but it is too late.

Her voice is slow, careful. 'You think I'd take sides with him?'

I sigh but say nothing.

'Listen,' she says, 'I know you're hurt. I know Timothy Squire is missing. I know this whole thing is a mess.'

'Oh, I thought it was because I was helpless? Now it's because I'm heartbroken. Maybe – just maybe – I actually want to stop rockets from killing my people.'

'Your people?' Joy's laugh is empty of humour. 'Or maybe you're feeling guilty. Maybe you feel guilty about your dad's involvement in making these things, and you see this as a way to make it right? Blow up some rockets, maybe blow up yourself in the process.'

I stare her in the eyes. 'Go back to America.'

20

TIMOTHY SQUIRE

3 August 1944

We have not eaten in twenty-four hours. We move faster than ever, and sleep even less. It is obvious the Germans are gaining on us, the bastards.

We pass a farm, which has been doused in petrol and burned. The bodies of the farmer and his family lie sprawled in the dirt. The Nazis forbid the burying of corpses.

More mutilated bodies swing eerily from the branches. There are German soldiers hanging there too.

'Deserters,' Wake says.

It's hard to care about dead Germans when not 100 feet away we stumble upon some of our own – fighters from other Resistance groups, each man shot in the middle of the forehead, their faces deliberately mutilated.

'Ambushed,' Bernard says, scanning the trees.

Oh, brilliant. We finally set up camp, putting a few miles between us and the ruined corpses. And, God willing, any bloody ambush waiting in the forest.

Above, the sky is flat and grey. Trying to ignore the cold spike of rain against my face, I watch Wake as she stares at an empty field.

'Ambush?' I whisper.

She shakes me off like I'm a mosquito. 'A field. And maybe the right one.'

'The right one for what?'

I imagine us all hiding in the bushes, before some horrible massacre unfolds.

'For our supplies.' She nods to herself. 'Full moon in 8 days.'

Parachute drops, I realize. Over the past few weeks, we've survived on the kindness of French peasants. I expressed my doubt when Wake first explained that the less people have, the more they are willing to share; but it seems she's right. *Even still, we have to get our own supplies eventually.*

She now gives me a long searching look before deciding she is willing to show me how a parachute drop works.

After we finally have some lunch – *or is it dinner? Does it matter?* – I sit on the log as Wake gives Denis a code name – Orange, Strawberry, Lemon – that matches a field on a meticulously detailed Michelin map. Then she adds a seemingly meaningless gibberish phase – Ding-dong-dell, pussy's in the well.

With that, she has apparently ordered more food – and explosives. So this is why she calls the wireless radio the Eureka machine. With the right code words, you can feed and arm a whole band of guerrillas.

The following day, we gather near the radio, listening

to the BBC news bulletin. The news is given, and then the voice announces 'some personal messages', and proceeds to list off a near half-hour of incoherent rambling.

When the rain's in the mountains the crow takes to flight. Clementine resembles her grandmother. Valerie Pringle's birthday is in October. Shake the trees to gather the pears.

Most of it is nonsense, Wake explains. But *some* of the phrases contain vital information for different Resistance groups across the country. After about fifteen minutes of wondering whether or not I've finally cracked, the phrase leaps out at me. *Ding-dong-dell, pussy's in the well.*

The drop is on.

Drops are only possible ten days before the full moon and ten days after, but we still must light bonfires and carry torches. Twenty men encircle the field, watching the dark trees. Sentries are posted further out, and Claude and the Alsatian sit up in the tall branches keeping an eye out for German scouts.

Several hours later, as the fitful moon peaks through the clouds, we are still waiting in the dew-drenched field. At last, the unmistakable sound of propellers echoes through the sky.

I glance over at Bernard. 'Who's in charge here? London, or her?'

Bernard shrugs.

Normally, we would silently retrieve the crates and get ready to hurry back the several miles to camp. But tonight something else has been sent.

Two giant men, in full uniform, parachute gently to the grass. Their faces are smeared black with soot, with streaks of white in fearful patterns. I've seen this type before, during the invasion launch. *Yanks.*

'Captain Trevor Reynolds and Captain Patrick Young,' announces one of the grinning giants. 'Now let's kill some Nazis.'

The two monstrous Yanks help us bury the parachutes and lug the crates back.

By the bonfire light, Wake helps unload the ammo, unpack and degrease the weapons, sort out the food, and hand out money. The Yanks have some fancy weapons with them, a whole load of bazookas – a gun that looks like a giant stovepipe. They must be rested on the shoulder, held with both hands, and fired from a kneeling position. Reynolds assures us there is no better weapon. I don't doubt the power of the thing; it's meant to be an anti-tank gun, after all. *Please God, keep us clear of any bloody tanks.*

Weapons training is scheduled for dawn, including introducing us to the new bazookas; but first everyone gathers round the fire to introduce our new friends to Calvados. Wake takes a long drink and passes the bottle down.

'Welcome, boys. We have a lot of rules around here, but one above all. The only good German is a dead one.'

Something else was dropped off in the crates. Folded up in a tight square is a British newspaper, which tells of the Allied advance across France. Once Wake is done with it, she hands it to me to read.

'The invasion is not going to plan,' she warns.

I nod, taking a swig from the bottle. Oh, it burns. 'Sometimes that's a good thing. If we'd launched the invasion to the original schedule, we'd have sailed into a great bloody storm and done Hitler's work for him.'

But the news isn't great. They still haven't captured Caen? The objective was to capture Caen on the first day. That was two months ago. Christ, is the invasion failing?

I can't think about it. I'll do all I can from here. Help sabotage German efforts to send more troops to the beaches. *That will have to be enough.*

The Americans are happily sharing their own bottle, and doing their best to learn a few key French words. They are properly amazed that some of the men used to be farmers and bakers before they joined the Resistance.

Wake hands me the bottle of Calvados. 'There are close to a million Allies on the beaches. They will break through. And we will help from our end.'

I take another long swallow. It burns a little less this time. Maybe the end is closer than we think. Maybe the bastards will surrender before summer ends. Well, they're sure as hell still here now, and no sense wishing them away. Only grenades will do that, I think with a smile.

But my smile slips, and as I take another sip I feel tears fill my eyes. Will I ever see home again?

Anna.

As my body begins to shake with sobs, Wake reaches over and not ungently pulls the bottle from my hands.

'Some things are unbearable,' she says softly. 'But we still have to bear them.'

I nod, force myself to stand, then head off to bed. Inside the tent, the chatter and laughter seems distant, part of another life. The wind in the trees sounds like the Thames from my bedroom window.

21
ANNA COOPER

24 August 1944

I have invited Cecil to the Stone Kitchen to apologize for storming out the Savoy. And because I am no longer welcome at Hamble.

'I wish I could have been there,' Cecil says again. 'Bomber Command needed me, bad leg or not. Things are turning sour on the ground, it seems.'

'It's fine. There's nothing you could have done.'

If only Timothy Squire had been here. I remember, just days after we met, he braved an air raid to switch shelters and be next to me, gripping my hand in the darkness through the worst of it.

Cecil shakes his head. 'Perhaps this is a blessing in disguise.'

'What?' I blink up at him.

'Anna, you have done so much. You are a proper hero to many people, including me. You don't need to keep fighting.'

'The war is still on. The V2 rockets are coming…'

'And the Allies will deal with them. Things are a bit difficult right now, but we still have the upper hand. You don't need to fly now.'

'I don't understand what you mean.'

'I only mean that at the moment, the world is – a different place. But soon the war will all be over, and things can return to how they once were.'

'Cecil.' I shake my head. 'I grew up in this world. I don't know any other.'

'You will, Anna. I promise you, there is a better world. A happy, safe place where everything makes sense.'

I sigh. I know he believes this. 'I don't want that world.'

For an endless moment he stares, then nods. 'You will.'

25 August 1944

Inside the bowels of the Tower, the outside world disappears into nothingness.

I am all out of grand plans.

I sit up straighter as I notice Yeoman Stackhouse, who is doing a passable job as the new Ravenmaster, approaching me on the bench.

'A lady here to see you,' he says, gesturing behind him with a gloved hand. 'Not too hard on the eyes, if I can say as much.'

Who is it? Before I have time to ask any questions, the

visitor mounts the steps and strides towards me. I barely recognize her in regular slacks and a hat.

'Bella,' I say. 'What are you doing here?'

'Getting what I was promised.'

I stare in confusion. Stackhouse offers a fairly ludicrous bow, and leaves us alone.

'I had a conversation with Gower,' she says. 'About how unfairly you've been treated in all this.'

Her eyes glint with excitement, so I lean forward. 'And?'

'And she's not willing to jeopardize the careers of any ATA pilots.'

'Oh.'

She grins. 'Luckily you and I aren't ATA pilots.'

27 August 1944

I may not have my wings any more, but I still have my uniform. It must have slipped Gower's mind not to ask for it back, I think with a smile. Will it be enough, though? Since my licence has been revoked, I can't legally be in the cockpit of a plane. And since the judge took my wings, it will be obvious to any pilot who sees us in uniform that I am not permitted to fly.

At a distance I still blend in, but I may have bigger problems here at White Waltham – Cam Westin is an engineer on the base. If he's lurking around, he'll notify the police and have me arrested for trespassing. *There's nothing I can do.* I simply have to hope he's in the Mess.

I stride across the tarmac, Bella at my side. As we get closer to the hangar, an uneasy feeling grows. I don't see any planes. And we'll need the control tower to be on our side for us to have any hope of making it out of here unnoticed.

Did Bella make a mistake? Is this a trap?

It looks very much like it is, as two men emerge from the east on to the tarmac, headed straight towards us.

Bloody hell.

I spin at the noise. More people coming, from the west this time.

It *is* a trap. I look at Bella, seeing her face in the sunlight. Does she know what we've gotten into? If she does, I've never seen someone so relaxed at the prospect of a gaol cell.

This is a disaster.

As they approach us the group of men slows. We are basically surrounded. There are six of us, standing in a semi-circle. No one says a word.

Then a short man in the centre clears his throat. 'You need two Spits, ready to take off on the south runway?'

I awkwardly cross my arms over my chest, hoping to cover where the wings should be above my left breast. 'Yes. That's correct.'

'Follow me.'

Two Spitbomber engines roar into life.

Our mysterious ground crew loads up the bombs, straps

us in, swiftly goes over the pre-flight checks, and waves us away. No one else is around.

One of the crew handed me a note, just before I got inside the cockpit. I open it now.

Damn the rules. This is a time of war.

I stare at the paper, the words she spoke to me years ago. *Thank you, Commander Gower.* Maybe I still have some friends after all.

I reach up and slide the canopy closed. Taking a long breath, I look around the cockpit, nodding to the different elements on the control panel in my strange pre-flight ritual. I test the microphone with a few whistles before I speak. I mean to say something inspiring, but different words come out.

'Thank you.'

A short pause before Bella's voice buzzes in my ears. 'Thank *you*, Cooper.'

For a final moment I stare at the dim glow of the instruments before opening the throttle and taxiing out towards the runway. It seems Gower couldn't stretch the miracle to include 500 lb bombs, but Bella and I each carry a 250 lb under both wings.

The Spits may look overburdened with their new load, but they fly just as smoothly, taking five minutes to reach 20,000 feet. We level off just above the clouds, headed towards the sea. I check and re-check the map, with Father's pencilled markings indicating possible sites.

It is cold up here. So cold that your tear ducts freeze up. I glance at the instruments to ensure the Spit is behaving properly. The altimeter holds steady, the air speed indicator at 300 m.p.h. I can't believe I used to fly without the controls. *Thank you, Joy.*

And thank you, Gower, for believing in me.

'You ready, Bella?'

'I've waited too long for this, Cooper.'

We flew through the dawn light without incident, veering far east of any landing sites. The French countryside flashes by green and empty below us; I try to match to the map. Even with Father's information, we will need luck on our side. The potential route is huge, and there is no guarantee that the rockets will be in motion today. And a Spit only has a range of 350 miles.

Timothy Squire is down there, somewhere – he has to be. Maybe he's re-joined his unit, and his letters home keep getting intercepted. Or maybe he's a POW. I don't want to imagine Timothy Squire in a cell – he is not as strong as Cecil, who scarcely complains about his time in a German cell. But they are not treated badly, Yeoman Sparks told me, and if anyone could find a way to sneak out of gaol and escape, it's Timothy Squire.

Most importantly, the invasion is working, so once our armies liberate France, they will free all the prisoners and Timothy Squire will come home again.

'Cooper.'

Bella's voice brings me back. There is something, off to the east.

'Looks like a convoy to me,' Bella says.

She's right. Now that she says it, I can see it as clear as day – one lorry under green canvas, and five trucks, moving west. It *is* a convoy, directly below us. *This is it.* They've spotted us and brought the vehicles to a halt, fleeing for the cover of the woods.

I know exactly how they feel. I have stood under a squadron of planes, as they peeled off and unleashed their bombs. I have stood, numb with terror, as the explosions echoed around me, as the surging smoke and the blazing heat convinced me that I was about to die.

My greatest fear was the rush of wings overhead.

I streak out of the clouds, my mind focused. I close the switch on the instrument panel, arming the 250 lb bomb. Some of the Germans are setting up gun positions from the trees. But I am not worried. *We've found them.* If we can destroy this convoy, we can stop rockets from firing on London.

'Time to move,' I say.

'You got it, Cooper.'

Our plan is well rehearsed. Except when we rehearsed it there were five of us.

Bella drops down to 7,000 feet while I stay above. Peeling into a dive, she tears down on the lorry, strafing it with cannon and a three-second burst of machine-gun fire. *Barcsay would be proud of that accuracy.*

Bella levels out of her dive and climbs quickly away,

forming up behind me minutes later. Black and red smoke climbs from the trucks below. *Bella became a pilot in order to fly from glamorous party to glamorous party.* The thought tugs my lips into a smile.

'You're up, Cooper.'

So I am. Over my target at 10,000 feet, I visually lock on to the centre truck. Shoving the stick forward, I drop to 8,500 feet. Targeting the now stationary trucks, I push the stick sideways, touching the rudders and bringing my wing up, rolling into a dive. *Make sure the angle is not too small; watch the maximum speed.* My speed breaks 390, inching towards 400 m.p.h, as my plane plunges vertically.

The shoulder straps catch me, pushing the breath from my body, but I never blink. Staring down the gun sights at the target, I glance continually at the air speed indicator, certain that the plane is already close to danger. At this speed a dive is twenty seconds from impact.

I rest my thumb on the bomb release, as the height pours away. Wind is always a factor, but I adjust my course as I scream through the sky, the trucks growing larger in my windscreen. *Impact is two seconds away.*

At 1,000 feet I drop the bomb smack among the three trucks. When it blows, the sides of the lorry wheel through the air. I pull the stick back and climb swiftly away.

The feeling is strange – the *sound* is strange. I know the sound of a falling bomb, the high whistle building into a whine. From up here, it is simply the clunk of the rack release. From up here, the ocean's roar of the explosion is nothing but a distant confirmation.

There is a slight problem. I managed a direct hit on the last truck, but I had actually targeted the middle one. My bomb fell a little short. *We never got to train with real bombs.* But the problem is fairly obvious – different lines of flight – and I get on the microphone before Bella drops a 250 lb.

'Pass over the target before release. If you aim directly, it will fall short.'

A cackle of laughter – excitement, or hysteria? 'Well, Joy missed that little detail, didn't she?'

I turn to watch Bella attack the convoy again, and however she is coping with all this, her final bomb hits the lorry dead on. I plunge down after her and release my final bomb.

We form up and admire our work. Smoke billows from a series of flaming craters beneath us.

'What do you say, Coop?'

I glance down at the instruments. We have little fuel remaining, and we're out of bombs.

'I say we've pasted them. Let's go home.'

But for another moment I linger over the forest, flying a low swooping arc over the treetops, my eyes straining for an impossible familiar sight, before I give up and follow Bella back across the sky.

IV

RISE LIKE LIONS

'Oh, the wind, the wind is blowing
Through the graves the wind is blowing
Freedom soon will come
Then we'll come from the shadows.'

The Partisan, Emmanuel d'Astier de La Vigerie, 1943

22

TIMOTHY SQUIRE

18 August 1944

Bernard and I place the bombs, hidden under bushes by the road, and run a long string from the trigger to the safe spot up the hill. Our convoy is due at noon. A much bigger one than last time, led by armoured cars.

Major's words echo in my head. *Keep moving. Never run standing up. Two shots. One to the stomach, one to the heart. Never look him in the eyes.*

If only he had taken his own advice, he might still be here.

The noise of trucks reaches me like an electric shock. *It is time.* I slip the grenade from my pocket, yanking out the pin. I breathe slowly, my thumb hovering over the safety lever.

A glint of light flickers in the distance. That's William, flashing his mirror from his lookout point in the far trees. We wait as the sound grows; we wait as the armoured car and first trucks rumble past. The Germans, helmeted and wary, stare into the woods as they pass. *Can they see us?* We hold off until the second to last truck appears – then

Wake cries out. The grenades fly, and before the explosion clears, both sides of the road unleash round after furious round into the shocked convoy.

I see the Alsatian rush forward and launch a petrol bomb towards the trucks. I race down the hill, screaming, and throw my grenade with all my force. Explosions ring in the air.

But the Nazis are bloody efficient. In seconds they are getting into position and returning fire.

Other Resistance fighters roar as they attack, the heat of their fury almost palpable. Reynolds is there, on one knee, blasting his great bazooka into the midst of the trucks. Wake, dwarfed by the weapon perched on her shoulder, fires alongside him, unleashing the heavy crunch of the rocket and the searing screech of blasted metal.

Despite the sustained fire from all directions, the Germans, bugger them all to hell, are mounting an offensive. Many of the roars are silenced by machine-gun fire, and from somewhere they have mortars. It looks like this battle is swiftly about to turn against us.

Wake gives the signal, and we start to pull back. Young, bazooka on his shoulder, smashes a flaming hole in the middle of the armoured car.

Another signal, and we dash madly for the trees. Desperate, I launch myself into the safety of the branches.

Gunshots follow us. This is not like the chaos at the farmer's field. The Germans move swiftly, low to the ground, like hunters.

But Wake has planned our escape. We withdraw in controlled waves, six members staying back to cover the escape, and then five staying back to cover theirs, and so on until the whole group has melted into the forest.

'You frogs can really fight. Christ Almighty, I've never see a farmer rush an SS battalion before.' Reynolds takes a great gulp of Calvados, his eyes shining.

The old man nods. '*L'esprit de clocher.*'

Bernard smiles, translating. 'The spirit of the church bells. One is always stronger when you can hear the church bells of your village close by.'

Young booms a laugh and takes a long gulping drink of the Calvados. He sports a great cut above his eye, but otherwise the two Yanks could have come straight from a Sunday roast.

The others are smiling too, but some look shaken. And, of course, some familiar faces are absent.

One of the Spaniards is dressing wounds, and using a swab of alcohol on a small man's stomach wound. Another boy was caught in the cross-fire, and since our medic is busy, the Alsatian wraps the boy's wounded arm with a thick bandage. Next to the white of the bandage, his skin looks almost black. His whole body is shivering, and his breathing is short and quick. *He will not last.* I look away, wondering when the Calvados will come my way.

We have found an abandoned farmhouse and decided to set up camp for the night. Wake has made her headquarters in the building, but there is good soft grass all around for the rest of us. We set up out tents and get the fire going.

When ten buckets need to be sent with ten men, I volunteer. I march to the river – where of course Bernard stands downstream, throwing water over his head. Further downstream, I am surprised to see Wake, kneeling by a turn in the river. She is washing a body – the boy – and gently shrouding him in parachute silk. I watch for a moment, trying not to be disgusted, before I fill my bucket and carry it sloshing back to camp.

The swinging bucket reminds me of Anna and her bucket for feeding the ravens. *Anything to not think about that dead boy Wake is burying.*

As we sit round the cookfire, the Americans grouse about the food.

'Sorry, gents. Grub's fallen off a bit,' I say. 'Usually we have mashed turnips *and* turnip soup.'

Reynolds gives a great guffaw, and turns to the booze to make up for the lack of food. I badger Young for news – has he heard of my division, or a sapper named Arthur Lightwood? He hasn't heard anything about any 'limeys', but he does have some welcome news.

'Rommel is out of the war,' Young says.

'Dead?'

'Hurt pretty bad. Spitfire attack threw him from his car.'

That won't hurt our chances, I think, as I scrape up the rest of my soup.

Soon, in the flickering light, the men talk about their past lives – the families and loved ones they have left behind, the homes they may never see again. A few of them speak in French, and I just nod along, but most of them speak in English, broken or otherwise, on account of the new Americans as much as myself, I'm sure.

One story, from a Frenchman who used to be a cobbler, inspires some confidence. 'We shot a German soldier in a field. The SS went from village to village, until they finally came to ours. They dragged out the parish priest to call the whole village together. If no one identified those responsible, punishments were imposed. No one ever did.'

I've heard lots of stories about the Germans rounding villagers up into churches and burning the damn things down. *How did you get free?* I want to ask, but another Frenchman is laughing scornfully.

'Don't get too romantic about the French,' he says. 'Yes, I am French, so I can say it. We are many of us here, in the woods, fighting back. But there are many, many more who stay, who turn a blind eye, who do nothing. See nothing, do nothing. Cowards.' He spits into the flames.

Sensing a dangerous turn in the conversation, I find myself wildly trying to change the subject. 'But the women – the French women – are rather beautiful.'

The women are rather beautiful? What the hell is wrong with you?

But Bernard laughs, seeming to take it up happily enough. 'You know a good woman when you see one, Tommy? I don't know that I can believe that. You ever been with a woman, boy?'

I feel myself turn red. 'Of course.'

'Yeah? Tell me about it.'

'Tell you about...?'

'You know. Tell me how it felt.'

'Well.' I cough. 'It felt like... I mean, the first time... Oh, Commander Wake. Hello.'

Commander Wake has returned from the river, and she sits on the log opposite. She doesn't look up, but takes a drink and stares into the flames. After a moment of silence, she glances at me. 'How many women are in this camp?'

'Just you, Commander.'

'Right. So you think I go round and wet-blanket camp talk?'

'No, Commander.'

'Then go on with your story, Squire.'

The Alsatian with no teeth smiles a wicked grin. But Wake shows mercy, and starts talking and passing round another bottle. I squint to see her, my vision dulled from the flames.

I realize again that I know nothing about these people. Wake is obviously some secret agent who would make Rockfist Rogan proud, and she curses like a docker, but the others? Bernard is an angry Frenchman, who bathes obsessively at every stream, no matter how small or cold. Claude says barely a word, and picks his teeth thoroughly after every meagre meal.

Wake is staring at me. 'Homesick for your castle, Squire?' She almost smiles. 'Ah, London. Like a stuffy old dowager. No worse than New York, of course. And nothing on Sydney. Oh, Sydney – a woman can't even get herself a drink alone without people thinking she's a prostitute.

I imagine London is much changed since I was there last. The bloody Luftwaffe.'

She pauses. 'Paris, though, I was there when they came. Paris was alive, a woman in full bloom, before these bloody Nazis rode in with their bullshit.' She smiles. 'I was a bit of a skylarker myself. Then I had to kill a guard with my bare hands. I remember, when they trained us, thinking the situation would never arise. We've all got guns and grenades and a bloody knife at least. But then it happened.'

Listening to Wake's talk of hand to hand combat sends Major Roland's words of wisdom crawling through my mind. *Never let them get that close. If you can see them, shoot them. If you see a puff of smoke, shoot at it. If you're worrying about where to kick some bastard, you're already dead.*

And her talk about home is even worse, conjuring twisted daydreams of Anna and Cecil. Not that she'd never fall for a sod like Rafferty. She doesn't care about pots of money and sherry and all that posh bother.

I find myself eager to talk to the Americans again. Reynolds is in the process of unveiling a cigar. 'From Havana,' he says with a wide smile. 'Dad gave me these in Boston.'

He passes it round, slapping more backs and laughing. Wake returns with the champagne, which draws a whole new round of cheers.

We will go back in the morning, once the Germans have moved off, and bury the dead left behind at the ambush. Wake insists that we set a stone at the top of each grave, and carve the words:

MORTS POUR LA FRANCE.

Died for France. It is the only bit of the blasted language I know.

And then we will move on.

Now, though, she is staring straight at me.

'Squire,' says Wake. 'Come with me.'

As I follow her to the farmhouse, some fool whistles.

She closes the door. My heart is thumping in my chest.

'We are very careful... but that business at the village. We have a leak. Maybe several. And I can't trust anyone.' She smiles. 'Except you. Because, whatever else you are, you're not a German spy.'

I breathe for the first time since she called my name. 'What about Bernard?'

'No one is safe.'

I take a moment to think how bad this would make old Bernard feel, fighting back a smile. 'Then why give me sensitive information?'

Now she laughs. 'I won't. I know everything; no one else knows anything. May not be practical, but it's the only way.'

A trained spy – the leader of a vast organization of spies – would not simply chat away with a stranger. *Everything she says, she says for a reason.*

'What do you need me to do?'

Wake grins. 'We rescued you. Now we need you to help us rescue another.' She rummages around, pulls out a bottle of wine. 'I need you to deliver this. To a prison guard.'

'I don't think I'm suited for this job,' I say, then swiftly add, 'Not that I'm a spy, obviously. We're on the same side, as you said.'

'Are we?' She cocks an eyebrow at me. 'You're just worried about your own skin. I'm worried about seven thousand skins.'

'I'm worried about other people, too. OK? I want this war to be over, so everyone gets to keep their skins.'

'And you get to go home?'

'That's the idea.'

She holds out the bottle. 'Well, this task could help end the war and get you home faster. Besides, we saved you from prison. One good turn and all that.'

I take bottle from her, holding back a sigh.

'And I need you to keep an eye on Bernard,' she adds almost casually.

'You really think he might be—?'

'I think he'll need someone to stand up to him,' she says. 'I need him, and he'll need you.'

I want to laugh at the idea of me standing up to Bernard. 'Seems like a lot of people to deliver a bottle of wine.'

'Just try to keep everything calm and easy.' Wake smiles.

This woman is going to be the death of me.

23

ANNA COOPER

27 August 1944

'I'm sorry I've been so busy,' Cecil says, swirling his wine. 'We've been sent out every night for the past ten days.'

I say nothing, taking a long sip of wine. My legs are cramped from spending all day in the cockpit. Even since we landed, exhaustion has vied with elation. The adrenaline from the bombing raid – and from landing safely on only a trace of fuel – still courses through me.

Cecil and I are back at the Savoy Grill, and this time I am committed to ordering the ice cream as a main. But at Cecil's polite insistence, I order the salmon in white wine sauce, while he orders something to do with quail eggs. It is a difficult adjustment, after all my meals in the Mess and at the Stone Kitchen.

More of an adjustment is my dress, which I knew was a bad idea from the moment Bella offered to lend it to me. I've never worn a dress with straps before, and I feel practically naked with my shoulders exposed. On top of it all, the straps are too loose, so I spend more time frantically adjusting them than I do eating. Leaning over the table is out of question, so it takes me forever to finish my fish, little bite by little bite. My lower back aches from forcing myself to sit up so straight.

'I hope you don't mind,' Cecil says once the plates are cleared away. 'Tonight after supper there is dancing in the ballroom.'

'Oh.' *Dancing?*

I don't have time to make excuses, and before I know it we are standing on a crowded dance floor, my mind racing. How does Bella do it?

The straps are too loose, and the dress is too tight at the waist for me to move. But somehow I manage it, as Cecil takes one of my hands in his and places a heavy palm on my back. We've danced together before, at the Lansdowne, and it feels natural.

A woman in a beautiful golden dress sings from the stage. Cecil smiles, laughs, points out members of parliament and various prominent figures I should probably know. The Langham and other posh hotels have been closed down, so most of the society crowd comes here. But I scarcely hear the words he says. The feeling of his forearms, firm around my sides, chases sensible thoughts away.

When the singer begins 'We'll Meet Again', our dancing slows and he pulls me closer to him. I can feel my face turning hot and I concentrate on moving my feet. Even before tonight Cecil had a way away of making me conscious of my hair, my smile, my body, but wearing Bella's dress makes me uncomfortably sure that he notices more.

'Anna,' he says quietly and my heart fails to beat.

'Yes?' I am forced to look up into his face, despite my brain urging me to turn and walk away.

'Anna.' His dark eyes are steady. 'You are beautiful.'

His arms tighten around me, and in an instant that seems to last forever he leans towards me and kisses me firmly on the lips. It is not the careful kiss of Timothy Squire, but an assured, inevitable kiss that chases away all thoughts of war or planes or rockets. He kisses me again, and his lips move, lightly, down to kiss my neck.

Guilt floods back in, and as he presses me tighter against him, I suddenly push away, covering my face in my hands and thinking only of Timothy Squire, helpless in a German cell.

'Anna.' Cecil places a gentle hand on my elbow. 'I'm sorry. That was not appropriate.'

'No, it's fine.'

The light drains out of his face. 'Are you all right?'

'Yes, sorry. I just – I could use some air.'

He nods, making a way for me through the crowd of dancers. My mind reels as we squeeze past the laughing tables and push through the door.

The cold breeze off the river is like heaven. I brush off Cecil's apologises, trying not to think about what happened, as we stand together in the fresh night air. *Oh, Timothy Squire. I am sorry.*

'I promise that won't happen again,' he says formally. 'If you don't want it to.'

I don't know what to say to this, so I say nothing.

Inside the singer pauses between songs, and the murmur of voices and clinking forks is the only sound. The silence stretches on.

Cecil coughs. 'The best air raid shelter in London.' He gives a forced chuckle. 'Right here in the Savoy. Air-conditioned, gas-proof, with maids and a bar inside. Mother got stuck here once when a raid was on. Said she'd never had better coffee.'

The singer starts up again, but I am not listening. I can hear something on the wind. I pause, leaning forward, sure I *can* hear something.

An eerie rumbling sound is growing on the wind. It is strange enough that Cecil stops talking to listen. There is a great rattle, then silence. It is coming. Fast. Straight above I see a sharp needle glinting in the moonlight, then a great whoosh.

Faster than sound. So this is it. The V2s have come.

I blink, my eyes staring up into the darkness. The only sight is a red flame, like a great blowtorch soaring in the sky, growing larger and larger.

With a massive blue flash, the explosion lifts and hurls me through the air. For a moment I am weightless, hanging above the trembling ground, before I am thrown with terrifying speed across the cobblestones.

Sound comes back first – a close ringing, likely something electrical. I blink against the darkness, push myself to my feet. Things are happening all around me. I move about, test my arms and legs, but the ringing stays. How does the rocket still produce that noise? The air?

Cecil is right beside me, watching me with a concerned look. And his mouth is moving – but I can't hear the words.

The ringing. It's me – my ears. Panic wells up in me, but I force it down. It will clear in time. The air, thick and hot, is difficult to breathe.

Cecil helps me to my feet. Bella's dress is ripped, my elbow shredded, but I wave away his concern. Instead I start walking towards the river, looking for the point of impact. The air has turned dry. A new wind blows across streets, and it feels – wrong.

'Anna,' Cecil hurries to keep up. 'We need to be careful.'

The streets glitter with shards of glass – the explosion blew out all the windows on the riverfront. People gathered on Waterloo Bridge to stare at where the rocket had landed. The vehicles on the road, stately and organized, burn and smoke. Headlights shine, then swiftly fade into the dark. I can hear distant sirens.

The rocket barely missed the bridge. The square is cluttered with ripped-off doors and roofing. Everything is smashed, broken, toppled, and black traces of smoke stain the remaining cobblestones. No chance anyone could have reached a shelter, whatever good that would have done. Bricks are piled everywhere, flames licking at the edges. There is no movement – not a single person – in the square.

A thick layer of red dust clings to everything. And, in

the centre, a smoking crater is gouged into the street, 70 feet across.

I can see – pieces – of what looks like an arm, horribly black and burnt. With a sudden rush of nausea, I realize what is scattered all around the streets. People, torn apart by the explosion. People who will never be identified.

People erased forever by my father's invention.

24

TIMOTHY SQUIRE

25 August 1944

Bernard shakes me awake and I hate him with my entire being. But I force myself to rise. Blinking in the sunlight, I realize only a few hours have passed. But the camp is now moving once again.

'Come,' he says.

I follow him, stumbling to the river. Kneeling down on the rocky bank, I throw the cold water on my face. It works.

'I'd take the opportunity to bathe properly,' he tells me. He strips down and wades into the water. I choose to stay on the banks. *I don't need this Frenchman appraising the length of my tackle.* But I am too dirty to resist for long, and soon I am stripping down and hurrying into the cold water, teeth chattering. The mud feels cool on hard, blistered feet.

Once we get back to camp, Wake is waiting for us. She explains the mission to Bernard, who doesn't take it well. 'They are scum.'

'Not all of them,' says Wake. 'There are glimmers of a human being in some.'

Bernard gives a hoarse laugh. 'You can't trust the guards.'

'I believe we can.'

'Then why don't you deliver the wine?'

'I've been seen there too much,' Wake replies, the patience in her voice clearly strained. 'You must believe, Bernard – if I could, I would send anyone other than you.'

The two stare at each other.

'Nazis.'

Wake shakes her head. 'One man. He will help us to pass on a bottle of wine. A gift that will be taken from him by the other guards.'

'And then he will free the prisoners?' Bernard gives her a hard look. 'At what price?'

Wake doesn't hesitate. 'We take him with us.'

'Ah, so he got tired of toadying for Hitler, did he? Needs a rest from burning families alive? I say to hell with him. If we need to do this, let's kill the guards and set the prisoners free ourselves.'

Wake shakes her head. 'This way is cleaner.'

Bernard smooths his beard, agitated. 'Cleaner? Working with this scum? Letting him join us? It's likely a trap – he's trying to infiltrate us. You can't risk everything to free a few prisoners—'

'There is one prisoner in particular. He knows something valuable.'

'He's still one man. We're bigger than any one person, Commander Wake. Even you.'

'Bernard. You must trust me. We have to do this. It is vital. And you won't be going alone.'

I see a reward poster in French, but I don't need to understand the words. It's a picture of Commander Wake. And the reward is five million francs.

No wonder she can't trust anyone.

Five million francs. I don't how much that is in pounds, but it's the rest of my life living in a proper home in the countryside. Anna would love a real garden – nothing too grand, but with some trees and space for flowers and all that. Even Cecil Rafferty doesn't have that kind of money. *Does he?*

I become aware of Bernard staring at me and I walk on, pretending I haven't seen the poster. I can *hear* his smirk.

I know he's taking us to a safe place, so I assumed we were headed for some trapdoor in a hayloft, but the building we are walking towards seems to be a proper home.

Bernard sees my look. 'Not like your house in London?'

For a moment I think of the top-floor flat in the Jewel House of the Tower of London. 'No,' I say.

As we wait outside, I look over and see my face reflected in the window. I am surprised at how much I still look like me. I expected an old warrior, lean but hardened, or at least a grizzled woodsman, but I just look knackered – half-asleep and very hungry.

We enter the cottage, wooden planks creaking under our

feet. A short old lady, kindly and smiling, brings us soup. I could marry her. It tastes like pre-war food.

It took us nearly two days to get here – including camping under the trees and getting no sleep (images of great German shepherds bursting from the night prevented any sleep), and I am hungry enough to eat forever.

Bernard is apparently familiar to the lady, who sends her regards to the White Mouse before leaving us to the fire. *The White Mouse. The Witch. Madam Andrée. Hélène. Nancy. Commander Wake.* Who is this woman, really? And who is this Frenchman across from me, who I'm not certain Wake even trusts?

'Why is this prisoner so important?' I ask quietly.

Bernard shrugs. 'The Witch knows everything. This guy has some kind of information, something that can hurt us or help us. We have to trust her.'

'Is she always right?'

He laughs. 'She knows all the demolition targets, all the safe houses, and every password. That's why the Gestapo has a five million franc reward on her head.'

I nod, trying to look surprised.

Once dinner is over, the old woman brings out honey and jam. I could cry.

Something occurs to me – what Wake said before she sent me on this little mission. She thinks there's a spy among us. And, more likely since it's Wake, she *knows* there's a spy among us. *Who?*

Bernard lights a fag from the stub of the one he just finished. He is also well into the wine.

'So what's the plan exactly?'

'Mr Nazi gets his shiny gift taken off him. Once the other guards are knocked out from our special wine, he releases the prisoners and then sticks the guards in the cell instead. We wait here at the safe house until they arrive, and then we escort the bastards back to camp.'

'How many men?' I ask.

'Thirteen.'

'Sounds lucky.' I take a long haul on the smoke. Bernard pours another tall glass.

'And one in particular – he's a boy, really. Bit of a runt, dark hair. Let's hope he's worth it.'

I'm not afraid of this mission, but on the whole I'd rather feed the ravens in the dark. *I mean, better here than hiding in a ditch waiting to ambush a German convoy.* Just being in the presence of a jar of honey seems like a proper miracle.

As the hours drift past, Bernard, well buttered now, smiles aimlessly around the room.

A knock on the door alerts us. Our guard is here.

A thin man in a black uniform stands before us.

Bernard hauls himself to his feet. 'So, you are going to help us? The enemy?'

The guard shrugs. 'We help each other. I get your prisoners out; you take me with you.'

'Grown tired of all the raping and killing, did you?'

'I was following orders,' he says flatly.

Bernard eyes him, though he looks a little unsteady. 'It was an order, to kill my son.'

The room goes quiet. I look at the closed door. Bernard said that the meetings usually take place in shabby cafés because Germans refuse to frequent such places. I wish we were in a café now – or somewhere a little more public.

Bernard has a revolver in his coat. The guard has a gun on his belt. This could end very badly.

'That was not me,' the guard says. 'I have killed no one.'

'You believe that? I have seen your prisoners. You think your hands are clean of this?'

The guard stands tall now, chest puffed out. 'What would you have me do? They will shoot me, as easy as they shot your boy.'

'My boy was five. He was too young to make a stand. You are supposed to be a man.'

'Take a stand? You mean hide in the woods?' he demands. 'We all have to learn to survive. My son is still alive because of me. Yours is dead because of you.'

'My son is dead because he was a Jew, like his father.'

'You're not wearing your yellow star.'

Without a thought I throw myself between them. But no one else has moved. Bernard is staring calmly at the guard, who has gone quiet, head down. My panting is the only sound.

The stillness is awful.

'All right, you two,' I say, for the sake of saying something. 'Bernard, give him the wine.'

He slowly hands it over. The guard, red-faced, takes it and slips it under his coat. It would be hard to have a worse feeling about this.

I look at Bernard from the corner of my eye. He has calmed down, somewhat, though I've never seen someone smoke four fags off the back of each other.

So he's a Jew. This is why Wake wanted me here. *Keep an eye on Bernard. He'll need you.*

She needed him to do the job, and she needed me to be his bloody babysitter.

'You think I should not have told the Nazi,' he says between hauls.

I can't help but nod.

'I have been to the camps,' he says in a cloud of smoke. 'I have seen them with my own eyes.'

I don't know what to say to this. He was imprisoned in a camp? I am afraid to ask, but Bernard goes on talking anyway.

'Even in the camps, they make Jewish prisoners fill the gas chambers. No one wants to be responsible, not even the Nazis have the stomach for what they're doing.'

Footsteps clatter outside, and the door creaks open. Four men stagger inside.

'Where are the others?' Bernard is on his swaying feet.

'We split into groups,' says a prisoner with scars across his bald head. 'Less noticeable. They will be just behind us.'

Bernard squints at them. 'Who told you to split into groups?'

'I did.' The guard steps forward.

'Oh good, the Nazi is in charge.'

Our boy is here, at any rate. He is small, with dark wavy hair the colour of a struck match.

Bernard smiles at him. 'Well, looks like you've been through hell. But the fact that you're still alive means you didn't talk. Whatever it is you know, I hope it's worth it. What's your name?'

He coughs. 'Ansgar.'

'Wait,' Bernard says, his voice far too loud. 'The *prisoner* is German?'

I put a hand on his shoulder. 'She said he was important. Let's go.'

He shrugs my hand away. 'We're bringing two Germans back with us?'

We stand in a circle, Bernard openly glaring at the boy. 'Why are you so important?'

The Germans talk to each other in low voices. I can feel Bernard's anger rising.

'No,' I say. I am so tired of people talking bloody languages I can't understand. 'If you want to come with us, you have to talk English. All the time. If you speak to each other in German, the lads'll start to wonder what you're really talking about. And everyone here is itching for a fight.'

I say the last bit with special emphasis, but the boy simply nods. 'I have information. Information that will help end the war.'

'Well, that's just brilliant,' Bernard says. 'What is it?'

'I can only tell Commander Wake.'

'*You* don't trust *me*?'

He stares at the red-bearded Frenchman. 'No.'

Bernard looks like he might hit the poor sod.

Keep everything calm and easy.

'Right,' I say. 'Let's make tracks. If it's so bloody important, Wake will want to hear it as soon as possible. Where's the second group of prisoners?'

The guard shakes his head. 'They should be here.'

I trade looks with Bernard. We can't afford to wait around for them. If we abandon them, they will be caught and give us away. But if they've already been caught, every second standing here is a second we're going to need to outrun these bastards.

Why is everyone looking at me? Christ, if only Lightwood were here – or Rafferty, or anyone bloody halfway sensible. Well, it's just me, and I've got to decide. It's either too late for them, or too late for us. Ansgar is the important one; he's the mission. Wake needs his information – it could stop the bloody war.

'We have to move,' I say, nodding to Bernard. 'Now.'

26 August 1944

We're forced to take a short kip in an abandoned barn. The Germans have been warned by Bernard not to speak – in any language – when someone can hear. I'm almost ready to agree with him. I keep fighting down the mad sense that the German army is just behind us.

The other group of prisoners is lost, one way or another. I can't think about them. I need to think about our group, about myself. Having come this far only to be shot in the back and left hanging from some tree…

'All right,' I say, rousing the figures huddled on the straw floor. 'Time to get moving.'

I go outside and leave them to pack up. We need to get a move on. I sneak a glance around to make sure no one is coming out of the barn, before I pull the honey from my bag. *If the Nazis have finally caught up to us, there's no way I'm not eating some of this.* For a moment I can only stare at it, then I slowly twist off the cap. The smell – I could simply inhale the whole jar.

'You bastard.'

The voice startles me, and, flustered, I drop the lid as I hurriedly try to fit it back on.

'You robbed that poor old woman?' Bernard is standing behind me, looking at me with open disgust. 'She risks her life to help us, to defy the Nazis, and you steal her food.'

'It's one jar,' I mutter, feeling lower than a cockroach.

He snorts and walks away. I twist the lid tightly back on the jar. I feel too guilty to even enjoy it now – at least until tomorrow, at any rate.

We make decent time. Morning light shoots through the high branches, easing the gloom. But I'm far from comfortable dragging prisoners through the forest. I am uneasy as we pass a clearing that links to a side road, but there is no army waiting in ambush. As the forest thickens again, I search the tree trunks for faces. When the sun glints off something metal, I full on scream.

Guns are furiously readied and the prisoners instinctively draw in to a circle behind us.

But it's all no use. Crouched in the trees is a German tank – a Tiger.

For an eternity we face off, Bernard and I pointing our guns. Sweat oozes between my shoulder blades. It is Bernard, ultimately, who inch by inch, lowers his gun. In a string of French words that are obliviously vulgar, he stalks towards the tank and gives it a mighty kick.

Now that the tension has drained away, it seems quite clear this tank is broken down and abandoned. I step forward, still a little wary. The forest has already started to reclaim it, with weeds sprouting through the caterpillar treads.

'Let's get moving,' I say, my voice gruff.

By noon we've made it back to the campsite. More sentries than usual stand among the trees. As soon as we return with the prisoners, they disappear into the tent with Wake. God knows what they're telling her.

A noise echoes behind me – did someone cry out? Wake throws open the tent flap, staring into the forest.

People fidget, watching the still trees. *Is there something out there? Have the Germans tracked us down?* I can no longer see the sentry that was watching from the distant tree. Did he climb down?

'Break up camp,' Wake says. 'We've lingered here too

long.' Her voice has an edge to it, and we immediately begin packing up, silent. I catch a glance at Bernard's face, which is pale under the unruly red beard. Claude has dropped any pretence of helping, and simply stares around like a spooked deer.

Wake at least is carrying on in workmanlike fashion, packing away crates and scolding those moving too slowly. She is keeping young Ansgar close by, however.

All at once noise blasts into the silence: a strange, unimaginable sound – music. It is actual, proper music, like being in a dance hall. Everyone freezes exactly as they are, but people's eyes are wild with fear. And I realize it is Glenn Miller, 'In the Mood'.

In the depths of the forest, it is terrifying. *I should have eaten the bloody honey.* No one moves as the song inexplicably plays. Reynolds stares into the trees like a madman. Even Wake looks terrified, all her energy and cunning rooted to the ground. Whatever is happening, it needs to get finished and over with.

The last frenzied trumpets melt across the crowded campsite, through the forest, and then die into silence.

A voice calls from the trees, bringing the nightmare fully to life.

'Did you enjoy your last dance?'

We all look at each other, eyes wide, still unmoving – except for Bernard, who just looks tired. He cocks his gun.

'Surrender. You are surrounded.'

As if to prove it, soldiers come tramping through the woods from the east and west.

Bernard catches my wild glance and slowly, deliberately, nods at me. Then, with an ungodly roar, he runs forward, firing. I am running too. So is the German guard, who Wake seems to have trusted with a Bren gun. My scream is lost in a blaze of gunfire.

Suddenly a voice cries out from just behind me. Stunned, I whip round.

Claude is standing, waving his arms and shouting for attention. Before I can figure out what the hell is going on, German bullets lace through the air. I stare at Claude, unable to make sense of what I see. He has someone before him like a hostage, gun pointed.

It is Commander Wake.

'Claude, you prick,' she hisses. 'Let go of me or you'll be pissing blood for the rest of your life.'

'It's over, Nancy.'

Unfortunately for Claude, the traitorous bastard, the Germans haven't cottoned on to his great plan, and they keep firing indiscriminately into our midst. I see Claude duck to avoid incoming fire, and that one moment costs him everything. Wake elbows him hard in the groin, and snaps back his arm to release the gun. I hear his arm crack over the gunfire.

Wake has her Colt automatic and does not hesitate to put a bullet in his head. She calls Ansgar's name and turns to run.

Released from the moment, we scatter, heading in every direction at once, not following retreat orders. Voices are screaming: *Vite! Vite!*

One of our Germans is shot through the head – the guard. Ansgar turns to face the shooters, raises his hands above his head. A burst of gunfire hits him. His arms fall as if someone has cut the tendons.

There go the secrets we risked our lives to get.

They shoot the bald prisoner too – I see his body tangled into the grass. I stare down at his blank face for an impossible moment before I turn at the angry roar of a bazooka.

Reynolds and Young are blasting an escape route through some unlucky Germans. Bernard hurries over to join the fray, spraying arcs of machine-gun fire, and in no time Wake is there too, Bren gun firing.

A momentary gap appears in the circle, and Wake is already rushing towards it at a sprint. Gunfire follows me as I make for the trees behind her.

I lean against a tree, too tired to take another step, but braced to run again if we have to. Bernard, who seems only a little winded from a endless dash through the forest, spits in the dirt. 'He was going over to their side. The second the guns started firing...'

I shake my head. I don't know what Ansgar was doing, other than being terrified in the final moments before he was killed. And I can't hold that against him.

A rustle in the trees and a modified bird call announces

a new arrival to our meagre gang of survivors. We have put at least a few miles between us and the Germans.

'Denis!' Wake turns to the man limping towards us. 'You're alive.'

He winces. 'I am.'

They stare at each other in silence.

'I thought they had me,' he finally says. 'I was sure they were on to me.'

'What happened?'

'I had to, Nancy. I had no choice.'

Wake narrows her eyes. 'What did you do?'

'I destroyed it. Threw the parts in the river.' He takes a long breath. 'And the codes.'

Silence reigns. He has destroyed the wireless – it basically kept us alive out here.

Finally, Wake nods to herself. 'Then we are on our own.'

25

CECIL RAFFERTY

28 August 1944

'Cecil, my boy, I'm glad you're here.' Sir Archibald shakes my hand, gestures for me to sit. 'As I'm sure you're aware, the situation has changed rather drastically.'

'Yes, sir. I was at Waterloo Bridge last night. The threat from the V2 rockets is real.'

I smile, almost melting with relief. Anna will be happy – and I owe her this much at least. I feel terrible for my behaviour at the Savoy. She is obviously still thinking about Squire, hoping that he might come back in some miraculous return. It doesn't matter that he's dead; my behaviour was improper.

Of course, the whole situation is my fault, for not having the heart to tell her that he is dead. *Or to tell her that he saved my life.* The man saves my life and, move in on his girlfriend. Father would give me a lengthy talk about the responsibilities of being a gentleman.

'What?' Sir Archibald leans across the table, fixing me with one of his stares. 'No, not that. Is that all you ever think about, lad? Rockets, rockets.'

He pours two glasses of whisky, sliding one across for me.

'The situation on the ground is worse than we feared,' he says. 'The Germans are pushing back. Rumour is they are about to launch an offensive in the forests of Ardennes—'

'An *offensive*? But that's impossible.'

'We knew the bastards would resist, but…' He shakes his head. 'Needless to say, it's taken everyone by surprise. Their oil and munitions productions have recovered. The war is far from over. But we're going to do our best to hasten its end. And we'll need your help.'

'Of course, sir.'

He stands, leaving his drink on the table, and walks to a map on the back wall. I follow, as baffled and uncertain as I always seem to feel in Sir Archibald's presence.

He points to an area of Germany, covered in pins.

'We have 722 RAF bombers,' he speaks the words quietly. 'And 527 US bombers, with 784 Mustangs. That's 4,000 tons of bombs.'

'My God,' I say, breathless. 'Berlin?'

'Dresden.'

I squint at the map. 'Dresden – is that a military city, sir?'

He looks at me with a frown. 'It's a German city, lad.'

'But, sir, with the Russians advancing in the east, the city will be filled with refugees.'

'But, sir—'

'Captain Rafferty,' he says, 'the Russians will breach the city in weeks.

'There are casualties in war,' he continues, moving back to his desk and leaving me trailing him like a dazed fox hound. 'If we don't bomb Dresden, the war drags on, and thousands more die. If we don't bomb Dresden *now*, the Russians will set up there, and we might be looking at a whole other war the moment this one is through. And how many more will die then?'

I nod, at a loss.

'We have to make Germany surrender and show Russia just who's in charge when the dust clears.'

The thought sinks like a weight. With one war ending, is another set to begin, between the victors? Is the promise of peace a lie?

Sir Archibald seems to sense my thoughts. 'Peace is never a thing done, lad. It is always something that people must be doing.'

'Yes, sir.'

'Cecil, I won't tell you father about your visits. I'm not certain he'll see that they showed the best of you. Just go on, do your duty, and help win this war. Can you do that?'

'Yes, sir.'

'Good lad. You'll be leaving soon enough. The long winter nights provide a safer operational environment for the bombers.'

I feel the opportunity slipping away. 'But sir, the rockets will come, no matter what happens in Dresden. The more desperate Hitler is, the harder will we get hit. I was there,' I say as I see him reach for his drink, 'that night at Waterloo Bridge. The terror it spread was worse than any explosion. Once they're launched, we have no defence. We must take out the launch sites.'

'I've told you already—'

'With all respect, sir, I have a proposition. Far be it for me to recommend 2nd Tactical Air Force, but with light bombers, even a small squadron, we can track the convoys that carry the rocket parts. We can destroy them before they ever launch, and snatch Hitler's miracle weapon out of his hands.'

Sir Archibald sighs. 'We can't spare 2nd – no, I'm sorry lad, nothing you say can convince me of that. But there might be something…'

'Anything,' I say as he stares, lost in thought.

'Perhaps it's worth looking into, Rafferty. We've heard about activity like this from the Dutch, and they are eager to snuff it out as well.'

'Thank you, sir.' I say, not quite sure what it is he is about to propose.

'Once we have a stronger foothold in Holland,' he says finally. 'I'll put 304 Group on it. Mind you, they're a Polish squad, and God knows if they're fit for purpose.' He gives me one final measuring glance, 'Is that sufficient to put this issue to rest, Rafferty?'

'Yes, sir,' I say, standing and saluting before he can change his mind. 'Thank you, sir.'

26

ANNA COOPER

'The situation on the ground is worse than ever, but he has agreed to send bombers to recce launch sites in Holland.' Cecil smiles as he delivers the news.

'Really?' I say. 'When?'

'Soon. As soon as the Allies have a stronger position in Holland.'

'A stronger position? What does that mean? When will that be?' I ask. 'Will you be with them?'

'No. Light bomber squadron only.'

'Only one squadron?'

'Yes, Anna. One squadron – the 304, he said. It's a Polish group.'

'A Polish group?'

'They are expert fliers and bombers. They use the new Mark XIV Spitfires. Sir Archibald handpicked them for the task.'

I pull him into a hug. After a brief hesitation, he squeezes back.

'I am sorry, Anna,' he says. 'What I did… I apologize.'

'Please stop. It was my fault as much as yours.' I draw a breath, wishing it was steadier. 'But I am in love with someone else.'

He nods, but his face is pale. He seems about to say something – another apology, perhaps – but instead shakes his head, offers me a bright smile.

'Allow me to call on you when I return, Miss Cooper. As friends.'

'Of course, Cecil.' I smile back. 'We will always be friends. Which is why I can never allow you to call me Miss Cooper again.'

He laughs. 'I'll write you as soon as I'm back.'

I watch Cecil stride from the room, the very image of an RAF captain, but my thoughts have moved elsewhere.

It's time to visit Polish squadron 304.

27

TIMOTHY SQUIRE

26 August 1944

Me, Bernard, Wake, Denis, the Alsatian, and our two big Americans sit around the campfire. Of course there is no time to recover the bodies or bury the dead.

'Our best bet,' Denis says, trying to remain optimistic, 'is to try and reach Gaspard.'

A low growl comes from Bernard. 'It's a hundred miles over dangerous roads, and we don't even know where Gaspard will be.'

Denis nods. 'But he will have a radio with him, I am certain. And a good operator.'

Wake agrees. 'I must get through to London, and pass this information on. It is too valuable to risk losing.'

She means getting killed by the Germans. At least she got what she needed from Ansgar, and if it will help end the war it might all be worth it.

'Let's move then.' Bernard stands up.

'No,' she says. 'I can find a bike in one of the villages.'

'Let me come with you,' he says. 'You cannot travel that far alone. A woman alone.'

'Sometimes that helps. There is always an advantage, if you look for it. I am merely a young housewife tootling along home. With you I will be far more suspicious.'

'I will go alone then.'

'Gaspard will only listen to me, and I have the password and codes needed to send the message. This message is too important not to deliver.'

She rises to leave.

Bernard spits. 'You can't defend yourself on a bike.'

'No weapons. A gun will take away my ability to bluff.' She slips free her Colt automatic, and hands it to him. 'Once I have the bike, I will change into my skirt, and at the first market buy some vegetables and carry them in a string bag. Just a housewife out shopping.'

Bernard frowns. 'What if a truckload of Germans drives up to you?'

'Then I will give a shy wave. And if they put a hand on me, I will break their fucking necks.'

She smiles at us. 'You will be in far more danger than me. Lie low in the village, and trust no one but each other. I will find you there. Good luck.'

And with that Commander Wake vanishes into the trees.

27 August 1944

Here the destruction of war is visible: huge craters from

shells, upturned trees, ruined vineyards, the rotting corpses of cows and sheep. Other, more horrid, smells reach us, but I don't think about what they could be.

We sleep, really just a nap, under the trees.

'We'll never get away from them,' Bernard says to no one in particular.

'Come on,' I say to the pale, exhausted men. The Alsatian and two other men have also found their way to us. 'We have to keep moving.'

Bernard doesn't budge. 'Hey, you're not the leader here, Tommy.'

He's right there. I am no leader. I think of Lightwood – how my mad ideas got him killed. But something in me snaps listening to this red-bearded whinger.

'My name is Squire. Timothy Squire. I don't give a toss what you think. And you made me the leader when you stopped having ideas and starting whinging.'

He stares at me hard. *Oh, Christ, he's going to fight me. It's like Rafferty all over again.* I get in more fist fights with lads in my own unit than I do with the bloody Germans.

'Squire's right,' says Young. 'We gotta move.'

Denis nods wordlessly.

Bernard isn't up for a fight after all. He snorts. 'Fine. You come up with the grand plans, I'll be in charge of making sure we don't get slaughtered wandering through the woods.'

Relief washes over me. 'Deal.'

28

CECIL RAFFERTY

29 August 1944

'I heard about the trial,' I say gently.

Cam Westin shakes his head. 'Not a bother,' he says, taking a drink. 'These planes are hard to control, and they need someone to blame when it goes wrong.'

I nod. 'Still, it's not fair that you have to take it.'

He shrugs. 'I'm glad it happened, to be honest. Let it get out there, the sooner the better.'

'What?'

'That these girls have no business in aircraft. I mean, it's clear as day as soon as you see it, but some people just nod along, thinking why not? Why not let the birds fly, too? Well, here's why, mate. You end up with stuck landing gear and broken engines and a risk to people on the ground.'

'Some of them are quite accomplished pilots, actually. Anna Cooper is an excellent pilot, no matter what happened to her landing gear.'

He takes a long drink in silence.

A WAAF officer walks past. 'And it's not all bad having the ladies around, is it?' I say, trying to lighten the mood.

He turns and gives her a completely inappropriate leer. He's had too much to drink.

'There was one,' he says, his words slurred, 'a right old bag. American, thought she was the greatest thing since sliced bread. Oh, she talked to me like I wasn't fit to shine her bloody shoes.'

I pause in my drink. West is well and truly drunk, who knows what he's on about.

'Let's call it an evening, shall we? I need to get back to base anyhow. We're headed back to Germany tomorrow night.'

'God, those Americans. They send their girls over here to fly our planes.' He laughs blackly. 'We'll fly our own planes, thank you darling. You'd better not test your luck on the new models, those big engines are tough to control. Trust me before you go up there and find out for yourself.'

'West, I should get you home, man.'

He waves me away. 'I've got a tab going.'

I try again, giving him my hand to help him up, but instead he clasps it and pulls it towards him. 'You make this country proud, Rafferty. You're a proper hero.'

I nod, tugging my arm slowly free. 'I don't fly alone, West, you know that. But I have to call it a night. You sure you don't want me to drop you off?'

'You give my thanks to your whole crew. Tell the boys, from the bottom of my heart, that Britain thanks them.'

29

ANNA COOPER

29 August 1944

Bella regards me with a smile. She is dressed for a night on the town and has demanded the same of me. Her dress is black silk and fits her snugly, and she wears a string of gleaming pearls. I have wisely declined to borrow another of her stunning dresses, choosing instead to wear my green silk dress again, which suddenly seems very prim.

'What are we doing again?' I ask.

'Getting back your wings.' Bella laughs.

'I don't understand.'

She loops her arm around my elbow. 'Well, you said there is a Polish squadron hunting V2 sites. I have no doubt that you mean to waltz into their crew room and demand to join them. But at the moment, I am merely a private citizen with a pilot licence – and you aren't even that.'

I nod. She's right, but how she intends to fix this problem is beyond me.

Bella laughs and clicks ahead in her heels.

'Can you at least tell me where we're going?' I ask.

She throws the answer over her shoulder.

'Where the officers go. The Lansdowne Club.'

The club is packed with fashionable people, sipping drinks and dancing. Waiters in white tuxedoes move gracefully though the crowds. The people here don't seem as hard hit by the war as most. In fact, they remind me of the diners at the Savoy. I scan the room for Cecil, but he is not among the confident men in uniform.

Bella leans across the bar and orders us champagne. She hands me the flute and I stare for a moment at the bubbles winking at the brim.

'Tell me you've had champagne before,' she says, aghast.

'How much did this cost?'

She shrugs, and takes a sip. I do the same – the taste is cold and fizzy and glorious. A jazz band, with the name *Haven Tweezer* written across the drum kit, loudly plays in the corner. By the sound of it, they've spent more time at the bar than the rehearsal room.

'Do we have to dance?' I ask.

'To this?' She raises an eyebrow.

I nod, grateful. Even in my appropriately fitting dress, I am in no mood for dancing.

We don't have to wait long before various officers begin to

surround us. Bella dismisses all of them, until two uniformed men approach. One I recognize – Duncan, who seems slightly less drunk than when Cecil introduced me to him a year ago. The other is a portly man who has overindulged in Brylcreem. Both have wings on their left breast.

'Good evening, ladies.'

Bella steps forward in time to absorb his leer. 'You are both pilots?' she says in tones of wonder.

'We are, indeed. And we would be happy to escort you and your lovely friend to the Astor, and show you an evening of dinner and dancing.'

'But we've only just arrived,' Bella says with a wicked grin. 'And I for one could use another drink.'

Duncan heartily agrees, and in mere moments his friend has returned with a bottle of wine and glasses. Bella has given me a cigarette, which I am still pretending to enjoy. The club is filled with the rich and stylish, but all I can think of is Timothy Squire, and how he would never want to come to such a place. *He would call them all toffs and laugh at the cost of the drinks.*

I turn back to Duncan, who is grinning at me. It seems he has no memory of our previous meeting.

'Are you also interested in aircraft, my dear?' he says.

'I think so,' I say, still unsure what exactly Bella is trying to accomplish with these two. 'They seem like amazing machines.'

'Well, if you ever want to take a joyride in a cockpit, I'm your man.'

My whole body shivers, but Bella gives a musical laugh.

'I think she's feeling a bit cold,' she says meaningfully.

'Of course,' he says, taking the cue and unbuttoning his jacket with impressive speed and draping it over my shoulders. It is heavy and smells of stale beer and aftershave.

It is already a warm evening, and in this packed room it is downright hot. Already I can feel the slide of sweat at my back. But Bella continues to talk and laugh for what seems like hours, before announcing that the girls need the powder room.

Once we reach the toilets, she tugs the jacket off my shoulders, tears the wings from the breast in a smooth motion, and bunches the jacket in the empty sink with a smile.

'Your wings, Flight Leader,' he says solemnly.

I take the small badge and slip it into my purse.

As we move swiftly towards the exit, I spot the two men across the room in a circle of giggling WAAFs, looking completely unfazed by our disappearance.

Bella hooks my arm, steering us through the sea of appraising officers. At that moment I spot another familiar face, this one moving to cut off our escape. Cam Weston. I would go back to the leering drunks in a heartbeat, I think as he walks towards us, smiling and carrying a glass. He holds up his free hand in mock defence.

'Please don't attack me, I've only just had dinner.' He gives a humourless chuckle. 'Listen, I've decided not to hold a grudge, despite your little witch-hunt against me. Your boyfriend asked me not to, and as a favour to him, I'll let it go.'

'What are you talking about?'

'Cecil Rafferty was just here. Asked me to go easy on you, on account of you being one of his women.'

'Did he now?'

I can feel Bella tugging me towards the door, but I resist.

'I think he fancies you,' he says. 'Though I feel duty bound to tell you that you're not the first girl he's fancied here tonight. But they've gone back to his hotel, so…'

'Go to hell.'

'Oh, the language on you birds these days.' He sighs loudly. 'Once the war is over, we'll all go back to how it was.'

He takes a drink, and looks me up and down in a way that makes my skin crawl, before Bella yanks me away and steers us to the exit.

30

TIMOTHY SQUIRE

29 August 1944

'What is Ravensbruck?' I ask. 'I heard Wake mention it, like it was a camp for female prisoners.'

Bernard glares at me as we walk into the afternoon. 'Don't go worrying yourself. Nancy will never be taken alive.'

What would Anna think of that if she knew – a Nazi prison just for women? I shake my head. What would she say? The emptiness that answers me is terrible. I see her, in my mind, but somehow it has lost the weight of memory. It is more like a dream than anything real.

We say little as we make camp and eat what few supplies we have left. Lately Young has been telling us wistful stories of his 'lady' back home, but today he is quiet. I made the mistake of asking Bernard about his boy, and we all sat horrified as he told us about the concentration camps. These Nazis are more vile than even I thought.

Bernard shelters the pot. 'Bloody crows are back again.'

'Ravens,' I mutter.

'What's that?'

My laugher comes out ahead of the words. 'Those aren't crows. Those are ravens.'

He shrugs. 'Well, they're tracking us now. We'll need to be careful preparing food. First sight of any food – anything edible and I'm including turnips – they come down. The Germans are wolves, they can hunt us by just following the flocks.'

I give a quick nod. 'They're proper smart.' I should know. I'm the one who turned Ollie into a kind of sinister parrot, only repeating the worst things he hears. Now I watch them, watching us. There are two more in the distant fir trees, not as hidden as they think in the dark branches.

'They're starting to creep me out. Always watching. I say we start shooting them off the branches. See how smart they are then. See how they taste at the same time. Can't be any worse than this soup.'

'Never kill a raven,' I say. 'It's bad luck.'

He smiles. 'An English superstition, perhaps?'

'Yes. King Arthur will come back one day. As a raven.'

'In France? Seems strange. But that's the British for you.'

The Alsatian laughs.

I frown, but Bernard does have a point. The bloody birds had better not give us away. To come this far and have the whole thing ruined by the ravens.

They're tricksters, Anna used to say.

They'll be bloody plucked and cooked tricksters if they lead the Germans right to us.

We enter a small village, where two old women watch us from across the square. We need a smart place to hide, at least for a couple days. This must be the sleepiest village in France. Covered in blood and dust, limping from the endless running, I must be a proper sight. People would run a mile from me, if there were any people, that is.

'Anyone else want to do the talking?' I ask, with a meaningful look at Bernard.

And that's when I hear the tank.

Earth sputters into the air. And I see the Tiger rolling towards us.

A great explosion punches my ears and I drop to the ground. Bernard drags me to my feet and we dash for the nearest stone building. The others clamber in beside us.

I can see from the window what we're up against. A battalion, likely doing a sweep of the area. Twenty soldiers at least, and one huge, 60-ton monster, its great gun swinging from side to side, arcing flames. And descending on us.

Bernard crouches against the wall beside Reynolds and Young.

'We have no hope against that Tiger.' I tear out my pack,

looking down at the plastic explosives in socks. 'Nothing we've got is even going to slow them down.'

A shell punches a 5-foot hole through the stone wall.

'Armour piercing!' someone cries.

The next shell goes clear through the building, from end to end. The shouts continue, but they're no longer words.

Bernard crawls over to me, his wild red beard singed from the flames. He points to the sudden gaping hole in the wall. A way out.

'The tank…' I say weakly.

'Forget the bloody tank. We have to get out of here.'

'Run? We won't make it a hundred yards.'

There're no forests, no trees, just bloody vineyards as far as the eye can see.

He nods. 'Let's start with ten.'

Young is first out, but we are right behind him. As we run, staggering, bullets fly all around us. The Alsatian is hit, straight through the neck, but I can't spare an instant to watch him fall.

'Run!'

We run, hell for leather, towards some imagined safety. But the soldiers are on to us, and the tank rolls ominously forward. I run, faster than I've ever run. The Tiger is just behind us now, zeroing in. We can't outrun a tank. *I will not die in this field.* I will escape these bastards and find my way home. I can see the trees now, but we'll never make it.

My bloody left foot catches my bloody right foot, my knees buckle beneath me, and I fall to the grass. I want to yell, to curse, to cry – but I don't have the breath. I am lying on my back, my chest heaving, staring up at the bluest sky I have ever seen. *Such a glorious day.*

How can it be so beautiful? This massacre in the sunshine.

All I can smell is grass, rich and heavy. Nothing has ever smelled so good.

I raise my head to see the sun glint off the armoured flank of the Tiger, crunching across the field. The German soldiers are advancing behind it, using it as cover while still firing on us. Reynolds is hobbling towards me, weighed down by his bazooka.

He falls to his knees beside me.

'I'm getting so tired of this shit,' he pants.

Fair enough, mate, but bazookas can do nothing unless you get a whole lot closer to the bloody tank, which is the worst idea in the world.

But no one seems to have told Reynolds this. I scramble to my feet as he turns and strides back towards the battalion – towards the *tank*.

I am frozen, watching the giant American as he marches towards his own death. Reynolds falls to one knee in the grass, not 10 feet from the armoured monster. Instantly a shot takes him in the gut. He crumples, but manages somehow to regain his balance. He is tottering on one knee like a drunk.

But the bastard is still aiming the bazooka.

Now they're all shooting at him; even the tank's gun swivels round to pulverize him. But through the hail of bullets and clouds of dust, the bloody mad American is still there, with the tank looming 5 feet in front of him.

The gun will tear his head clean off.

But he is faster. With a hollow boom, the bazooka launches its rocket. The world explodes in fire and steel.

I close my eyes, feeling the heat of the distant flames. But as I blink away tears, I see Bernard staring back at me. He looks like the devil, covered in ash and dirt. *At least he's finally lost that beret.*

The tank explosion burned away all the grass, leaving a bald brown patch of ground all around us. I rise to my feet, coughing and hacking.

But the Germans are still shooting, and I've given them a nice little target.

'Bernard,' I croak, stumbling over to him. 'Up you come, mate.'

We race back into the shadows of the trees, my legs hollow as gunfire splits the air all around us. It is a bloody miracle none of them hit us, as we reach the first trees of the forest, turning wildly to avoid offering a straight shot.

Once we reach the forest proper, there is a long silence. The Germans fight back hard. That's a lesson I never quite seemed to learn. Even after Reynolds blew up their tank, they don't let up. *Reynolds, you mad bastard. Thank you.*

The wind is loud in the branches. From behind a large oak, I realize the village must be engulfed in flames. Ink-black smoke pours into the sky above. Where are Young and Denis?

'You all right, Squire?'

I reach down, touch my side gently. Something is stinging, hot. What happened?

'You're in shock. Just breathe. We'll fix you up once we lose these buggers.'

'Fix me...?'

Gently, he pushes me until my back presses against a tree. I slide down to the base of the trunk, my thoughts coming slowly. *What is happening?*

'You've been shot, Tommy. Don't worry, just stay down, don't move. I'll be back, yes?'

'Where are you...?'

But Bernard is already gone. Shot? Oh, God. I try to relax, focus. There is no pain, somehow, just a stinging, which grows the more I think about it.

Shock, he said. I am in shock. But my wandering thoughts finally snap into place, and fear takes over.

I am alone in the forest, with a bullet in my side.

I am going to die.

My lungs feel hollow, empty, as I try to breathe. In a sudden rustle of leaves, Bernard returns, all smiles.

'OK, Tommy. I've found a place where we can keep you safe. It is not far.'

I groan, trying to rise to my feet. 'As long as I don't have to run anywhere.'

'No running. Just fast walking. Then you can lie down for a rest.'

A rest? I follow the mad bastard, wondering what I ever did to deserve being captured, *shot*, and abandoned in the forest with a Frenchman.

He slows and I realize the trees are all starting to look familiar. I must be losing blood. No, I have seen this clearing before. We passed through here a few days ago.

'What are we doing?'

'There,' Bernard whispers, and for a moment I can see nothing but more trees.

Then I see it, crouching under the branches.

The abandoned tank.

Bernard lowers me, cursing, inside the great reeking belly of the tank. I slump into the seat, staring blankly at the steering wheel and various levers. The driver's slit is dark, blocked by overgrown weeds. It is cramped and hot, the stench of oil heavy.

I hear the ping of metal and Bernard darts back up the ladder. Someone is shooting at us, I think, but the idea is distant. I fight to stay focused. I am hiding inside a tank as Bernard exchanges fire with soldiers.

A voice reaches me. 'Squire. I will close this, and you just rest.'

I look up to see Bernard's face in the hatch opening. 'I will come back for you once it is clear.'

'What if?' Words, thoughts, come slowly. 'What if they find me?'

'Then you'll be fish on a dish.' He is smiling, the mad bastard is smiling. 'Don't make any noise. I will return.'

The hatch snaps shut and darkness crashes down.

I am helpless. *Fish on a bloody dish is right.* It's darker than a sewer in here, and my eyes never seem to adjust. Even the putrid stink of oil won't stop dogs from sniffing me out. They will find me.

No, I just have to wait. Bernard's coming back. I just have to wait here, and try not to bleed to death. All manner of horrible bugs crawl over my legs, and after a while I stop fighting them off and save my energy.

Misty memories of flightless ravens and stone castles and uniformed guards reach me, along with thoughts of water and light. *Anna.*

Distant sounds pull at me – what's that noise? Barking? – before everything goes dark.

My eyes blink open and the truth rushes back to me.

I have to get out. I force myself to stand, clinging to the side. The tank is low, and bloody hard to move around in. I never want to be a close dark space again.

I'm not thrilled about the prospect of trying to climb out of this thing, but at least the sky will be above me again. You only need to spend a few hours buried inside a tank to never want to be in the dark again.

Has it been hours? Has it been days? My throat cracks with thirst.

I grip the ladder, my thoughts racing. You are too reckless, Anna would say. She's not wrong. This is mad. The second I pop my head out, some SS sniper is going to take it off.

And even if they're not waiting out there, I can barely move. Where am I going to go? The dogs will smell the blood, hunt me down in minutes.

Machine guns and bombs and tanks, and I've spent the whole bloody war being scared of dogs.

To hell with Bernard, and Wake, and bloody everyone telling me what to do. I am not going to die hiding in some dark box. I have to get out of here.

I take a few steadying breaths, reach for the hatch, and push it open with a great clang.

Blazing fresh air, light all around.

I pull myself out of the hatch, blinking up at the burning blue of the sky. No crack of rifle fire, no bullets ricocheting loudly off the armour. Slowly, pitifully, I climb down the side of the tank, but drop to the earth with a punishing thud. I lie there, without breath.

The silence of the forest is heavy, as if the trees smother sound. I can't seem to stand, and fight to stay upright on my knees.

A voice calls out. I don't know what he's saying, but he's saying it in French. After a second time, he switches to English.

'You are the Resistance?' he says to a scatter of laughter.

I don't speak. *Just where did these bastards come from?*

I am not going to die on my knees. With a strength I thought long gone, I force myself to stand. Time has never moved more slowly.

Three large men stride into the clearing, their rifles gleaming darkly in the light. And two slathering German shepherds are at their heels. Even if I wasn't at death's door, I'll never get to my gun in time, and both of my remaining bombs are in my pack. Still, Major's advice comes back to me. Two shots. One to the stomach. One to the heart. Never look him in the eyes.

I gather my voice with effort. 'You are the Milice.'

Their leader nods, his face expressionless. 'Once, yes. No more.'

'What?' My mind is jammed. They haven't raised their guns. *But what about these bloody dogs?*

His eyes are wide as he searches my face. 'You have heard the news, yes?'

I shake my head, unable to look away from the great

pointed ears of the dog. But the words he says are so staggering that I'm half-tempted to stumble over and pat the great monster's head.

'Paris has been liberated.'

I'm not sure whether to laugh or scream. *I can finally go home, only now I'm bleeding to death.*

At that moment Bernard, Young, and Denis step out of the trees behind them.

'Tommy.' Bernard nods at me. 'Sorry about the wait. Our new friends here had to reconsider their loyalties.'

He waltzes over, gives me a shoulder to lean on. 'We'll get you to a medic, OK? You'll be fine.'

My teeth are chattering, I realize, and speaking words has become a new and complicated challenge. 'But the Milice.'

'Told you the bastards had no souls,' he mutters. 'Soon as they heard about Paris, they were roaring "*La Marseillaise*" and helping us finish off those Germans.' He spits. 'Cowards.'

Young comes over to my left side, puts an arm around me, and mercifully takes my weight. The two men carry me back to join our new allies. If it weren't for the searing pain in my side, I'd wager good money this is all some mad dream.

31

FLORENCE SWIFT

25 September 1944

We packed our things, knowing only that we were being loaded into a plane and taken across the Channel to set up a field hospital. The past three months had seen us, the nurses of 29th General Hospital, following in the wake of the Allied advance, setting up field hospitals outside battles in France, or inside recently liberated towns in Belgium.

Our latest military hospital has been set up in an old convent, in the small town of Eeklo, west of Antwerp. After months of living inside a canvas tent, I am blissful about the walls. If I never see mud again, I will be happy.

The mutilated bodies, though, keep coming. The German defence is strong, and the battle to open up the port of Antwerp rages on.

I will always see them. Even when I can find sleep they are there – dead and dying, amputated legs and arms. There are Russians and Germans, but mostly Canadians. I talk to them about chewing gum and ice cream, and all the things I learned about in Montreal. It helps that I know about ice hockey, which gives me something to chat to them about as I pass through my usual wards.

'Still no ice cream today?' a young soldier asks with a smile. He wasn't smiling when they amputated his leg.

'I'm sure it's on the way.'

'Nurse Swift,' another calls. 'Any news on our Maple Leafs? Is Syl Apps scoring any goals?'

'I'll have to check, Sergeant Lowney. But I'm sure Syl is still scoring.'

I move down the beds to the new arrivals, a Norwegian and a British soldier. Both look pretty banged up.

'I'm Nurse Swift,' I say. 'How are we feeling?'

The Norwegian is muttering something in his own language, but I don't speak a word. The British lad with a long face smiles up at me.

'I don't understand him either,' he says. 'Fifty miles, with him going on like that. Imagine. I didn't think a man could be more annoying than Timothy Squire, but—'

My smile freezes. 'What did you say?'

He shakes his head, closing his eyes. 'Ah, nothing. An old mate, talked your ear off. Kristian here isn't so bad. We met up on the road and decided not to kill each other. I mean, I've had second thoughts since—'

'Did you say Timothy Squire? From London? From the Tower?'

Slowly, his eyes open. He is looking at me in the most

peculiar way. They all do, happy to see a woman amongst it all, but this is different.

'Nurse Swift.'

'Yes,' I say.

'He told me you were beautiful.'

'What?' I say.

'You're Flo. Florence Swift.'

'What?'

He closes his eyes again, but the grin on his face is huge and full of mischief.

'Squire told me all about you. I'm Arthur Lightwood. Now what are the damn odds of that?'

32

TIMOTHY SQUIRE

29 August 1944

After some eternity, I open my eyes – and instantly wish I hadn't. My head is in agony and my thoughts spin in circles.

Bernard is carrying me, like I carried Rigby all those months ago.

'Looks like Sleeping Beauty is up,' Bernard says. 'You OK?'

I shake my head, an action that makes my stomach go south. 'Doctor.' I manage to say.

'That's the plan,' he says. 'We should be there in an hour. Young, can you take a turn with this bag of bones?'

Young lifts me off the ground with no apparent effort.

I turn my eyes to look up at him, and focus. 'Did you bury him?'

He shakes his head no.

I say the next words very slowly. 'I can help you. Marker. Later?'

Before I slip away again, I think about how I would have liked to honour Reynolds properly. Bring his body down to the river, and wash it, just as I saw Wake do, and shroud him in the parachute silk that was once his tent.

This time when I open my eyes I don't want to howl in pain.

I can smell iodine, heavy on the warm air. And the pain in my side has been dulled. But this is no hospital room that I have ever seen. In fact, it is a downright palace. But most of all, my head is resting on pillows. *Pillows.*

'You must be used to this sort of place,' a voice says. 'Feeling right at home, Squire?'

I look over to see Wake standing in the doorway, a terrific grin on her face.

'This is more like it.' I agree, my voice sounding slow and hoarse. 'Where am I?'

'Vichy, the traitor capital,' she sits in the chair opposite the bed. 'You came here surrounded by traitors. A great bloody triumphant entry.'

'How?'

'The news from Paris had a bit of a knock-on effect. The Germans started evacuating every town they held. Our new friends in the Milice helped chased them off.'

I nod, finally understanding. Once the battle was lost, the Milice defected to our side. And now they get to be heroes. The thought should sting, but I am only thrilled that it is over.

'So you got the message off?'

'No.' She smiles. 'I just buggered off for a bike ride. Of course I got the message off.'

'And it will help end the war?'

'That depends.' She lights a cigarette and fixes me with a long look. 'I'll have to go back to London and see.'

'I can come, too,' I say, trying my bravest smile. 'I am feeling practically normal again.'

'You need a hospital bed. And as far as hospital beds go, this isn't so bad. Good news is you haven't punctured any major organs.'

'That does sound like good news,' I smile up at her. 'So they'll be sending me home?'

'That's the bad news, I'm afraid. You won't be getting out of this bed for a few weeks, and it will be several months you are fit to travel.'

'Months?'

'Afraid so.'

'I'll be stuck here?'

'Could be worse.' She smiles. 'This is the mayor's house. I fought to get you in here, Squire, so don't start whinging on me.'

'Thank you, Commander. It's just hard to be happy about... getting shot...'

She shrugs. 'On the bright side, the armed forces won't send you back out after a wound like this. Your war is over, Squire.'

I can't help but smile at that.

It has hardly been a week, but Wake helps me to my feet and takes me out to get some air.

'Don't tell the doctor I got you up,' she says, passing me a cigarette.

I nod my thanks and light the fag, inhaling deeply. The pain in my side is vicious, burning, but somehow the tobacco eases the sting.

Now that the Germans are gone, every man, woman, and child sports a tricolour armband, smiling smugly like they haven't been hiding for years. Posing for photographs in front of an abandoned German 88 mm gun. You'd think they ousted the Nazis with their bare hands. It's like bloody Borough Market all of a sudden.

I stare at the sound of a woman screaming, as three angry men drag her into the square.

'What is happening?'

Wake shakes her head. 'They accuse these women of sleeping with German soldiers. So they will shave their heads to mark them as traitors.'

I watch, and see the men screaming right alongside the women. The anger is almost visible in the air. They want to shame these women, but they too are ashamed.

'It is the war,' Wake says finally. 'It has made them hate themselves.'

'Someone should stop this,' I say, feeling a weak flare of anger.

'There is no one.' She shrugs. 'The Germans are gone, so the police are gone.'

I stare for another moment until Wake gently nudges me with an elbow.

'Come, let's get you back to bed before the doctor gives me an earful.'

The mayor's house turns out to be where all the celebrations are held. Which means I can *hear* all the parties taking place in the ballroom below.

Tonight the sound is the clinking of glasses and the shouting of toasts.

There is still no power in Vichy, so I can imagine the great ballroom is lit by hundreds of candles. A very different type of castle from the one I grew up in.

Someone with a heavy step is coming up the stairs. My door is pushed open and even in the dim light of the candle I recognize the red-bearded man standing there.

'Tommy.' Bernard waltzes in and plops down on the chair opposite the bed. 'I could use a nap, too, my friend. I mean, there is only so much champagne a man can take. And the beef? It is too rich.'

He laughs, and then proceeds to tell me how he has unearthed hidden stores of wine, fruit, bread, and various wondrous meats. He also announces his intention of keeping me abreast of all the feasting and toasting I am missing out on.

If he didn't hand me a napkin filled with cheese and bread, I might have killed him there and then.

The sun is high at the window, and a new feast is in full swing downstairs.

There is a noise, hidden by all the cheering, in the distance. Loud, rhythmic – boots, and lots of them. Even beneath the floor, I can hear Wake's voice.

'Everyone down! Away from the windows! Now!'

I prop myself up on the pillows, staring wildly out the east-facing window. What seems like the entire German army is coming up the drive. *They didn't simply bugger off after all.*

They must be evacuating nearby cities, and the sheer number of the bastards is enough to turn my bones to water.

I watch the tops of their helmets march through the streets. It is different, not leaping out of ditches or hiding in trees. Now I know what it feels like to see them – relatively – face on. They are a force capable of crushing us like a bug. They are terrible, even in retreat.

But there is something even I can tell. This is not an army in retreat.

I remember what Wake once said when I asked her what happens next. *Same as always. The bloody Germans come kicking back.*

I may be out of it now, but the war is far from over.

16 September 1944

With a cane and very slow steps, I am able to move around the palace now, and even pop in to some of the parties in the ballroom. But I am uneasy, picturing the German army moving off.

Outside on the balcony, the sky is vast and empty. Anna is somewhere up there. The memory returns to me, the scene as I have imagined it so many times since I landed in France. Anna and I sitting on the battlements of the Tower, looking out over Tower Bridge, giddy and happy just to be alone together.

The pink sky has turned golden – time to get back upstairs before the doctor arrives.

But it is Wake who is waiting there, and she has come to say goodbye. I do not bother her with my pleas to join her on her trip to London. She has promised that when the doctor deems me fit, a ship will take me home – but not a moment before.

We didn't keep you alive this long just to kill you sending you home.

Instead, I have another request for her.

'Will you do me a favour, Commander Wake?' I hobble over and pull the letter from the side table. 'Can you see that this letter makes it where it's going?'

'The censor will read it, so you'd better not have any sensitive information in here.'

'I know, Commander.'

She looks down at the letter and for a moment I think I

see her eyes widen at the address – *Anna Cooper, The Tower of London* – but then she nods and slips it into her pack.

'It's as good as done. Goodbye, Squire.'

'Goodbye, Commander Wake.'

V

THESE GREAT HEIGHTS

33
ANNA COOPER

16 September 1944

We've arrived by train at RAF Coltishall, in Norfolk. My ATA work rarely took me here, so hopefully there's little danger of running into anyone I know. And I certainly don't know the skinny blond man with a huge Adam's apple standing in front of me now. Most pilots and soldiers are young men, but this man must be at least 25.

'I'm Flight Lieutenant Wroblewski – everyone calls me Double Whisky.'

We shake hands firmly. 'Anna Cooper and Bella Jensen.'

He looks at us with a critical eye. 'And the Air Ministry sent you?'

We are both wearing our full flying uniforms, stolen wings proudly displayed. 'Sir Archibald told me to report to 304 immediately.'

'First he cuts our pilots, now he sends us new ones.' He shakes his head. 'Word is he is looking to cancel our mission.

For a minute I thought that's why you had come – to shut us down.'

'No, sir. We're here to help stop mobile V2 launches.'

He nods, slowly. 'And how are you going to do that?'

I take a long breath. I can persuade this one pilot to listen to me.

'Aggressive reconnaissance over the area, and shoot anything that moves – or doesn't. Bridges, railway tracks – any way these rockets can be transported will go up in flames.' He is silent, so I keep talking. 'I was thinking skip bombs with eleven-second delays. You can dive low and then climb out of the way without too much risk to the aircraft.'

'You've done some divebombing?'

'We've hunted convoys in France, sir. Successfully.'

'How old are you?'

'Nineteen,' says Bella, though the question is for me.

'Eighteen,' I lie smoothly. I have been adding at least a year to my age since the war started. The next question, though, catches me off guard.

'You're the proper height, aren't you?' He glances at Bella, who is an inch or so taller. 'Tempests are too big. Spits are perfect. Bloody good timing too.'

'What do you mean?'

'The Mark XVIs are ready. You two will need to do a familiarization and air test straight away, unless the ministry's thrown that out, too. Let's get you up there.'

I impressed him enough that he shook my hand and led me into the crew room. *No need to tell him I was flying the Mark XVI when it was still in the test phase.* Bella seems to have made an equally favourable impression.

'This is Fearless – Fearless Pullman. One of the few Brits we have here – you can tell from the moustache. No Polish man would do that to himself.'

Fearless grins at me and I wave back.

Double Whisky continues his introductions. 'Royal Canadian Air Force is here too. Flying Officer Jimmy Farrell. Jimmy-Farrell-the-human-barrel. Hell of a nice guy. And some Indian pilots – Ankit and Hamza over there by the card table.'

They are so old; every pilot here must be twenty or older. These men, proud and dignified in their uniforms, remind me of Cecil. Many of them even have their hair slicked back in his style. At the back of the room, I meet the crew of Squadron 304, the all-Polish unit. They seem to take our sudden addition to their squadron in their stride.

'We've still got a green light for this mission, but I don't need to tell you that the ministry is not happy. They could pull the plug any day. I assume adding you to our group will help gain the ministry's favour.'

'Well, they didn't say as much…'

'They never do.' He laughs, and the others join in. 'These British. Hiding behind everything. They never just come out and say what they want.'

I cough, eager to change the subject. 'What have you found so far?'

He points to a table top map covered in button pins. I look closely, and see the map is a detailed study of a forested region.

'As you said, a large part of the operation is to deny the Germans their ability to supply the launch sites and factories. We've been targeting shipping, railyards, trucks, anything that could possibly help assemble a rocket. The launch bases are hidden, but we destroy everything we can.'

I nod in agreement.

'Today we've had some vital intelligence. Socha spotted a white exhaust trail shooting vertically into the sky above northern Holland at 10,000 feet. He watched the contrail rise high above, arcing west.'

That sounds like a rocket. 'So we have a firing point?'

He gestures to a button pin. 'And now we've got two new divers. You'll be Yellow 3 and your friend is Yellow 4.' He frowns. 'You know a lot about these weapons, yes? They say the rockets are unkillable.'

I nod. 'We don't have to kill the rockets, just the launch bases.'

'You're a damned good pilot.' Double Whisky smiles. 'Good angles on those dives.'

'Thanks,' I say. 'I had a good teacher.'

We spend the morning on precision bombing training. The Poles are very skilled divers, and we exchange tips on angles, speed, and timing. Double Whisky is thorough enough even for Joy's liking.

'Remember,' he says, 'if you can't see a target, don't bomb it. But there's no excuse for not finding the target.'

When the weather turns, we spend the afternoon in the lecture room, watching combat films. Before dinner, we listen to the station armament officer discuss the fusing of time-delay bombs.

The men of 304 are serious, efficient, and able pilots. For the first time in a long time, I feel a glimmer of hope.

I barely have a moment to savour it, though, as I cross the tarmac towards the Mess. In the far hangar, I am certain, is Cam Westin. I would know him anywhere, and the sick feeling of dread comes over me.

I thought he was sent to White Waltham. What is he doing here?

He must be attached to the Scottish squadron operating out of the east wing of the airfield. I won't let him ruin everything. They have a separate mess and crew room – so as long as I move across the main runways like a ghost, he'll never see me or know I am here.

21 September 1944

I scurry into the crew room under the morning sun, confident that for another day I have avoided Cam Westin.

'Hey, Cooper.' Bella calls from across the room. She sits on the edge of the table, parachute slung over her shoulder.

She is utterly at home, surrounded by adoring men from all around the world.

'So, what are things like with you and Rafferty?'

It's a bit early for all this. 'We are friends, Bella. As I've told you.'

She shrugs. 'You'll have to tell the society ladies too, then. They are begging for scraps, and Hugh Rafferty's son – he's a proper steak. It has been a dreary war for the club girls. Well,' she smiles, 'not all dreary. But they'll go wild for this.'

'There's nothing to say.'

'I believe you, Cooper. I mean, if you have a lot of men paying court to you, you'd best keep your options open.'

'Bella, I don't have anyone paying court to me.'

I realize I am staring directly at Jimmy-Farrell-the-human-barrel, and quickly look away.

'I'm going to check on the plane,' I say hurriedly. 'See you in a minute.' I head to my locker, gather my things, and slip out to the hangar.

Though I am certain Westin doesn't know I am here – or that I am flying planes anywhere – I can't help the urge to check the engine on my Spit.

A quick glance tells me everything is fine. I will test all the instruments before take-off, but I am mostly satisfied.

I catch myself staring at Double Whisky's plane. Why would Westin sabotage these planes? Women aren't flying them – he's got nothing to gain by killing Polish pilots. Still, I slip over to the plane and have a peek. I do a slow walk round it, looking for any evidence of tampering, but everything is as it should be.

'What do you think?'

I almost shout in fear.

'Oh. Double Whisky,' I say turning to face him. My mind races. 'I'm sorry – I just wanted to see…'

He nods knowingly. 'Yes. Painted it myself. Isn't it beautiful?'

It isn't until that moment I realize he is taking about an illustration on the nose of the plane. Nose art, pilots call it, is usually reserved for the heavy bombers and thought to bring good luck. Except in this case, the painting is of a baby in nappies wielding a hammer over the crying head of Adolf Hitler. It is many things, but beautiful is not one of them.

'It's… lovely, Double Whisky.'

He smiles with great pride. 'That's my son, Aleksy. And that's—'

'Hitler.'

He nods. Mercifully, the rest of the squadron is now entering the hangar, and the armed recce is set to begin.

Rain streams down the windshield. Winds buffet as we climb, finding good visibility once we pass the cloud base at 7,000 feet.

We form up over the North Sea, then climb to 20,000 feet, setting a course for the Dutch coast. Double Whisky wants to take advantage of favourable winds at 20,000 feet, despite it meaning we have to don the horrid oxygen masks at that height. We could comfortably fly at 11,000 feet – it wouldn't be nearly as cold – but I hold my tongue. *I'm not in charge here.*

We fly in silence. Once, Oakes forced me to listen to a symphony by Sibelius, insisting that it captured the sensation of flying. Now there is no Sibelius, no proud swaying trumpets, just the slow song of the wind. We reach Holland in thirty-five minutes, and drop down to 10,000 feet, locating a possible target only a few minutes later.

Our plan is well rehearsed. Our first priority is to recce the convoy and establish its destination: the storage bunker. From here I can see the three camouflaged trucks and a 3-ton lorry with a trailer. Intelligence has us seeking long vehicles called *meilerwagen*, which are specially constructed for carrying rockets by road.

The formation always moves under Double Whisky's lead, and he gives the signal to pull back and let Socha, his wingman, shadow the convoy alone. If he can track the convoy to its destination, we can discover where the rocket materials are being picked up or delivered. But as he tracks them along a narrow road, heading into the forest, the lead truck in the convoy screeches to a halt.

They've spotted him. The whole convoy stops, and soldiers pile out and immediately begin to set up anti-aircraft weapons. I curse loudly. *Where were they going?*

Double Whisky's voice comes over the radio. 'Lets make the most of good visibility. Stick to the guns. No need for bombs against this lot.'

Double Whisky leads the attack, descending to 7,000 feet while the rest of us remain above. Then peeling into a dive he tears down on the lorry, strafing it with cannon and machine-gun fire. He levels out of his dive and climbs quickly away, forming up with the squadron minutes later. It is smoothly done.

Yellow 4 targets the lead truck, which he leaves stationary and smoking.

The next pilot, Yellow 2, attacks in a shallow dive, and two soldiers are killed before they reach the safety of the woods. Some return fire is coming from the trees.

'Yellow 3, you're up.'

That's me.

I peel into a dive at 10,000 feet. The world drops away, and I rest my thumb on the firing button. I make cannon and machine-gun attacks, giving the trailer and the lorry equal share of the ammunition, but enemy guns chase me back up to 12,000 feet. The trailer is smoking badly, and a dark brown liquid is pouring on to the road.

Bella does a fine job to avoid getting hit on her dive through a curtain of return fire.

The soldiers have vanished into the woods, but the convoy is now ruined and in flames. Double Whisky calls for us to head home. As it's far too dangerous to attempt a landing when equipped with bombs, as we fly back we jettison the unused 500 lb bombs in the cold sea below.

34

ANNA COOPER

30 September 1944

New target material gives us a hint of the German plan. A photographic mosaic shows a track through a wooden area in the south is being used for the transportation of V2 rockets to the sites around the area.

We are flying over the area now, discovering side roads cut through the trees. The Germans are hiding under the cover of trees, and launching rockets from these hiding places. There is a pattern to their movements that makes no sense. There *must* be a storage bunker hidden somewhere in these forests. If we can destroy the storage bunker, we can stop the rockets.

And we are running out of time. Only this morning we heard the news that a V2 struck Smithfield Market in Farringdon Road, killing 110 and injuring 123. No warning, no siren. People were slapped to the walls of buildings by the pressure and left hanging there.

We have endured enough. It has to stop.

I drop my first bomb at 4,000 feet, and turn tightly, bringing the Spit back round on to the target and thumbing the firing button. As I come back to level, there's a glimpse of white on the distant road.

'I see another one,' I say. 'Moving west.'

'Yellow 3, that's a tractor,' comes Bella's voice.

'It has a trailer.' *And the trailer could contain liquid oxygen.* It's hidden by a green canvas. If more fuel makes it to the bunker, more rockets will fire at London. I keep my thumb over the firing button.

'It's too small, Yellow 3. That's half a ton at the most.'

'Permission to engage, Leader?'

The air crackles around Bella's voice. 'Cooper. That's not the lorry we're looking for. There's not even any gunfire.'

'I'm not asking your permission, Jensen.'

Double Whisky settles it for us. 'If you see a target, Yellow 3, engage.'

Peeling into a dive, I am dangerously close to the 457 m.p.h. maximum speed when my cannon bursts into life, and I score a direct hit on the trailer. As I pull up, the black fury of smoke climbs behind me.

1 December 1944

Bella and I have just suffered through the indignity of lying to Double Whisky about us needing to go on leave. I fought against the idea, but Bella insisted it would start to look suspicious if we didn't take a leave like everyone else.

So now the Tower, lightly dusted in snow and cold as a tomb, is my home for the next three days.

I've barely had time to get comfortable on my bench when I see a woman striding across the Green towards me. Something about the way she carries herself, I don't think even Yeoman Brodie would dare to tell her to keep off the grass. She is holding a letter.

My heart jumps, but the envelope is not blue. A hundred times I have imagined the telegram boy delivering the terrible news. But this is not it.

'You're Anna Cooper?'

I nod as she comes closer.

'Nancy,' she says, shaking my hand. 'Nancy Wake.' She is looking around with a small smile. 'He really does live here, huh?'

The ravens flap over, intrigued by the new visitor.

'Can I help you?' I ask.

She turns back to me, her eyes sharp and focused. 'I don't usually play delivery girl, but this seemed like the sort of news you don't want to get from just anyone. Timothy Squire is alive and well.'

Without a second of warning, I am sobbing, my eyes watering, gasping for breath. It is not until I feel the strong grip of a hand on my shoulder that I nod, force my breathing to settle long enough to speak.

'Alive?' I squint up at her through blurry eyes. 'How do you know?'

'I was with him, in France, a few months ago. He is recovering in a military hospital.'

With another long intake of breath, I speak. 'Recovering? What happened?'

She looks at me steadily. 'He was shot, in the side. He will be fine, and safe to travel home in a few months.'

'Months?' I repeat, desperate.

She gives a half-smile. 'That's what he said, too.' She reaches into her coat. 'He asked me to bring you this.'

She hands me the letter and I take it in a daze.

'The French Resistance. We pulled him out of a prison train back in July.' She looks at me with concern. 'Here, take a seat.'

I sink slowly back onto the bench, the unread letter gripped in my hands. The croak of ravens fills the cold air.

I stare down at his handwriting on the address – my name. Again I am crying, and my mind is blank of anything but *He is alive.*

'He's been a good fighter,' Wake says gently, 'and a handy chap to have in a tight spot. He's a brave enough lad, but a dense one – kept trying to send messages to his sweetheart over Special Operations radio. I'm afraid this is the first one that's been able to make it to you.'

I look down at the letter, terrified to open it. 'Thank you. This means the world to me.'

She seems ready to leave, but squints her eyes at me.

'He told me you're an ATA pilot. That's an admirable job. I could never master flying a plane. Prefer to jump out of them myself.'

'I'm not an ATA pilot anymore.' I say. 'Apparently the RAF isn't so keen on female pilots.'

She laughs. 'They never stop buggering you. You just have to show them who's in charge.'

'Commander Wake!' A voice calls from the gate.

She sighs. 'My driver. I must go. Unless you care to fly me to South Africa?'

I laugh, and stand to shake her hand. 'I'm afraid I'm due in Holland tomorrow, on the hunt with a squadron of Polish pilots.'

'I love a good Polish man. What are you hunting?'

'A storage bunker. If we can find the V2 storage bunker, we can stop the rocket attacks.'

Her hand drops slowly to her side. 'Rockets? In Holland?'

'Commander!'

She takes one last look back at me, and she seems lost in thought. But I am already tearing open the envelope.

Magpie,

I am coming home as soon as I can.

I told you I have my own plans for us.

I love you,

Timothy Squire

VI

MEMORY OF LIGHT

35

ANNA COOPER

11 February 1945

Timothy Squire is alive. He'll be home soon. I need to make sure there's still a home for him to come back to. I can't shake off the news from yesterday. A Woolworths was hit by a V2 rocket – the entire building collapsed into the basement, and 168 people died.

To make sure another rocket never reaches us, today 304 is targeting the railway wagons that transport the rockets. And Double Whisky has led us right to the mark.

Socha peels off to take out the upcoming bridge. Bella and I take off to attack the locomotive, each of us carrying four 250 lb bombs.

I drop my first bomb at 4,000 feet, and pull up to see the red glow of a direct hit on the train. I think of the Blitz in the early days, the Thames shining red in the flames, the clouds of smoke blotting out the sky. The people screaming in fear as bombs suddenly fell from the skies above, tearing their world apart with fire and death.

'Yellow 3, you alive over there?'

I shake myself. 'All fine, Yellow 4. And I'd like to see you copy a direct hit like that.'

We re-join Red Section north of the river, and turn back for home. As we fly across the forest, a heavy explosion rocks the sky.

'Sweet Christ.'

Suddenly a huge great rocket appears, like Nelson's Column, rising effortlessly from the trees. Fast, graceful, deadly. Climbing vertically above the tree tops, it must be 50 feet long.

Father's words come to me. Five storeys high. A steel cylindrical body tapered to a sharp point which contains the warhead.

All at once, in mid-air, a huge stream of exhaust appears, arching across the sky. I stare in horror, dimly wondering at the unbelievable power of the thrust, and where the gyroscope and compass must be to control the rudders and guide the missile. And the speed – Father warned it could exceed 2000 m.p.h. That may well be the case, because it is now going too fast to be seen.

And then the words of Double Whisky fill my mind, and I am terrified that they are true.

A rocket is unkillable.

Jimmy-Farrell-the-human-barrel nods as I enter the crew room.

'Someone came to see you,' he says with his grin. 'Woman. Left this note. Told me in no uncertain terms that I wasn't to read it.'

'Thank you... Jimmy.' I take the note and slip it into my coat. I hurry to a table at the back of the room before I break the seal and unfold the letter inside.

It's all numbers. No, it's coordinates.

> 50.8286° N, 2.1837° E
>
> Jackpot.
>
> – Wake

I throw open the door to the Mess. Pilots, hungry at the end of a long day, gaze up at me without expression.

'I have the coordinates. I know where the storage bunker is.'

Double Whisky puts down his fork. 'What do you mean?'

'New information from Special Operations. I'll show you on the maps.'

'Now wait a moment,' he says, getting to his feet. 'We can't move on, not yet.'

He's bursting with arguments against changing our plans as we hurry down the corridor to the crew room. In truth, he doesn't stop talking for a moment until I show him the note.

He stares at the coordinates. 'This isn't Holland.'

'No.'

Together we stand in silence over the detailed illustration of a forested mountain terrain. I draw my finger down the map.

'Maybe,' he says, 'that's why the convoys were all moving south, and then turning west.'

As I look at the map it all miraculously seems to make sense. *That's* why they were moving south. They were trying to avoid the areas of heavy fighting, and sneak up behind us. Why would we even think to look in France, now that the Germans have been pushed out?

Another thought occurs to me. That convoy that Bella and I destroyed in France – it could have been headed to the same bunker. *They've been there all along.*

But Double Whisky isn't so sure. 'It seems a damn bit insane to me. You're sure this is dependable intelligence?'

'Positive,' I say, smiling wide. 'This, and what we've uncovered. Everything points to the rockets being stored and launched here. So we're going too.'

Now he is smiling too. 'Tomorrow morning.'

The sun shines. Even the weather is on our side today. I march into the crew room, knowing that today is the day we finally strike a killing blow against the rocket soldiers.

Double Whisky stares back at me, armed folded over his

chest. The men of 304 are standing around the room, many frowning openly.

'What's going on?'

'You may be going alone.' Double Whisky's voice is empty, hollow. Not one of his strange attempts at humour. Before I can ask what he means, the door bangs open behind me.

British military police enter, guns drawn.

My mind reels. They've found me out. *It's Cam Westin.* He is having me arrested. And the pilots will be in trouble too. Oh God. *Anna Cooper, you selfish monster.*

The officers spread into the room, led by a tall man with a crooked nose. The Polish pilots stand unmoving.

'Your sidearms,' the lead officer says.

'You want our guns?' Double Whisky says slowly.

'Wait,' I say, holding up my hands. 'This is my fault.'

The officer with the crooked nose barks a laugh. 'If you're Joe Stalin, I'm Mae West. Now step aside, miss. You men give us your sidearms.'

I stare around in confusion, but I am the only one. Whatever is going on, the Poles are not surprised. *Stalin?* Why did he say that?

The officer doesn't smile. 'There is talk of mutiny, and we can't risk it.'

'The Polish government has stated that we are to follow orders and fly your missions,' Double Whisky says.

The officer nods. 'Well, the British government has decided that we can't take that risk. Squadron 304 is to be disbanded, effective immediately.'

Gravely, Double Whisky hands over his gun. He looks at me, and smiles a weak smile. 'You see. They give you something, and then they take it away.'

The officer snatches it. 'This is the price of peace.'

'Is it? To have your country carved up by your own Allies? I was born in a town in Poland that Churchill has handed over to the Soviets.'

I say nothing. I heard from the news that the leaders were meeting in Yalta to sign some new agreement. I remember Cecil's words. 'Our soldiers are firmly stuck west of the Rhine. They've been stuck there since November. *Only the Russians can end this war now.* We need them.'

The officers have finished relieving the pilots of their weapons. The man with the crooked nose takes a final look around the room, before turning back to Double Whisky.

'Clear out your lockers.'

'I'm sorry,' I say, knowing how pathetic it sounds. The pub is almost empty, and the only sound is the clattering of glasses behind the bar.

'Squadron 304 is finished.' Double Whisky bows his head.

I mutter in agreement. I have no idea how it must feel to be so betrayed.

I take a drink, and Double Whisky mirrors the gesture. 'They are coming to collect our planes tomorrow morning.

That's how much they trust their allies.' He laughs, takes a long sip from his whisky. 'And just when we finally cornered the bastards. I'd like to have finished the job.'

I stare at him, slowly pulling my hand from my glass.

'Who? Who is coming to collect the planes?'

He shrugs. 'The bastards at the ATA.'

I reach out and grab the arm that is throwing back more whisky. 'Don't. You need to be clear-headed tomorrow.'

'I think we have different plans for tomorrow, Cooper.'

A smile spreads across my face. 'Your planes will still be ready for take-off at first light. We are going to finish the job. Tell the others.'

'But how?'

'Leave that to me.'

28 February 1945

'Would you look at what the cat dragged in?'

I smile at the ATA pilot standing on the tarmac. Flakes of snow drift from the morning sky. 'Joy.'

'Anna Cooper.'

We look at each other. The distance between us is like a physical object – a mountain, maybe. And it's my job to start the climbing.

My breath clouds out ahead of the words. 'It's good to see you.'

'Is it?'

I smile.

'Well, it's good to see you too, actually. Surprisingly.' She looks down. 'I wanted to visit you, but...'

I wait for more, but that is all.

'I'm glad you're here now.' I smile, huddling my shoulders up against the cold. 'Who else is with you?'

She narrows her eyes at me. 'I brought the girls in the Anson. Barcs, Minx, Canada. To take these Spits back to Hamble. '

I nod. 'Funny that you'd have the whole crew with you.'

'We need four pilots to collect the planes.'

I hold her gaze. 'The same four pilots we trained with?'

A hint of a smile. 'Word is you've been hanging out here, illegally flying with some Polish pilots.'

'That's true.'

'Did you give them your speech about fighting for your homeland?'

'No,' I say. 'They fight to bring peace. Just like you, Joy.'

'Damn right.'

We smile at each other and the mountain between shrinks to a hill.

'So,' I say. 'You have a taxi full of dive-bomber pilots. Will they remember any of it?'

'Gower hasn't exactly been listening to the RAF.'

'That was never her strong suit.'

'We've kept up the training. The girls are good – Minx has never listened to another person in her whole life, but the others have learned most of what I could teach them.'

'So you'd say that they're ready?'

She nods. 'Looks like they're going to have to be.'

It's all I can do to laugh. 'Sometimes, Joy, you got to live like your hair's on fire.'

Double Whisky squints at me across the crew room. He definitely finished that drink last night, and likely went for another couple more. 'The planes are still here?'

'Even better. We have an extra formation joining us.'

He makes some confused sounds as we exit the crew room and step out on the tarmac. The Ravens stand in a semi-circle, helmets in hands.

Double Whisky's eyes go wide, and he sets to fixing his hair. The rest of 304 emerge behind us in a straightening of backs and puffing out of chests.

I move to stand between the two groups.

'This is Joy Brooks – she is an expert diver, and she's my wingwoman. I've shown her the maps, and our route to the final site. With them on our side, we can take out the site in a single raid.'

Double Whisky laughs. 'Because that's all we'll get, one chance, before the police take us all away.'

I nod. 'We could end up with the police. Or worse.'

Double Whisky looks from the Ravens to me and back again. 'She is a lot of trouble, yes?'

Joy nods. 'You could say that.'

Socha smiles. He's also looking more pale than usual this morning. 'So we're are all going to Holland?'

'Not Holland.' I shake my head. 'France.'

Double Whisky calls over the squadron armourers, who wheel out more bombs. The men begin equipping the four additional Spits, and in under an hour we are armed, fuelled, and ready to go.

Until an all-too-familiar voice shouts across the tarmac.

'Stop! I knew it!'

Cam Westin comes strolling up, his face an almost worrying shade of red. I'd forgotten, in all the excitement, to keep a low profile. *I've been standing in the middle of the tarmac chatting with Joy for ten minutes.*

'This woman – this girl – is not legally allowed to fly,' Westin proclaims. 'A judge has revoked her licence. She is not permitted under any circumstances to pilot RAF aircraft!'

Double Whisky steps calmly forward. 'Me neither.'

Westin eyes him, uncertain. Then he takes a step back.

Having marched up to me, the situation is only slowly dawning on him: twelve pilots, standing together. Bella's glance alone could wither an oak tree.

Westin looks at me with pure fury, gesturing wildly to the aircraft. 'For you to fly an RAF Spitfire – you – it is an insult to the British!'

'I'm Polish,' says Socha.

'Us too.'

'Canadian, actually,' adds Canada politely.

'USA,' Joy says.

Barcsay smiles. 'Kolozsvar.'

Westin is losing steam in a hurry. It seems a new judge and jury have ruled in my favour.

'This time you're going to gaol,' he says darkly. 'Wherever you land this plane, I will have the police waiting for you.'

I take one last look at Westin before I don my helmet. 'Have a tea waiting for me too, would you, love? Try to rustle up some milk if you can. Come on, squadron, we've got a job to do.'

We seem to fill the sky, wing to wing. In a dropped-down V formation, I stare out at the angry North Sea beneath us. Snow falls heavily from the clouds below.

Glowacki, one of the younger Poles, flies above, providing top cover, but we don't expect to run into any trouble in the air.

It takes a whole squadron of Spits to carry the same bomb load as a Lancaster, and our smaller planes can only travel much shorter distances. But we're fast, agile, precise, and – hopefully – ready to dive. *This is our only chance.*

'Now, pilots,' I call out into the speaking tube, 'I know we're all still getting to know one another, but I've had the pleasure of flying with every pilot here, and I couldn't ask for a better squadron. Thank you, Ravens, for coming to our aid and supplying the aircraft. And thank you, 304 Squadron, for fighting on.'

Double Whisky's voice crackles. 'Our country is occupied by the enemy. We are going to get it back – or as much of it as we can. We are freedom fighters.'

I give his message the moment it deserves, before taking the microphone back. 'We all have the same goal today – demolishing this bunker.'

Joy's voice comes. 'If he's going to have police waiting, we're all in for it, girls. And if we'll be in prison tomorrow, let's be sure we smash this place.'

Minx laughs. 'Oh, the *Daily Mail* is going to love that.'

Bella and Barcsay take turns cheering into the microphone.

'No one's going to gaol,' I say. 'We'll land at Hamble and figure something out. Gower won't let Westin within ten miles of the place. But first, let's destroy the target. There may be a battalion of Germans hiding out in there, and they'll be ready to defend it. We have one chance. We need to give it everything we have.'

36

ANNA COOPER

The bunker is a grey stone fortress. It makes the Tower look like a welcoming cottage. There are no windows, no doors, just a great impenetrable rectangle.

We found it easily enough using Wake's coordinates, roaring over the forested site and doubling back to prepare attack formations. But the Germans must have spotted our approach, because anti-aircraft guns have been wheeled out.

The soldiers have set up three 88 mm anti-aircraft artillery guns, and flak is racing towards us thick and fast. We've learned all about these weapons; there are few more dangerous to pilots. The guns can pick us off as far as 20 miles away, and they track us all the way through the straight line of a dive. Each strike we make will be under constant fire.

'All right, Ravens,' I call out.

The Ravens move into their diving positions and tear down on the target at the forest edge. While on the run-up,

I arm the 250 lb bomb, and release it at 1,000 feet, before pulling the control column back hard, dragging the Spit into a steep climb. Anti-aircraft fire chases me into the sky.

'Heck of a dive, Coop,' comes Joy's voice. 'Finally sorted out your angles.'

Glancing in the mirror, I see the other four Spits coming up swiftly behind me.

Orbiting the target area, the Ravens dive again and again, dropping their 250 lbs, followed smoothly by 304 Squadron unloading their first round of bombs. But this bunker was built to withstand massive impact, and our attacks have little effect aside from palls of smoke. Snow continues to fall thickly, making it harder to see the bullets rushing at us. We'll keep hurling bombs at them until it cracks open like an egg.

We form up, chased off by the flak. There must be a fourth gun down there.

I edge closer to Joy, who grins at me through the windscreen. I hold up my thumb and grin back.

'Joy,' I say into the microphone. 'How low do you think you can get?'

'How low do you need?'

'I'm headed for the middle section. Can you follow me through and hit the same spot?'

'Just watch me.'

I bark a laugh, and peel into a dive, the nose of the Spit racing to meet the bunker. Bullets fly past. The air speed indicator reads *450 m.p.h.* Forcing myself not to pull out of the dive until the last second takes all my willpower. But my 500 lb bomb hits the crack dead on.

Joy swoops in behind me and hits the exact spot. Columns of grey and black smoke twist into the air. The bunker might be cracked, but nothing like the amount we need to empty the place out. It's difficult to see the target through the inferno of flames. We will need to get extremely close.

'Bella,' I say. 'Remember that truck in France?'

'I'm on it, Cooper.'

Bella dives down. I wait 30 seconds before I follow.

Flak is heavy. I stare at the target, just past Bella's diving Spit. Bullets race silently past. The heavy 88 mm gun is trained on us. The shots are close.

It is because I am staring straight down the nose of my Spit that I see it happen. The bullets racing towards her. One direct hit knocking her into a wobble, and another that must catch her 500 lb bomb.

Bella's plane explodes in a great flash.

I am diving too fast to pull out. I am headed straight for Bella's plane. But there is nothing there. No smoke, no heat, no aircraft. On I dive, passing through a cloud of debris clinking like hail against my wings. *Bella.*

After a direct hit, and with the explosives attached, she vanished.

I turn at the last moment, targeting the closest gunner. Without even giving the order, I feel the planes forming up behind me. The Ravens attack in a tight, stepped-down V formation, bringing the massed firepower of our machine guns to bear on the 88 mm guns.

'Control your bursts,' warns Barcsay, but I don't listen, using a long five-second torrent that leaves the 88 mm gun in ruins.

Fuel is running low. We have to get back on target soon, or we'll never have enough fuel to make it home.

'All right, Ravens. That's our target. Not an inch to the left, not a centimetre to the right. Show us what you can do. Let's do it for Bella.'

We swarm the bunker like hornets. Like ravens.

They peel off and dive, the barest time lag separating each dive – and each bomb a direct hit. There is little wind to offset the trajectory. We re-form, and below us the crack has definitely opened up. *But not enough.*

'OK, 304. You're up – crack this bloody thing wide open.'

Double Whisky plants his 500 lb perfectly, and the others follow suit. On the last drop, the crack widens, and part of the roof buckles.

There's a cheer from both squadrons, but it's restrained. The damage is not enough. Even if we all came back on another run and all hit the same spot, it's too little.

The far plane in the Polish formation is hit in the wing, staggering through the air in a cloud of grey smoke. It is Socha – he is an easy target now, his speed gone and broadside exposed to the gunners.

Voices scream in Polish over the radio, but there is nothing we can do. The next spray of bullets punches the side of his Spit, and one hits the cockpit. Socha's plane pitches to the earth, a flaming heap in the snow.

Double Whisky leads his men in the destruction of another of the 88 mm guns. Only one remains, but the bullets are accurate and constant. We have broken formation, circling independently.

'What do you say, Coop?' Joy asks.

The Ravens hover, waiting. But there's no choice. We're out of bombs, low on bullets, and the mission is not complete. *We have to turn back.*

No. Bella didn't die so we could turn back and leave this bunker standing. Socha didn't die so we could abandon the mission.

Without giving notice, I tuck back into a dive. My cannon bursts into life, and I strafe the length of the area with cannon and a five-second torrent of machine-gun fire. Turning tightly, I bring the Spit back round even closer and blast the target again. As I roar away, climbing, I notice movement in the far corner of the roof. An escape hatch opening? I move back into a steep dive. Before the sound reaches me I know what a terrible mistake I've made.

In a sea of flames, a huge black and white bullet erupts from the bunker, climbing slowly into a perfect vertical climb. A great tail of fire follows, as long as the weapon itself. *Five storeys high. A steel cylindrical body tapered to a sharp point.*

A rocket.

Father's words come to me. *It is impossible to destroy a rocket. Blindingly fast, it turns supersonic at 10,000 feet and is impossible to track.* But this isn't 10,000 feet. And the rocket is directly in my gun sights. There is no time to make sense of it. Squinting, unable to see in the fire and smoke, I press forward into a screaming dive. I may only have a few seconds of machine-gun fire left, so I must be close. *455 m.p.h. 460 m.p.h.* The Spit is rattling, the wings shaking, and the propeller threatening to snap off. Too much faster, and the plane will be torn into pieces.

A rocket is unkillable.

In that blinding instant I see the ruins of Woolworths, of Smithfield Market, of the Tower, of the houses and lives suddenly and instantly destroyed. Other thoughts flash past, a warning. Timothy Squire. Oakes, Father, Cecil, Gower, Cam Bloody Westin – they are not safe, not with this rocket launching at them.

'Cooper – watch your speed!'

470 m.p.h., and the stick shudders in my hand. I am not thinking about destroying the bunker, or completing the mission, or my own safety. I am thinking one thing only. *This rocket will not reach London.*

'Anna! For God's sake!' Joy's voice crackles in the distance.

475 m.p.h. Every part of the plane rattles, threatening to snap. A crack forms on the cockpit glass, spidering outwards. The engine roars in panic. The voices in the headphones are drowned out by the wrath of the disintegrating Spitfire. But the pain in my head dulls, releases, as I press forward, unleashing the machine gun in its final burst of gunfire.

Then the world vanishes, and I am buried in light.

37

ANNA COOPER

'Joy?'

I say her name again but she doesn't answer. It takes a moment to understand that the word didn't make it out of my mouth.

I am lying in the snow. I am alive. I remember, mainly from memory, that I landed the Spit in a field. I can see it, just in the distance, the wing bent, cockpit window shattered, engine likely fried.

Gower is going to kill me. Again.

The ringing in my ears – I remember that. But I'm not certain it's ever going away this time. I see another shape, tall and thin, moving towards me. Double Whisky. 'Can you hear me? Anna?'

I nod. His voice is the barest whisper over the ringing, though I'm sure he's shouting. The look on his face is as disapproving as I've ever seen it.

'You fired at a ballistic missile, Cooper. Jesus, you could have killed us all.'

I reach into my memory and see it – yes, the flash of light I flew into, gun firing. 'What happened?' I mouth.

'What happened? You shot down a bloody V2 rocket. That's supposed to be impossible. And you're lucky that plane held together at the speed you were going.'

One thing I know for certain. *That rocket never reached London.*

But the darkness is returning, and as Joy asks me another question, I drift off.

Bella.

VII

THERE'LL BE BLUEBIRDS

‘Before us stands yesterday.’

Ted Hughes

‘Women of ability are held down because of a subconscious Hitlerism in the hearts of men.’

Lady Astor, *The Times*, October 1940

38

ANNA COOPER

10 March 1945

Turns out Cam Westin did have the police notified. Despite the success of our mission, all of the ATA pilots involved have been placed on suspension. The Polish pilots risk gaol.

I will have to explain to Gower why she's getting back three fewer planes. But first we must spread the word about a funeral for Bella.

'You're doing remarkably better.' Cecil smiles. 'I heard all about it. You are an amazing woman, Anna Cooper. They say the V2 rockets have stopped – that you destroyed a storage bunker.'

I try to smile. No one outside of the squadron knows about the rocket, and I think it's best if it stays that way.

He nods. 'I commend those Poles, for taking you under their wing. They are brave men – and the pilots from the ATA, too. But you…' He cuts off, laughing.

'I am mad, I know.'

'What are we going to do with you?' He smiles. 'As Wellington himself said, *next to a battle lost, the greatest misery is a battle gained.*'

I stare. 'I don't know what that means.'

'The return to civil life will be dull.'

Today is hot, almost a summer's day, with the sun pouring down. I am happy to be in civilian clothes again, a white blouse and navy skirt – but it doesn't feel right. 'I'm not sure I'll ever be able to have a civilian life.'

Some mad part of me thought the problem of headaches, the darkness, would go away after I flew into that rocket. But it's part of me, and no great gesture will ever eliminate the pain. I will have to cope with it, that's all.

Cecil shakes his head. He can't believe my recklessness, but he is also struggling to adjust to the news I gave him earlier. That both Timothy Squire and Arthur Lightwood are alive.

All morning he has been regaling me with the tale of when the two sappers broke him out of gaol.

'"Meet me at the Fox and Hounds," he calls out, as if any of us were going to make it out of there.' Cecil smiled at the memory. 'He risked his life to save me. The man is a hero. I'm sorry I didn't tell you the truth, Anna. I just thought that he must have died. I didn't want to take away your hope.'

'I understand,' I said.

Now we look at each other and realize we are saying goodbye.

'Thank you for all your help, Cecil.' I smile up at him.

He nods. 'I've not been the greatest help, I can admit that. But I think I can give it one last try. Goodbye, Anna Cooper.'

'Goodbye, Cecil Rafferty.'

39

CECIL RAFFERTY

10 March 1945

'Cecil,' Sir Archibald says. I notice the chill in his voice. He is tired of me coming here. That makes two of us.

'Sir, I am sorry to take more of your time.'

He shakes his head. 'Drink?'

I nod and he pours two whiskies.

'Sad business,' he says after a moment. 'The editor should be fired.'

This newspaper article is on everyone's lips, raising questions about bombing raids on non-military targets. The piece contained many details, including the thousand-degree heat, and the desperate civilians jumping into fountains only to find the firestorm boiled them dry.

Archibald grumbles. 'No one is allowed to use the term *terror bombing*. Not if it's us doing the bombing. He's doing Goebbels' bloody work for him.'

'I'm sorry to hear it, sir.'

'To call it terror bombing,' Archibald shakes his head, 'knowing full well what that means, is an insult to the Air Ministry. But I know why you're here, Rafferty. You're here to fight for your Polish friends, aren't you?'

'They did help end the war, sir.'

'Through illegal actions. I shouldn't have to remind you of the importance of the chain of command.'

'No, sir,' I say. 'But the information was urgent. From Special Operations.'

'Special Operations?'

'Commander Wake, sir.'

He sighs. 'Wake, eh? She's got a reputation for starting trouble. And for getting things done. It was a success, you say?'

'Assuredly, sir. Without a single civilian casualty.'

'Not likely to make it into the papers then,' he grumbles.

'I don't know, sir. But London has not seen a rocket since.'

'Fine.'

He said yes. I savour the victory for a silent moment, finishing my glass and working up my courage.

'One last thing, if I may, sir.'

He is visibly concerned by my continued efforts. 'What is it, lad? I feel badly, always having to say no to Hugh's boy, but you're pushing your luck here.'

'I know I am, sir. But it's about a fellow RAF man.'

He looks at me, waiting.

'A flight engineer. Cam Westin, working out of White Waltham.'

'What about him?'

'He's a traitor.'

Sir Archibald slowly sets his drink down.

'He sabotaged some female ATA pilots last year,' I say.

'I remember this business. He was cleared of charges by a judge. Donald, I think, had that case.'

'I'm afraid Cam Westin lied.'

'Are you quite certain?' He looks at me until he's sure I am. 'A second trial would be costly, and could prove an embarrassment. You will stand against him, your words versus his?'

'I will.'

'Thank you for bringing this to my attention, lad. And send my regards to your father.'

'I will,' offering a firm salute. 'Thank you again, sir.'

40

FLORENCE SWIFT

20 April 1945

The past nine months had seen us, the nurses of 29th General Hospital, following in the wake of the Allied advance, setting up field hospitals outside battles in France, or convents in recently liberated towns in Belgium.

But then we were heading to Germany. The Allies had crossed the Rhine, and the war would soon be over. It should have been a happy time.

I arrived at Bergen in the evening of 18 April, only three days after the British 11th Armoured Division's eastward advance. An army truck brought us here, to the gates of the Bergen-Belsen concentration camp.

Nothing I have seen in the past nine months is close to the horrors of this place. The skeleton living, nearly identical to the dead. The disease, the starvation, the cruelty – the evil. Bodies heaped in mass graves, grotesquely stacked in lorries, children murdered in cold blood.

The Allies are freeing concentration camps all over Germany.

We are here for another eleven days. Then, before we are sent home, every inch of our bodies must be sprayed with DDT for decontamination.

I rub my eyes, red and aching from the scalding tears, and get back to work. I know one thing for certain. For the rest of my life, however long it may be, I will wonder how such cruelty can be allowed to exist.

I saw the photographs in the *Sunday Pictorial*, the smug, unabashed faces of the female guards. *They do not repent.*

I feel my eyes growing hot once again and force myself to move onwards. But one thought I cannot shake. *How long have the German people known about this? And how long has the British government known? The Americans?*

Black eyes, so thin. Bones showing through skin. How have these people not died?

Home leave is allocated by lottery. But how can any of us go home now? How can we return to our old lives knowing this?

41
ANNA COOPER

30 April 1945

A fierce but mostly friendly game of chess is in progress, with Oakes currently getting the best of Father. Both men sit surrounded by folded newspapers.

Father makes us listen to German radio – 'better music' – a concession Oakes surprisingly makes. I was also touched to learn that Oakes dug up an old violin from the White Tower storeroom, and gave it to Father to practise on, 'so long as he takes requests'. Oakes has a much bigger heart than most people know.

'You did a brave thing, Anna,' Oakes says, his voice almost a shout.

I nod – *I can hear you* – and respond in a deliberately softer tone. 'We did what we had to.'

He laughs, a great high bark of a laugh. 'You broke about every rule there is.'

Father smiles at me. 'I'm proud of you, Anna.'

'Well.' Oakes clears his throat. He is still very protective of me around Father. 'It looks like you've stopped the V2 rockets coming in. And the Allies have finally crossed the Rhine.'

But the mood does not feel celebratory. I am still shaky from the encounter with the rocket – and maybe a little deaf – but at least I kept all my teeth this time. My head is also clear.

We have already learned that Mussolini is dead. He and his mistress were strung up in a town square for people to spit on. Italy has surrendered.

Berlin is surrounded. The Russian and American armies have met. Hitler is raving, everyone says. Either that or he is dying.

It is all happening so fast. It took forever to come, and now it is all happening at once. One can hardly keep pace with it.

Father makes a move that seems to irk Oakes no end.

I still feel a little out of place. The novelty of wearing Austin Reed skirts and nice civilian clothes has already worn off. I can't spend my days watching old men play chess.

A new song comes on; there are slow strings. With a strange grunting noise, Father leaps to his feet, spilling the chess pieces across the board.

'Oh come now, Will. I had you in two moves—'

But Father is a thousand miles away, holding up his finger and listening to the slow strings coming from the speaker. The strings swell, beautiful and full.

'It is so sad,' I say, to fill the silence of voices. What is wrong with Father? Is he ill?

Father closes his eyes, lets his hand drop. 'It is the happiest music in the world. He is dead.'

'What? Who?'

'Listen.' He gestures to the speakers, the sound of swirling strings. His voice is a whisper. 'If you hear Bruckner's Seventh, it will mean the end is upon us.'

No one speaks as the long piece of music unfolds. It must be almost ten minutes, but it feels like seconds.

Abruptly the music stops. A drum roll is followed by another, and another. There is a moment's silence. Then a dry, cracked German voice enters the stillness.

'What is he saying, Father?'

But Father is laughing, and crying, and he doesn't need to say a word.

Hitler is dead.

4 May 1945

Finally, German forces in north-western Europe surrender to General Montgomery. It is the end of the war in Europe.

No one has announced anything. It is over? It is truly over? Then why not say as much?

Why not tell people to blow the trumpets and get out the flags? The hesitation keeps everyone on edge. What are they waiting for? Treaties to be signed? Must we all delay celebrations on some negotiations and formalities?

Perhaps they are waiting for Sunday, or for June. But surely we have endured long enough. After everything, after Dunkirk, after the Blitz, after D-Day, after the V1 bombs and the V2 rockets – it is almost too much to wait.

Is it over? Is this peace?

I shake my head at the sky and walk up the stairs to my bedroom in Bloody Tower. For years I lived here, with Uncle's room just down the stairs. I would sneak down to the Stone Kitchen, where it was a not-so-secret secret between us that the biscuits were hidden behind the great suit of armour.

Sliding under the pile of blankets, I let my eyes relax in the darkness. Wind breathes through the room. I pull my knees closer – the cot is far too small for me now.

For the first time in months, I let myself think of Mum – of her making cheese on toast, or reading the newspaper in the back garden, the sun flashing in her red hair, redder than mine. *Fox red*, she called it.

I close my eyes, breathe deeply, and dream of laughing foxes.

7 May 1945

Today I travel to Hamble. No one raises the alarm to see me, even if they don't run over to say hello. The girls had their suspensions lifted thanks to Cecil's word with the Air Ministry, but my licence has not yet been restored.

Joy smiles her great wide smile. 'Come on. I don't think they'll toss me out of the ATA for bringing a civilian into the Mess.'

We sit down with plates of boiled potatoes. *Well, that*

hasn't changed. I watch her eat, my own appetite having vanished on the journey here.

'What would you have done,' I ask, 'if there hadn't been a war? Would you have stayed at your dad's air circus?'

She shrugs. 'Maybe. Maybe started my own. Don't know what, but it wouldn't be on the ground.'

I nod, stabbing the potato with a fork. I remember Joy once told me flying was the future. *Flying is scary, Coop, no two ways about it. But it's also the future, and women can have a part in it, same as men. Black or white, young or old.*

'Miss Cooper,' Gower enters the room, and I stand and salute.

She sits down and I hurriedly do the same.

'I'm sorry about the Spits, Commander—'

'I've heard all about it, Cooper, thank you. It's a shame to lose the machines, but a much greater shame to lose such a remarkable pilot. Bella was one of us, even if she went her own way in the end.'

I nod, feeling the hot sting of tears in my eyes.

'In fact, none of us will be ATA pilots soon,' Gower goes on. 'The organization is to be shut down. My last act as head of the ATA will be to have your flight licence reinstated. Apparently a number of other pilots – at the persistence of an American pilot named Joy Brooks – came forward to give evidence of tampering and negligence by Cam Westin.'

I smile at Joy across the table.

Gower continues. 'It seems Mr Westin has recently got into some hot water with the Air Ministry, so this latest evidence got him suspended until his trial.'

Having delivered her news, Gower leaves us to finish our lunch.

'Thank you, Joy.'

The fork clatters on the plate as I drop it in shock. Barcsay has raced into the room, and she is screaming. The noise echoes through the Mess, reaching a wordless, ear-splitting pitch.

So this is it.

Joy reaches across the table, sending potatoes spinning to the floor, and crushes me in a hug. 'Tomorrow,' she yells, her eyes bright. 'We're going to London.'

8 May 1945

The ATA pilots are off duty for the celebrations. Everyone, it seems, is off duty to celebrate.

And they have all come to London. At the connecting station, Churchill's victory speech blared over the station's loudspeakers:

> 'The German war is therefore at an end. The evil-doers are now prostrate before us. Our gratitude to our splendid Allies goes forth from all our hearts in this island and throughout the British Empire.
>
> We may now allow ourselves a brief period of rejoicing. Advance, Britannia! Long live the cause of freedom! God save the King!'

I stared out of the train window, Joy babbling beside me, watching as every house, every cottage, every battered old building, flew a Union Jack. Curtains were thrown wide; people were smiling. Church bells pealed and town bands played.

Now we are here, inching our way towards Trafalgar Square, as bunting flutters on lamp posts, pubs overflow on to squares, gramophones on street corners blare dance-hall music. Women are baking and cutting sandwiches, chalking *Welcome Home* and *I Love You* on house walls. Everyone is happy.

No, not everyone: there is a woman not smiling among the happy wives, and another. They have a look of bitterness, of resentment. There are thousands – hundreds of thousands – who will never come home, who will have no party thrown in their honour, no bunting, no cut sandwiches, no conga lines, no ecstatic kisses.

For those thousands, there was only pain, then silence, then being left behind in some European field. And the wives, the girlfriends, the mothers, will do what they can to carry on.

And the fight in the Far East is still on.

The nightmare has passed, but it has left a heavy trace.

Father's words come back to me. *Survivors pay with their conscience.*

'Hey, Coop. You'd think we lost the war, looking at your face.' Joy pushes a bottle of gin into my hands. I take a painful sip; the taste is horrible, like swallowing searing pine cones.

'There you go,' says Joy, taking it back and hoisting it for a long mouthful.

With each horrible sip, I can hear the bombs fade away, replaced with music, and laughter – and life. I give in to it, and feel transported by the relief all around.

We push through the forest of crowds, and pass by a group dancing and singing 'Land of Hope and Glory', and I am sure some of the Polish airmen are in that group, arm in arm with British officers. *The war is over, all is forgiven.*

Trafalgar Square is bursting with men, some in uniform, some in their Sunday best, all swaying blissfully. Women wear bright floral dresses, with red-white-and-blue ribbons around their waists, some with children on their arms, some staggering with pewter tankards.

The square is a riot of colour, as though the world before now was made up of only greys and blacks. The screaming-laughing faces crush us in, and there is nothing for it but to scream right back.

As night falls people dance and sing Vera Lynn songs. The feeling of joy, of a freedom won, shimmers like electricity. People dance down to Whitehall to hear Churchill, or sway to Buckingham Palace to see the royal family appear on the balcony.

'Anna Cooper.' Nell's beautiful smiling face slides out

of the crowd. She is wearing cornflowers in her dark hair, which curls down to her red lips.

And then those red lips kiss me. She squeezes me in a great hug. Then she kisses a startled Joy, and throws a hug round her, and after a brief hesitation, Joy squeezes back.

We drink together. I have not seen Nell since she visited me in the Tower a year ago, to make peace after our fall-out at Cecil's midsummer party. Cecil is the furthest thing from either of our minds at the moment.

'Nell Singer. It is good to see you.'

She looks me up and down. 'Looking snappy, Cooper. *Very* snappy.'

In my first months at the Tower, I idolized Nell for her effortless fashion sense and charm. She taught me how to put on lippy and how to dance in heels. She taught me, without meaning to, how to never let a boy get in the way of a friendship.

Nell laughs, rich and smoky. 'Looks like we're all redundant. The WAAFs, the WRENS, the ATA.'

'You're all welcome in the circus.' Joy laughs, hands her the flask. 'Gin?'

I scan the crowd, the smiling faces blurring into one unknown face.

But there is no Timothy Squire.

I thought he'd be here. It would be just like him to turn up at the last second, still smiling, with some great excuse.

Where is he now?

Flo meets us, like she promised she would. She looks very pale and thin, but her eyes are bright and happy.

Joy wants to go to Rainbow Corner, that little bit of the USA on Shaftesbury Avenue. But I am in no mood for a packed club – Americans or not – and the idea of jives and jitterbugs is enough to make my temples throb.

Nell shakes her head too.

Joy heads off to the US servicemen's club alone. I say goodbye to her, and she folds me in a hug with drunken grace. Nell, Flo, and I walk slowly through the happy night. Once, the three of us went to a film together – a film about Anna Neagle – and it seemed impossible that we could all be friends. But the smiles tonight are the smiles of friends, bound by suffering and joy.

Somewhere, someone plays 'Auld Lang Syne', and when Nell starts to sing, low and deep and surprisingly heartfelt, we join our voices to hers.

We follow the crowds, walking amazed under the returned street lamps.

People pass round bottles, and I think of the old woman I met years ago in a doorway, who resisted my offer of a slice of bread until I pushed it into her hands.

We arrive with the crowds at Green Park to lie down in the grass. Nell has cheese and some sweets, but I'm fuller than a shark at a shipwreck.

Timothy Squire used to say that. *He should be here.*

Small bonfires light up the night. Again I remember baths from the days before the war – no 5-inch rule, no measly single tablet of soap per fortnight. A proper bath will be bliss.

Big Ben chimes midnight. It is warm, no one moves to go home, but stays smiling into the darkness. It is mostly young people out. In fact, I saw few older faces in the celebrations. It's hard to imagine the Warders down here – they're far too dignified. Oakes, though, seemed happy when I last saw him, lecturing Father and playing chess. He's even started researching again, heavy leather books alongside the heaps of newspapers. He claims he is ready to finish his book on prisoner graffiti in the Tower.

Nell lights another cigarette. 'They've got us all attending EVT classes.'

'EVT?' I say.

'Education and Vocational Training. Looks like it's back to being a typist for me. Though I can't imagine going back to £15 a week.' She smiles again. 'Guess that's why most of the FANYs were so quick to volunteer for the Far East.'

'What about you, Flo? Oxford in the autumn?'

She shakes her head. 'I'm going back to Germany. I leave on Tuesday, actually. They need all the nurses we have. The things...'

She stops, forces herself to smile. *Not tonight*, she seems to say, and silence falls once again except for the laughter that carries on the breeze.

42

TIMOTHY SQUIRE

21 May 1945

The West Gate unguarded, the battlements unmanned, the Parade Ground empty. Only a raven, fat and healthy, flaps across the cobblestones, landing at my feet. He tilts his head, curved beak catching the light.

Yugo.

'Good to see you too, mate.'

It may not have been the submarine journey Wake threatened me with, but the ship journey was close to a nightmare. I am staying right here, on the bloody ground, for the next ten years. My wound hasn't fully healed, and I'm forced to use a walking stick, at least for a few more weeks.

I am back at the Tower, I am home. The sky is grey again, the wind is cool. Everything is frighteningly the same – and somehow slightly different. The Tower is an old ruin, almost looks like no one's looking after the place – at least from the outside.

Inside, though, it's not all bad. The old prisons and lordly chambers have long since been divided up into flats, mostly for the Warders and their families. It wasn't designed for a man with a cane, I'm certain, as I hobble up the steps to the Green.

Anna is not with the ravens. The Green looks bigger, somehow, until I realize it's because the old trees were destroyed in the bombing and new saplings have been planted in their place. Trees will grow back; the flats and buildings outside the Tower, now rubble, are gone forever. War has changed the face of London.

Anna could be around any corner, I think, my mouth dry, my palms slick with sweat. *She could be at the airfield.* No, she is here – I am sure of it.

'Come on, Ollie. Let's get a move on.'

A woman's voice. A voice I'd know anywhere in the world. And, now that I can see a glimpse of it from the corner of my eye, hair glowing red in the sun. Anna stands on the Parade Ground, feeding the ravens, bucket in hand.

I manage to choke out the word. 'Magpie?'

She nearly drops the buckets and whirls around to face me.

Ollie the raven starts croaking madly, and other ravens soon swoop in to join his commotion. But I don't care, about the ravens or anything else. I am staring, in the middle of the Tower, at Anna Cooper.

'What are... how are you...?' I can't find any words that make sense.

The whole world is paused, holding its breath for her to speak.

She swallows. 'You came back.'

'I did,' I say, finding my breath. 'For you.'

This is the part where the big hug and kiss is supposed to be, but she just keeps on staring. She stares for so long that even ravens fall silent, as if wondering what's happening.

'Nancy Wake came to see me,' she says. 'She told me you were wounded. Are you OK?'

I shake my head, having lost the sense of her words in the clear, miraculous sound of her voice. Her voice, which I heard over and over in my head as I hid in an impossible forest in the middle of an impossible war. Anna Cooper.

'I'm OK now.'

She smiles, that great wide grin I worried I'd imagined. 'Then what are you doing standing way over there?'

My cane hits the cobblestones as I race to her, and she is lighter than a feather as we float through the air.

I feared seeing Anna was likely to be the last happy encounter I had today, as Mum and Dad would be furious that I only sent them one quick letter saying I was on the mend and heading home as soon as I was able.

But they're not. Mum hugs me for an hour – she's not upset that I failed to bring her back some French cheese – and Dad keeps gripping my shoulder like he's trying to leave a handprint there. When we finally sit down to dinner – Brussels sprouts and boiled potatoes, but no grousing from me this time – the questions come in an onslaught that would make Rommel proud.

'Parachutes dropping food in the forest? I don't believe it…'

Trouble is, they really *don't* believe it. Or maybe it's that they can't. Either way, I can tell Mum's just being polite and Dad's all but lost interest.

They just want you home, and safe. You can't fault them for that. And just the feeling of being in proper clothes again is enough to keep me happy.

Dad spoons some potatoes into his mouth. 'Shame about Grampa's watch, though—'

'William,' Mum cautions.

'But I suppose it got you home safe, and that's all that matters.'

Rommel committed suicide, they say. *He was part of the plot to kill Hitler. He wasn't a Nazi at all, just a proud German and a wizard on the battlefield.* Well, I don't know about any of that, but I do know it's possible to be a German and not be a complete devil.

'A lot of the boys are heading to Malaya,' Mum says.

'Or Java,' Dad adds.

I shake my head. 'Don't worry. They won't send me out. My time as a soldier is over.'

'And what will you do for a living, dear?'

I can only shake my head. I was dying to get in as a sapper, but it took next to no time before I couldn't wait to be out. The regimental life isn't for me any more than the Resistance life. But what is?

And then Dad goes and says it. 'You'll find something, lad, even if you never did manage to finish up school. And now that the smoke's all cleared, what about you and the young Anna Cooper?'

'She's a wonderful girl,' says Mum, as always. 'I'll bet Anna is all ready for a good spring clean. Assuming you two had a nice little place to set up.'

I cough. 'I think the war might have changed things, Mum.'

'War is men's work. Peace is women's work.'

'OK, Mum.' I nod. 'Can someone put the kettle on?'

I'm the only one who ate their meal at a sprint, but then again I'm the only one who's been living in the woods for the better part of the last year. Mum puts the kettle on. There is no sweeter music than the hiss of a gas burner. I could listen to it for hours.

But Mum isn't content to let me have the silence. 'Believe me, dear. Women are caring, and a woman's home is central to her life. It's more than just her duty to keep the home fires burning. It's her instinct. It's who she is.'

Now Mum is so sincere, so genuine as she lays down her advice, that I don't have the heart to tell her that while she was talking I was thinking of Wake leading our bleeding men from a machine-gun ambush, or hearing about Anna firing directly on a V2 rocket in mid-air.

'Besides, it's not seemly for a married woman to work.'

Grateful, I take the teacup with a grin.

And it isn't long before that topic comes up with Anna. We are up on the battlements, where we once stayed all night to watch the sun come up over Tower Bridge. Today it is grey morning light. *But no bloody snow in sight.* In truth, the days are already growing longer. Spring has returned.

The sounds of the docks echo up to us. Once you could smell the Spice Docks, the hint of nutmeg on the wind. Those days will come again too.

I should have brought her back something – lavender soap, maybe. I got her some for her birthday once and she seemed to like it well enough. *And lavender comes from France, doesn't it?* Well, it's too late now, at any rate.

'Well, Magpie, do you want to go and look at the ravens? And then grab some lunch in the Stone Kitchen?'

I offer an arm, and with a laugh, she takes it.

We sit down in the Stone Kitchen to a Spam sandwich and coffee. The gods don't eat as well. I chew, grinning through mouthfuls, remembering Anna promised we can go down to Borough Market later in search of the perfect sausage roll. But Anna isn't smiling.

'What is this?' she asks as Oakes slides a newspaper across the table with a hopeful look.

'A notice for a traineeship,' he says. 'To be an air hostess.'

'A what?'

The temperature in the room plunges but, bless him,

Oakes carries right on talking. 'Civilian flights are starting to resume, flying out of the Croydon Aerodrome. You could be an air hostess for British European Airways – that could be a great job for you. I know it's not *flying* the aeroplane, and obviously it would only be temporary, but, well, you would be flying...'

Anna tries and fails to crush out a frown. 'An air hostess?'

'It's very glamorous, but you would have an edge, being that you have so much experience, you know, in the air. You would fly to Paris, to Madrid.'

'Serving drinks to politicians?'

Yeoman Oakes has mercifully cottoned on, and hides his face in his teacup.

'Didn't this room used to be Henry VIII's bedroom...?' I try, but no one's having it. Anna openly scoffs.

The fire crackles, giving more smoke than light. Oakes sips his tea loudly, turning his attention on me. All the lines on his face are frown lines. 'A wild adventure you've been on, lad.'

He does his best to crack the tension, chatting to me about the Resistance and the comforts of sea travel. Anna is like a raincloud sitting next to me. Eventually Oakes tries his luck again. 'I'm sure it's not so bleak, Anna. If anyone can find a way to become a pilot, it's you.'

'I've heard from Commander... from Mrs Gower,' she corrects herself ruefully. 'The ATA is closing forever. There is no requirement for female pilots.'

Oakes reaches out a hand. 'There will be, Anna. Commercial flying—'

'The boys need their jobs back, Yeoman Oakes.'

I cut in. 'You're a far better pilot than any of them.'

Anna shakes her head. 'Gower thinks she won't live to see female pilots fly again. She says it will go back to how it was before the war. Women in the kitchen, or secretaries in the office. Or air hostesses.'

'It's not fair,' I say. 'You were in the Great War, Yeoman Oakes – what happened when all the men came home?'

Oakes coughs. 'I'm afraid it was rather similar. Women and girls had been used to fill the gaps when the men went away. Once they came back...'

In the silence Anna stands, heads off to make more tea. The only sound is the hostile bustle from the kitchen.

I don't know what to say. All my clever ideas have long bailed on me. What happens now?

My eyes start to prickle, likely on account of all the smoke. It is so unfair. Anna is a bleeding war hero; she flew a squadron of Spitfires into enemy airspace and blew up enemy convoys – not to mention shooting down a bloody V2 rocket. She's saved hundreds, maybe thousands of lives.

Oakes looks at her, adding a new frown line to his creased face, as she sits back down.

'Forget about all that,' I say, waving a hand like a fool.

'It's not so easy,' she answers.

Suddenly Oakes laughs, shaking his head. 'You two will make a right pair. Both deaf as a post. Shouting at each other across the kitchen table.' He stops when he sees we're smiling at each other, completely at home with the image.

I can't imagine anything more perfect.

Of course Lightwood is waiting at the West Gate as I leave.

'Fox and Hounds?' he says, as if nothing out of the ordinary has happened in the past two years. Both of us are wearing our good tweed coats and caps, and for once my cane feels properly dapper.

'First pint's on me,' I say.

The Fox and Hounds is good and quiet, just the local lads having a quick pint after work. So we've only made it halfway to the bar when we spot the strange man in the too-nice suit at the corner table.

Our eyes meet. *Cecil Sodding Rafferty.*

'The wine takes some getting used to,' he says with that public-school smile.

'You should be used to it then,' the barkeeper interrupts, before turning to us. 'He's been here all week, like a bloody bump on a log.'

'I've been waiting on some friends,' Cecil says. 'Who have only just arrived. I'll take the first round, shall I? Let's move on to the beer, though, if that's OK with you gentlemen?'

That's about all I remember, aside from the three of us, drunk as lords, staggering over the cobblestones of a free city. Many of the destroyed flats have stayed destroyed, but some are being rebuilt, brick by brick. We even took a moment to stare out at the Thames, the smooth river a far cry from the growling waves of the North Sea. *It still didn't feel real.*

Lightwood had lots of questions about Flo, seems to

think he has a chance. Imagine, old horseface Lightwood with the stunning posh girl? Madness.

He did tell me Rigby is alive, though not quite the same bloke. Who is?

After Lightwood says his drunken goodnights, Cecil lingers for a moment. The night air is cool, the breeze fresh off the river.

'Goodbye, Squire,' he says, putting out a hand. 'Thank you.'

I shake his hand firmly and watch him walk away, making his way through the streets like some king.

'Rafferty!' I call out.

He stops, watches me approach, my cane slipping on the cobblestones. Even in the darkness, the state of me is obvious.

'Thank you.' I try not to slur too much. 'I know how hard it was.'

Rafferty stares at me. 'What are you thanking me for?'

'For looking after Anna. I know how hard it is… I know you love her, too.'

His eyes shine bright. *He is a handsome bastard, I'll give him that.* He clutches my arm, and when he speaks his voice is almost a whisper. 'You're a good man, Squire.'

'You too.' I say the words as clearly as I can, and mean them. 'You are a good man.'

43
ANNA COOPER

26 July 1945

Timothy Squire has been recruited to help the Warders carry overfilled crates of armour and weapons up from the White Tower basement.

His father, as curator, oversees the whole process, and I smile to see Timothy Squire sneaking off for a breather and looking genuinely miserable doing physical labour. *He has not changed so much then.*

But the Tower definitely has, and the reason for the all this sudden influx of work is just around the corner: the Tower of London is getting ready for its grand reopening to the public.

Another great change has come, and I for one can't quite believe it.

'Attlee has won.' Oakes smiles.

'Attlee? The Labour Party? But, Yeoman Oakes, even you must have voted for Churchill's government – after they won us the war.'

His smile widens. 'The war is over. This is a chance to change for the better. To create a new, freer, equal society out of the ashes of war. Churchill is not the man for that job.'

I remember how rude Oakes was when Churchill visited the Tower during the Blitz. 'Clearly we owe him that chance. It's unpatriotic.'

'Anna, you didn't grow up in the thirties. But for those who did, they will never forget the poverty, the slums, the Jarrow marches. Attlee will launch a National Health Service, providing care for all. He will guarantee Welfare for those in need and a Family Allowance, and do away with our frightful class system.'

Oakes always did sound like a boring politician. 'It is easy for the people who didn't fight to worry about society.'

He smiles kindly. 'It was the soldier vote that wiped out Churchill. People need food, not tanks. A new world, a new day, is dawning.'

I nod, without words. I can't shake the feeling that Churchill saved the world and we turned our backs on him.

'All the soldiers will get their jobs back,' he says. 'Whatever they were doing before they joined up, that employment has been kept open. Attlee will guarantee it.'

I nod. *But not for the women. My job is gone, vanished. Nell's job no longer exists.* It doesn't sound so much like a new world after all.

At least Father has a new opportunity. Despite how well Father and Oakes seem to be getting along, Father is getting ready to move away.

'America,' he says. 'They want scientists.'

'For what, exactly?' I ask.

'Space travel.'

Convinced he was in danger of arrest, he was shocked to learn the Americans, in fact, wanted him, and they have eagerly taken many of the V2 plans and scientists back to the United States.

My own future, however, seems far less certain.

30 July 1945

Flo is deeply affected by what she witnessed at the concentration camps. I only saw the Pathé newsreel at the Odeon Cinema, and I can scarcely recall those images without my stomach turning. For Flo, the sight of it, the smell... and she had helped, with her own hands, to save those she could from death.

And now she is going back.

'Berlin is gone,' she says, sitting across from me in our usual spot at the raven graveyard. 'It is rubble. Far, far worse than London. It is a city of nightmares. And the Russian soldiers behave like beasts. The stories the German women tell, of rape and brutality...'

We sit quietly, occasionally glancing up at the clouds. The air is full of rain.

'You spoke to them?' I ask.

'Yes. Non-fraternization rules have been imposed, but I didn't care. Our troops – and the American and Russian occupiers – throw lavish parties, with fancy gowns and unlimited consumption. The Allied Control Administration building hosts endless balls, with bands and mountains of food. Of course they make the starving German women act as waitresses. You should see their suffering.'

'Defeat has its cost, Flo.'

'So does victory, she says quietly. 'It brings responsibility.'

Many of them were Nazis, says a voice in my head. *But all of them are humans.* Mum told me what was at stake during the war: our common humanity, she said.

'At Buchenwald, American troops forced SS prisoners to exhume the hundreds of murdered Jews. Then they forced the residents of Nammering to tour the site and rebury the corpses.

'And when the Russians came the German women – the mothers, the daughters – ran for their lives. The Red Army...'

I move over to her and grip her in a hug. She squeezes back, firmly, and for a long moment neither of us lets go.

7 August 1945

There is no news of politics in the papers today.

'*RAIN OF RUIN*,' reads *The Times*. I grab another paper, the *Daily Mail*, and start reading.

> Hiroshima, Japanese city of 300,000 people, ceased to exist at 9:15 on Monday morning.

An atomic bomb. Destruction such as the world has never seen. My vision swims, the world tilting around me. Nothing I have heard – about the V2 rockets, about the firestorm of Dresden – had prepared me for this.

Weapons of peace. That's what Cecil called our bombs.

During the Blitz the fear dragged on; we lived in a state of panic. This bomb – there was no fear, no prolonging of agony.

They are all dead. Obliterated.

Ceased to exist.

10 August 1945

ATOM BOMB ON NAGASAKI –
SECOND CITY HIT.

Father stares, open-mouthed, at the newspaper on the card table. His great fear has been realized. If we could create such weapons, then something would be changed forever. *How can we live in a world where this weapon exists?*

'Father, you saw the papers, when Dresden happened. You see the papers today. People are seeing the cost of this, truly. Now that we know the consequences, countries will not use it.'

He has the ghost of a smile. 'Hope, is it? How can we live our lives in the hope that feuding countries and mad politicians won't simply launch a weapon that wins their war?'

'Hope is all we've got,' I say.

'What about the next time Germany and France fight? Or maybe next time it's Italy who wants revenge? Europe is always at war. Or if we make the same mistake as we did with the Treaty of Versailles? Hitler would have used this weapon in a heartbeat – he's been trying to develop it for years. Why won't it happen next time? You think the threat of the bomb will keep the peace?' His voice cracks.

I shake my head. 'Threats can't keep the peace. Only a shared future can.'

He smiles, and after a moment something like a laugh spills from him. 'You are turning out more like your mother than I thought. Yes, she saw the problems without having to live through them. She was not hopeful for the future, and I dare say she wouldn't have been optimistic about a nuclear one.'

I lay my hands flat on the table. 'But we have to be, Father. It's the only way to move forward. With hope.'

15 August 1945

The bunting is back out, the street parties once again in full swing. People gather at Buckingham Palace, the royal family appears on the balcony, and parades march past, filled with demobbed soldiers and laughing girls.

Or so I hear.

Timothy Squire and I sit alone on the bench in Tower Green. 'They have jellies, you know,' he says, eyeing the cabbage in his hand. 'And cakes.'

'You're welcome to go to a street party if you want, Timothy Squire.'

He sighs, chewing the cabbage. 'And leave you to fend off Malcolm's advances?'

Soon there'll be plum pudding; I have to believe that. One of the Wives clicks across the battlements, flowers in her hair, off to some party. Her son has been a POW in the Far East for three years. He'll be coming home now.

But so many won't. And now, with the atomic bomb, can we ever feel safe again? They did not all die, when the bombs fell. Timothy Squire told me all about it, once I had chastened him for trying to hide the details and treating me like a child.

Those who escaped the blast – those who were unhurt – began to fall sick. Then there was bleeding, and vomiting, and rotting flesh. And then, only after the suffering, came death.

'Timothy Squire, do you think the world is a hateful place?'

'Sure as hell seems like it.'

Father's words come back to me. *We will always live in the shadow of this new weapon.* I push them aside. I can't bear to think of this news alongside all that Flo has told me about the concentration camps.

'Some things are unbearable,' he says after a long pause. 'But we still have to bear them.'

I nod. 'I think there is a chance for peace, real peace. I have to think that. A normal life.'

Timothy Squire glances at me, and I notice that his eyes

are bluer than ever. 'I didn't think you wanted a normal life.'

'I don't know. I've never had one.' I shrug. 'And you? What do you want?'

I know Timothy Squire too is standing on the threshold of a new world. The sense of purpose, the motivation for peace – it is gone. His urgent mission, his vital service, to defend his friends and kill his enemies – how must he feel, suddenly unimportant and irrelevant?

There will be no more air-raid sirens, no more gas-mask drills, no more hiding underground. But at least, then, there was always an All Clear to come, to look forward to. What is there to look forward to now? So much time has passed; so much has changed.

It is all wrong. The promise of peace – has it all been a lie? For one thing, bananas are *not* back, and I haven't seen any silk stockings in the shops.

Timothy Squire tosses a strip of cabbage to an attentive raven – Ollie. The bird makes his strange *yips* and clicking noises, but speaks no words today. 'They seem pretty happy,' Timothy Squire says. 'Maybe we can learn from them.'

'Yes.' I rest my head against his shoulder, closing my eyes. 'We just need some outdoor space, and someone to come and feed us every day.'

'Malcolm would do it if you asked.'

I shift, trying to find a comfortable position. He is skin and bones. 'I knew you'd come back, Timothy Squire.'

'I wouldn't have, if it wasn't for you.'

'Next time I'll come get you myself.'

I open my eyes to see a huge smile on his face. 'I love you, Anna Cooper.'

'I love you too.'

15 August 1945

The night air is warm. I took my bike down to the market, and cycled through the empty roads, before going to Bow Cemetery to visit Uncle's gravestone. No one was around, so I felt only a little foolish telling him how the war has ended, and the six ravens are safe in the Tower. And that Yeoman Oakes is doing a lot better these days.

'I never did find Grip or Mabel, Uncle. Maybe one day they'll come back. And there will be wild ravens in London again.'

It is late as I push my bike across the West Gate bridge, and head up to the Green. Something tenses at the edge of the Parade Ground, a fox perhaps, and I pull up and stare.

At the roost, a single figure stands under the lamplight. Every time I see him, it's like seeing him again for the first time. *Father.*

War changes people, I know that, even the civilians. As I walk closer I see again how thin he is now, how small. His short hair is as pale as moonlight, his high cheekbones drawn in, and – something new – his eyes bright with purpose. But when he turns to me he is grinning from ear to ear.

'Goodbye, my dear.'

'Goodbye, Father.'

When I squeeze his body against mine, he is not so thin, not so frail, and his heart beats loud.

EPILOGUE

44

ANNA COOPER

1 January 1946

The dry, insistent croak of the ravens echoes off the stone walls.

Stackhouse has decided to move on. There's a new Ravenmaster, Yeoman Skaife, who seems to know more about the ravens than even Uncle Henry did. He's filled with all sorts of ideas. He wants to let the birds fly. He has plans to build bigger, open-air cages. No raven should live in a box, he says, and I couldn't agree more. They are wild animals.

Following the sound of happy ravens, I make my way to the top of the Green, and sit there beneath the saplings. I sit on my bench in the familiar – if cold – swarm of mist. Suddenly a woman sits down next to me, and then a man next to her. I have never seen a stranger on this bench before.

As I look up, a family comes round the battlements, two children screaming as they race across the grass.

'Mum! Look at these fat crows!'

'Stay away from those birds, dear. They could bite.'

More people crowd up the stairs, turning on to the Green or flooding into the Chapel behind us, and queueing to see the Crown jewels in the Jewel House. Flashblubs fire off, and it seems everyone has their own camera in hand.

Warders wander among them, leading tours and stopping eager visitors from entering personal homes. Yeoman Brodie, Malcolm's father, will have a proper fit if he sees all these people walking on his precious grass.

'I told you life would return to normal,' comes Oakes's voice. He stands beside me, looking out over the swelling group of visitors. It's *worse* than Piccadilly Circus in here.

'I've never seen it like this.'

'Wait until summer,' he says, smiling.

I had never visited the Tower before the day that I was brought here to live with Uncle. By then the Blitz was under way and the Tower was closed to the public. It has always been a quiet, empty place, filled with echoes and silences. I knew today was the grand reopening to the public, but this...

'Gus! Do not touch that bird!'

Oakes and I watch as the new Ravenmaster leads a group to the roost, and gestures with a gloved hand to the birds, the snapping beaks and flailing wings.

'Always there have been six ravens at the Tower,' Yeoman Skaife says, his voice crackling with excitement. 'Legend has it, if the ravens ever leave the Tower, Britain will fall.'

I look out over the astonished faces, and I smile.

11 March 1946

'Build a school for flying aeroplanes? Anna, no one has that kind of money.'

Except Cecil Rafferty. I bury the thought, worried he can somehow hear it. 'Father has moved to America,' I say instead. 'He sold the house on Warwick Avenue – we both knew I couldn't live there. He gave me the money.'

'All of it?' he blurts out.

'Enough to get started. I have a barn that I can turn into a hangar. And a Moth from Gower – it was her old Trainer when she started out. I'm not going to break any speed records, but...'

'Good,' he says with relief, then swiftly tries to hide it. 'And just where is this barn?'

'Are you asking me to show you?'

Timothy Squire is thinking. When he thinks, his forehead wrinkles with lines. *There are more lines there than before.*

For an answer, he slips his hand into mine. His fingers are rough and calloused. I squeeze, hard.

'Can you hear me?'

He presses the speaking tube against his mouth. 'I can hear you.'

'Are you nervous up there?' I ask with a smile.

''Course not,' he says, adjusting the strap once again.

'It's just... another wooden box. Last one didn't treat me so well.'

'Well, I'm flying this one, so don't worry.'

I fix my goggles, breathe in the smells of wood and petrol, the leather of the helmet, and lead us down the grass of Hamble runway. Since the plane was Gower's personal plane, no clearance was required. Just a quick hug and a spin of the propeller to get us started. She agreed to endorse my Flying Instructor certificate, and promised to come and check up on the school in the autumn.

The engine is loud as we taxi away. I peer over Timothy Squire's helmet, down the long runway. The airfield is practically empty as we bump along. No barrage balloons, no jumble of RAF fighters and bombers, no queue of aircraft with urgent missions.

I haven't flown an open cockpit bi-plane in more than a year. No breaks, no flaps, no control panel. No roof. As I throttle for take-off, the feel of the spring wind is exhilarating. For me, at least.

Gaining speed, I open the throttle and the wheels push off. The little green Moth slides into the sky – and stays there. *A miracle every time*, I think, as I begin the climbing turn.

'All OK?' I ask.

There is a long pause as we level off. 'Just a tad cold, to be honest. I'm not going to be sick.'

'Great news.' I grin, in case he's looking in the mirror. I throttle back so he can hear me more clearly. 'Well, we're on our way now. Just a slight change of direction.'

He makes alarmed noises for a while before surrendering to the view. *Just like I did on my first flight with Joy. Though she was a fair bit more pushy about it.*

I bank right, turning us north-east, the gleaming blue sky on all sides. We keep along the bottom of the clouds when the odd one does appear, with the sun at our backs. The slipstream snatches at my helmet.

'Are you sure you don't want to try the controls—?'

'Not for me, thanks,' he says hurriedly.

I nod to myself, pulling back on the stick, warm from the sun. Under twenty minutes and we are here, following the bright reflection of the Thames as it snakes into London. As the Tower rises in the distance, I hear his intake of breath through the microphone. And I understand the feeling.

For the first time, I am flying over the Tower of London. Home.

A wide descending turn hardens the features into shape: the ancient sprawling castle, its solid turrets reaching for the sky, the great White Tower at its heart, proud and unyielding. A thousand years it has stood there, as Uncle always reminded me. And still it stands.

Approaching at 60 mph, throttling back to lose more speed, we are alone, silent, hovering above the medieval walls. I think of the smooth stone passages, which lead to flats, Warders' homes – once even a small school, where Timothy Squire ignored me day after day; the dry moat that became an allotment, and ensured we had a lifetime of carrots; the Green, where I spent my days on the bench, hoping Nell would come and talk to me.

I see squat Develin Tower that I showed Timothy Squire how to climb, and the even stubbier Brass Mount, where I disastrously scaled a drainpipe in order to escape, then Salt Tower, where Hew Draper carved his map of the night sky. There too is the massive Jewel House, where Timothy Squire's parents live, now besieged by tourists, then Bloody Tower, with the gas mask under the bed and the occasional mouse, and finally Traitor's Gate, with its glistening sharp teeth, where I first saw Father when he returned.

And down there, somewhere, are six croaking ravens.

'This place kicks,' comes the voice. *Yes, it does.*

I turn west, into the cross-winds, and open the throttle, chasing the sun across the sky. Beneath us, sunlight breaks in waves across the ancient stone.

15 September 1946

It is autumn, my favourite time of year, and the leaves are turning a buttery yellow. Butter – it will have been worth it all to have butter back. Soon, Oakes promised before I left. Soon. I stand in front of the rickety barn. One day, with a little help, this will be a proper hangar. For now, the Moth sits patiently on the grass runway, its name freshly painted along the side. *Bella.*

'Ouch!' comes the voice of Timothy Squire from inside the barn.

'Are you OK?' I call.

'Yes. Just this bloody hammer....'

Smiling, I turn back to the main building – the lecture room, eventually. For now, it is our house. It is small, cramped, and the furthest building from the Tower imaginable. It is perfect.

I've offered instructor positions to all of the Ravens. Minx laughed at the idea of a post-war job, but Barcsay seems to be considering it. And I could sure use the help. Joy claims one day she'll expand her air circus to Britain, and build on the plot of land opposite. Canada has returned home with promises to come and visit soon. Everyone agrees to spread the word around their flying clubs.

I smile, eager to begin, to share the one thing I know to be true: the thrill of achievement, the confidence of skill, and the utter freedom of soaring above the clouds.

The Ravens Flying School will have Joy's words as its motto: Flying is the future. Man or women, black or white, young or old. Learn to fly.

We have a few actual ravens in the area, that swoop down to feast on the scraps Timothy Squire leaves out for them. He's even given them names, calling one Bernard and carrying on long bantering conversations with him. I still like to imagine that any of these birds could be Mabel and Grip, the Tower ravens I let free so many years ago.

A loud bang brings me back to the present. The farmer who sold me the barn tosses the last of his things into his truck. 'Well, good luck, Mrs Cooper. Though I can't say it's not an unusual thing to hear about. A flight school in Devon? And run by a boy so young?'

'It's Miss Cooper,' I say smoothly. 'And I'll be the flight instructor.'

He scratches his chin, eyes wide. 'So the little lady's a pilot, is she?'

'Yes, sir.'

He shakes his grizzled head. Now he's heard it all. 'You going to teach men how to fly?'

'I'll teach anyone who can pay.'

He smiles at that, but wants to impart some seriousness before he goes. 'You know, there were quite a few young men who flew during the war. Saved Britain, they did.'

I nod in agreement. The sun, still bright, is on its way down.

'Well, maybe they had some help,' I say.

As his truck pulls away and Timothy Squire's hammering resumes, I stand fixed, smiling at the gleaming sky above.

THE END

Acknowledgements

This novel was written in memory of my grandfather, Colonel Harvey Edward Theobald, who landed at Normandy in a Sherman tank. He fought for the liberation of France, Belgium, and the Netherlands, and for his bravery was awarded the Military Cross.

My special thanks to the Arts Council England for their generous support of these novels. I am exceedingly grateful for the partnership of Megan Gooch and Ceri Fox at Historic Royal Palaces, who combine their expertise and determination with enthusiasm and good humour.

My thanks also to Chris Skaife, the real Ravenmaster at the Tower of London, whose knowledge of and passion for the ravens earns him a special shout-out in the last pages of this story.

Thanks to the great team at Head of Zeus, particularly my publisher Nicolas Cheetham, for his feedback, perception, and patience, and to my editors Helen Gray and Sophie Robinson for their insight and efficiency. And a special thanks to my agent, John Richard Parker.

To Bill and Jill, for their continued support and grace. To my parents, Greg and Bronwyn, for forcing my novels on book clubs around the city.

And a special thanks to JJ, just because.

And, as ever, to my wonderful wife Jackie, who knows the characters better than I do and who was instrumental in bringing the whole thing to life.